"A beautiful book . . . whose careful cadence follows
the necessity of maintaining a stilled surface . . . a reach
toward Proust, the evocation of significant feeling and
memory out of the commonplace."

—*Lambda Book Report*

"Elegant and moving. . . . Love and death make
dramatic entrances in this elegiac first novel."

—*Kirkus Reviews*

"An urgent, closely observed, deeply conflicted but
somehow elegant account of the illness and death of a
mother . . . a winning blend of emotional intensity and
elevated lyricism."   —*Los Angeles Times*

ANDREW SOLOMON was educated at Yale and
Cambridge universities and now lives in New York and
London. He is a contributing writer for the *New York
Times Magazine* and a frequent contributor to other peri-
odicals, including *The New Yorker*. He is the author of *The
Irony Tower: Soviet Artists in a Time of Glasnost. A Stone
Boat*, his first novel, was also published to great acclaim
in England.

by the same author

The Irony Tower:
Soviet Artists in a Time of Glasnost

ANDREW SOLOMON

A STONE BOAT

A PLUME BOOK

PLUME
Published by the Penguin Group
Penguin Books USA Inc., 375 Hudson Street,
New York, New York 10014, U.S.A.
Penguin Books Ltd, 27 Wrights Lane, London W8 5TZ, England
Penguin Books Australia Ltd, Ringwood, Victoria, Australia
Penguin Books Canada Ltd, 10 Alcorn Avenue, Toronto, Ontario, Canada M4V 3B2
Penguin Books (N.Z.) Ltd, 182–190 Wairau Road, Auckland 10, New Zealand

Penguin Books Ltd, Registered Offices: Harmondsworth, Middlesex, England

Published by Plume, an imprint of Dutton Signet,
a division of Penguin Books USA Inc.
This is an authorized reprint of a hardcover edition published by
Faber and Faber. For information address Faber and Faber, Inc.,
50 Cross Street, Winchester, Massachusetts 01890

First Plume Printing, February, 1996
10 9 8 7 6 5 4 3 2 1

Copyright © Andrew Solomon, 1994
All rights reserved

Excerpt from "At the Fishhouses" from *The Complete Poems 1927–1979* by Elizabeth Bishop.
Copyright © 1979, 1983 by Alice Helen Methfessel. Reprinted by permission of
Farrar, Straus & Giroux Inc.

 REGISTERED TRADEMARK—MARCA REGISTRADA

LIBRARY OF CONGRESS CATALOGING-IN-PUBLICATION DATA:

Solomon, Andrew, 1963–
A stone boat / Andrew Solomon.
p.   cm.
ISBN 0-452-27498-2
1. Mothers and sons—United States—Fiction.   2. Cancer—Patients—
United States—Fiction.   3. Americans—England—London—Fiction.
4. Gay men—England—London—Fiction.   5. London (England)—Fiction.
6. Domestic fiction.—lcsh.   I. Title.
PS3569.O589S76   1996
813'.54—dc20   95-37579
CIP

Printed in the United States of America

PUBLISHER'S NOTE
This is a work of fiction. Names, characters, places, and incidents either are the product of
the author's imagination or are used fictitiously, and any resemblance to actual persons,
living or dead, events, or locales is entirely coincidental.

BOOKS ARE AVAILABLE AT QUANTITY DISCOUNTS WHEN USED TO PROMOTE PRODUCTS
OR SERVICES. FOR INFORMATION PLEASE WRITE TO PREMIUM MARKETING DIVISION,
PENGUIN BOOKS USA INC., 375 HUDSON STREET, NEW YORK, NEW YORK 10014.

For my father and my brother

Contents

It is like what we imagine knowledge to be:
dark, salt, clear, moving, utterly free,
drawn from the cold hard mouth
of the world, derived from the rocky breasts
forever, flowing and drawn, and since
our knowledge is historical, flowing and flown.

Elizabeth Bishop
'At the Fishhouses'

I

My Mother's Paris

I need to write this as quickly as possible, because it is about my mother. I want to write it while we can still remember how we hoped that she would get well. That is sentimental and extravagant, I know. I once told my mother that I would never forget her because there is so much of her in me, but this year, I'm not so sure that I can rely on myself to recall everything about her, and I need to remember everything I possibly can. Did I get this sentimental and extravagant streak from her? Five years ago, I would have said that it came from my father, but now I'm not so sure.

Yesterday I was on a plane. I remember when that was an event in my life – to take a plane somewhere – but now planes are the most regular occurrence of all; I am the emperor of baggage-claim, the king of check-in, the prime minister of in-flight meals. I am as savvy as a flight attendant, with a profound knowledge of the location of the emergency exits and an aficionado's grasp of the technology of seatbelts. I can guess within a fraction of a second when the 'No Smoking' sign will go on. I have figured out how to angle myself so that the overhead reading light illuminates my book and not my hair, and I know where the further extra pillows are stored when the first cache of extra pillows has been distributed. I have mastered the look that bores customs officers, and even when I am carrying great misshapen boxes and large cumbersome suitcases, I am not stopped on my way out of the airport.

On Friday I will take a plane to Istanbul to play in a Brahms festival in the gardens of the Topkapi Palace. No doubt the piano will be sliding out of tune. Next Monday I will return to London. Next Tuesday I will go to New York, and then for a few days to Berlin to play Schubert, and then the following Friday I will go back to New York for an indefinite period of not more than nine days. That's the plan, unless my mother needs to go in for surgery.

If my mother needs to go in for surgery, I'll just go straight to New York and miss some more of the rest of my life and stay for as long as I have to and cancel all my performances. I've done it before.

This is what happened when my mother got sick: we were in Europe, on one of those family trips we had been taking since my childhood, one of those exquisitely conceived and impeccable holidays into which my mother poured – so it seems in retrospect – more energy than she could afford. 'Just think, Harry,' my mother had said a week before, her voice lilting. 'Four days of Paris, August sun, the city almost empty, and then we'll go down to the château – you'll love the château – and we'll eat breakfast looking across the valley, and we'll go for walks, and we'll swim a little if it gets really warm, and we'll go see all the Matisses. There's a piano at the château, so you can practise, but no one is going to make you perform for a whole two weeks. Just come along and relax and have a good time.'

I was living in London then, and my parents flew across the Atlantic three or four times a year; my father's bank had an office in the UK, and since my move to Britain he had taken an active interest in supervising the local staff, and came over for regular quick visits. My mother and I would spend the afternoons together while he worked, and then we would all meet for supper. Sometimes my parents came straight to London, but often enough I met them on the continent so that we could all travel together. A few days before breakfast looking across the valley, my mother got sick in Paris.

I will not forget my parents' arrival in Paris that time. My old friend Helen, my brother Freddy, and I had been sitting for at least an hour in the bar at the hotel, waiting. When Helen and I left the bar (we left to see whether my parents had arrived yet, while Freddy went off to the bathroom), there they were. My father was at the front desk discussing the rooms in his familiar way, and my mother was sitting nearby. The reality of my parents' checking in that day is so strong that it overwhelms me: it seems more real to me than anything that has happened since, as though it was the last moment of my own life, as though the life I've been living since is on loan from someone else. My father was standing at the desk, talking to the man at reception. My mother was sitting on a gilded baroque chair. She sat slightly forward – at ease, but poised. She was wearing a pale grey wool suit with a soft off-white silk blouse, and you would never have guessed to look at her that she was at the far end of a long day's travel: she looked as though she were newly dressed to go out to lunch. She had a small square bag, her little travel bag, which she always took on flights, next to her feet. She was wearing shoes with slight heels, and she had crossed her legs at the knee. She was looking up: her hair was set neatly in a twist at the back of her head, and her clear blue eyes were fixed on my father, and that skin of hers, that clear and soft skin pale as titanium, seemed to rest as gently on her high bones as it must have done the day she married him. One hand rested on her lap, holding a blue felt-tip pen, which she absentmindedly clicked open and closed. The other hung over the arm of the chair. She wore little sapphire earrings and a necklace of beaten gold, and on her hand her diamond ring fragmented the neutral hotel light into all its hidden colours.

She was watching my father check in with the particular expression she wore in Paris with my father, an expression of trust, of pleasure in the luxury around her, of certainty and self-assurance, and most of all of love. Every time we went to Paris, she fell in love with us all all over again, and you could see it in the lightness that came to her walk, in her new delight in the same old restaurants and museums, in the way her hair was brushed, and in the particular tenor of her laughter. You could see it in the way she would sustain her energy for long strolls, in the way she would get dressed quickly after her bath and her nap, in how utterly sure of herself she suddenly was and how utterly sure of all of us. My mother always looked younger than she was, in the way of glamorous women, but in Paris she became really young again. I used to feel, there, that I had been given the opportunity to be with my mother as she might have been before I was born, before she was married.

I went to France for that terrible trip planning to have a long-overdue argument with my mother, but when Helen and I came out of the bar the evening my parents arrived, I found all at once that I could have just stood forever, looking at her in that pale grey suit on that gilded chair; it was as though seeing her made me whole. I had grudgingly agreed to go on this holiday to vent my anger, to settle the terrible differences my mother and I were having at that time. But when the moment came, the holiday seemed to stretch in front of me like a piece of music whose delights, obscure on the printed page, become perfectly obvious as soon as you touch the keys. I felt lucky, as lucky as I had always felt in my childhood, when I believed my mother to be the envy of all the children with preoccupied, or plain, or distracted women uncertainly calling their names.

Helen and I paused for a moment, and then my mother turned her head and saw us. 'Harry!' she said, 'and Helen!' as though she were surprised, though no meeting had ever been planned in more detail. And then she smiled, a smile I knew well, a smile that was her particular smile for me, and it was as though the emotion that had been just behind her face while she watched my father checking in came all at once to its surface. We were in a hotel, and it was ten o'clock at night, and so I just walked over to give my mother a kiss on the cheek, but there has never been any meeting in which there was more urgency or delight than there was for me when I crossed the infinite space, up the three stairs, past the concierge, across the front of the elevator, to where my mother sat on her chair, with her square travel bag by her feet. I would like to be able to live in that moment forever. It passed in a few seconds; there was some question about getting the luggage up to the room; my mother asked Helen about her flight; I remembered how angry I was at my mother; she was tired; that particular August day settled in with all its irritations. But for a moment, when I saw my mother, reality itself had stood at bay.

The city in which my mother got sick was one in which I had spent a lot of time on my own. I knew it on foot and by métro as my parents, driven by hotel chauffeurs, could never know it. But Paris remained my mother's city. In my mother's Paris we would devote hours as short as minutes to the roses in the garden of the Musée

4

Rodin, or we would stroll along the Faubourg Saint Honoré and contrast this year's elegance with last year's, or we would sit in the sun (it was always radiant sun in my mother's Paris) in the Place des Vosges and consider Victor Hugo. Sometimes we would go to the Jeu de Paume to look at the heavy apples in the Cézannes, or to lose ourselves in the colours of the water lilies under the Japanese footbridge. At dinner, we would perhaps gaze at the Tuileries from our table at a restaurant untouched by time, our faces dimly lit by the heavy light of candles reflected on an Edwardian ceiling of pleated rose-coloured silk. Oddly, there was never impassable traffic in my mother's Paris; and the French were never rude to us, or even brusque; and the streets were always as clean as though they had been swept in honour of our coming. 'Look,' my mother would say at the end of an evening. 'It's our moon over Vendôme.' In my mother's Paris the moon was always full, the better to cast that fairy-tale light in which we would return to the hotel near midnight.

There was always music in my mother's Paris. Once or twice we were all there when I was performing, and my parents would come to some remote concert hall or church to listen to a recital. Even when I had no such engagements, music seemed to follow us. The piano-player at our favourite bar would recognize us as we came in, and would play the tunes my mother liked best, tunes that I had learned after listening to him, and that I sometimes played for her at home, trying to imitate his light fingerwork and symmetrical arrangements. We knew why he was playing what he was playing, and my mother would shoot him an unforgettable smile; but everyone else assumed he was inspired only by the time of night, the sight of a waiter with four glasses, and the shifting light that drifted through the old glass of the windows. Secret recognition is the best kind of recognition, and my mother's Paris was full of it; it seemed to me that everyone, from the chauffeurs who drove us around town to the vaguely aristocratic men and women who took tea in the hotel garden, turned to pay silent tribute to my mother when they saw her. The city was not so much a place as an eternal coronation.

In my mother's Paris sickness itself seemed aberrant. It was so unlike her to leave a trail of restaurant reservations not claimed, walks not taken, conversations not had. It was out of character for her to suffer in that city, the face of which seemed to say that suffering was gratuitous. In New York we often fought our way through the weeks. In New York it was impossible to pretend that all was pleasure and light. In New York – well, in New York we had raw edges, flashes of anger. In Paris, we regretted nothing; in Paris there was nothing to regret. My mother was never angry in Paris (except, perhaps, if I was very late for an appointment; but that anger soon passed). She was never sad in Paris. She was never overtired after the first two days of jet-lag. She was never tense, or irritable.

When my mother was little, her favourite film was *Love in the Afternoon*, in which a girl has an affair that takes place entirely in a vast suite at the Ritz. My mother dreamed when she was twelve that she would go one day and stay in that suite in that hotel, and when she married my father, he took her there. Is it fair to say that my mother's life, which has sometimes seemed so easy to those who don't know her, was more than half the painstaking realization of a plan nearly perfect for herself and for the rest of us? I think it is. My father provided more than the means; my grandparents might have taken her to the Ritz if there hadn't been a war, and if their taste hadn't led them to other hotels, and if my grandfather hadn't died young, and if a thousand other dramas hadn't interfered. But they didn't take her there, and my father did. Love in the afternoon, love in the morning, love in the evening: that was my mother's dream for herself, and so it became my father's dream for her too, in the end a family dream for our ever-dreaming family. My mother loved the Ritz, where we always stayed, because it was beautiful; but she really loved it because, for her, being there was an affirmation of love itself.

'Well here we all are,' said my father, after he had finished checking in, that first night. He turned to my mother. 'Back in your hotel,' he said.

'My hotel is suffering from threadbare carpets,' my mother replied with a laugh, looking at a worn patch near the stairs. 'But otherwise it seems to be in pretty good shape. Glad to be here?'

We were all glad.

The porter held open the door of the tiny elevator. 'Should we go upstairs?' said my father.

The year my mother became sick, I was not interested in the perfect world of my mother's Paris. She had been so disagreeable about my lover, Bernard, that I had decided to let the family slide altogether. I had long since moved to London; but geographic remove had proved insufficient. She drew my very self from me on the telephone and with occasional postcards and with opinions I could not avoid knowing, whether she voiced them or not. My sleeping with Bernard was an event in her life as much as it was an event in mine, and this was unlivable. I went on that trip to France to sever the ties of our intimacy. I set off to Paris in anger, determined for the first time to act upon anger.

We were five in Paris. My younger brother, Freddy, had in the end *not* brought his girlfriend, Melanie, a short blonde girl with blue eyes, a turned up nose and a blandly chilly manner. She broke up with him – with her star-gazer knack for timing – right before the trip. I suppose that I was not at that time in love, with Bernard or with anyone else, though for purposes of argument I insisted that I was in transports of passion. I still wonder what the true extent of Freddy's devotion was, whether he too had attached himself to the rhetoric of infatuation in part to escape the exhaustion that my mother's attention could engender; but it's more likely that if Freddy said he was in love, it was true. I was, at best, trying to see my life as separate from my mother's, trying for an involvement that was not essentially about her; and though that attempt was a flop, to try at all was something. For Freddy these matters were always easier.

'Calm down, Harry,' Freddy had said to me. 'Just live with Bernard if that's what you want to do. Mom's not going to come over there and try to move you out of his apartment. She hasn't even said she wants you to break up. She just doesn't want to hear about it all the time.'

But I felt that she had to hear about it.

'If you want her to get out of your life, then just talk to her about the weather when she calls,' said Freddy. 'It's not that complicated. I mean, you're in London.'

'But I'm in Bernard's apartment,' I said. 'We see the weather together. I can't edit my conversation all the time. I don't want to live a double life.'

'Everyone leads a double life with their parents,' said Freddy.

For better or for worse, when my mother was planning our trip to the south of France, I was living with Bernard and trying to love him, and Freddy was stepping out with Melanie. Melanie was as much interested in the rest of the family as she was in the theory of special relativity. I disliked that girl partly on my mother's behalf, but I disliked her also for her icy self: it was bipartisan antipathy. Freddy announced that he wanted to bring Melanie along to France, and my mother, aware that one of the two women in Freddy's life was likely to seem small and anxious lest it be she, acceded. Holding fast to her notion that fair was fair (that equality was equivalence), she said that if Freddy was allowed to bring a girl on the trip, I was allowed to bring a girl as well. If I'd had any dignity I would have refused, but I was still proud of my mother's Paris, and so I asked Helen, who had a few months earlier broken off her relationship to a man who worked in film, and was now rather at loose ends. I asked her to come stay at the Ritz, to travel to Saint Paul de Vence, to bear witness to the infinite lightness of our attractive family discourse. I invited her also because I felt that I needed someone on my side for this trip, and that Helen, though she admired my mother, would always be behind me, whether I was right or not.

We all met in Paris. Helen and Freddy and I arrived variously in the course of the afternoon; we were all coming from different countries. Helen and I checked into our room; Freddy was to have his own. We had dinner in the Espadon, at the back of the hotel, and then went for a drink in the bar. I had just been given a contract to make a recording, my first recording, with the label I had most wanted, and I knew how much this would mean to my mother. They were going to let me do the Schubert and the Rachmaninoff; I had signed the contract an hour before leaving. I did not mention this over dinner with Helen and Freddy, nor did I plan to tell my parents that night. In some angry part of my heart, I was considering keeping this success completely secret, to punish them.

'I really hope we aren't going to spend this entire vacation talking about you and Bernard,' Freddy said, picking at his feuilleté. 'I hope you're not going to fight with Mom every day. I have to go back to medical school at the end of this trip, and I want to have a holiday.'

Helen cut him short. 'I think Harry's going to settle whatever he feels he has to settle with your mother, and then he's going to relax for a little while and get a tan and hear some music, and not go spinning out of control. Isn't that true, lambchop?' She turned to me.

'I wasn't planning on spinning out of control,' I said.

'Good,' said Helen, acidly businesslike. 'So, Freddy,' she asked, 'how are you doing? Was it a bad break-up?'

And for the next forty-five minutes we discussed the ins and outs of Freddy's relationship.

And then my parents arrived. My mother had felt odd on the plane, bloated, and wondered, while she unpacked, whether it was just a problem with the cabin pressure. My father thought she should see a doctor (my father believed at that time in doctors). 'Settle whatever it is,' he said. 'Don't spend a week in Saint Paul being uncomfortable.'

'Perhaps it was just the plane, Leonard,' my mother said to him.

My father thought it was best to be sure. 'You've never felt odd on planes before,' he said. 'It was a very smooth flight.'

My mother wavered.

'Better to see a doctor in Paris than to get stuck with a doctor in Saint Paul,' said my father. And while my mother continued unpacking he telephoned friends in Paris and in New York so that he could select a duly qualified physician.

My mother started on that thing she did, ordering flowers and putting out the odds and ends that somehow transformed the place into *her* room. The square travel bag on the desk, and the silk bathrobe thrown over a chair, and the felt-tipped pens and a book on an end table, and the make-up brushes in the bathroom, reflected forever in facing mirrors, and the dry-cleaning papers in the wastebasket, and the little travel clock and the manicure set with two emery boards by the bed, and the great suitcase in the corner – it was all at once ours. Even the smell of bath powder and roses and clean silk blouses conjured home. Other guests who came to stay in that room found only the Louis XV furniture, and never saw how it looked when it was really lived in and full of my mother, how its whole quality changed when, by the end of four days, it was softened further by roses just beginning to drop their petals. My mother had to stop the maids from throwing away those roses; she loved them when they had opened too far and always kept them a day longer than the French staff thought fitting. In fact, that last day of the roses was her favourite.

After my mother had unpacked, my father went downstairs to confirm the week's restaurant reservations and car bookings with the concierge. Freddy was sitting on my mother's bed and she was looking for her reading glasses when Helen and I stood up to say goodnight. We both kissed my mother and Freddy, and then we headed for the door, where we paused for a second while Helen checked to make sure that she had our room key.

'So Freddy,' said my mother in an off-hand way when she heard us opening the door. 'Any news from Melanie?'

Helen looked through her purse.

Freddy squirmed a little bit. 'I talked to her on the phone yesterday,' he said. 'She sounded fine.' You could tell from his voice that he would have liked her to sound any way but fine.

'The fact that she sounded fine doesn't mean that she's feeling that way,' said my mother reassuringly. 'Melanie was always very good at sounding fine.'

'She wasn't – not with me,' said Freddy. 'You had to know her really well to get the other side of her. Sometimes she sounded completely miserable.'

There was a pause.

'Is she still working on lighting design?' asked my mother. 'Is she still working on that same musical – the one with the pig in it?'

'Of course she's doing lighting design,' said Freddy. 'That's what she does, is lighting design.' He began to play with the hotel notepad next to the telephone. 'I don't know whether she's doing that musical anymore. She should have finished it by now. In fact, she should have finished it a month ago. I just don't understand why she let it drift on and on that way. It wasn't such a big project. I could have finished it by now, and I'm busy full time with my own work.'

'Freddy, please stop fiddling with that notepad. I'd like to have it there in case someone calls,' said my mother.

'She's an amazing designer,' said Freddy. 'She's having some kind of a block with that musical, but you know her work is terrific.' He put down the notepad. 'I learned a lot about lights from her. She understood them.' He turned around and saw Helen and me. 'I thought you two were leaving,' he said sharply.

'Yes, Mussolini, we're going,' I said. 'Helen's just looking for our key.'

'You left the key in the living room next door. It's on that end table with the ugly Empire lamp,' my mother said. 'Remember breakfast is at 9.00 sharp. If you come late, you may find your croissants eaten and all the marmalade gone.' Helen and I kissed my mother goodnight again. 'Sleep well,' she said as we left.

We closed the bedroom door. But the voices trailed after us as we stopped in the outer room of the suite to find the key, which was not in fact on the table with the Empire lamp.

'Freddy, you know that Melanie wasn't my kind of person. Insofar as I came to be fond of her, it was because she made you happy and I loved to see you happy. Now that she's making you unhappy, I don't have a lot of affection for her to fall back on, and I won't miss her, not for herself. But – I'm sorry things ended this way, and especially that they ended right now, right before this trip, which I thought could be a really good time for all of us. I want you to know that I admired your loving her, and your loyalty to her. I want you to know that I tried my best to love her too.'

Helen picked up the key, which she had located on another end table. I pretended to be preoccupied with an article in a magazine my father had left in the room. We didn't leave quite yet.

'I know you did, Mom,' said my brother.

'Freddy, each of us loves in his own way,' my mother's voice filtered through the closed door. 'You give to people what you have to give. You can't give them what you don't have. And you gave Melanie everything you had to give. Maybe what you had wasn't right for her, and she needed something else. And maybe you needed to feel loved in a way she wasn't capable of, or that she wasn't capable of sustaining, anyway. Somewhere out there is a girl who wants just exactly what you have to give, and who will give you everything you need. There's someone out there whom you'll make happier than she ever imagined she could be. You'll make each other that happy. Remember what your grandmother used to say? "For every pot, there's a lid." The right person is out there, Freddy, but it takes time.' There was a pause, then my mother's voice again. 'Freddy. You are loving, and kind, and loyal, and very few people have that. It's . . .' her voice drifted off. 'It's the best thing there is, just to be the kind of person you are. Be patient for a little while, and try not to be too sad now. I know it's hard, but it's important too, not to be so sad you miss the other things and the other people life has to offer you.'

'I'll try,' said Freddy.

My mother's voice suddenly rose sharply. 'And would you please also try not to destroy that notepad?' she said. 'I'm sure there are notepads in your room. I'd like to have that one so that I can write down a phone number if I need to. We are no longer seven years old, Freddy.'

Helen and I walked quietly out of the suite and back down to our room.

The day after we arrived in Paris, I went out with Helen and Freddy for a long walk. We had ice cream at Helen's favourite place, and we strolled past Notre Dame. I had bitten my lower lip and had an irritating cut inside my mouth, which the ice cream inflamed. On the Ile Saint Louis we passed a shop selling amusing socks (Helen vetoed the ones with cherubs on them as too amusing), and I bought three pairs for myself and one for Bernard. Then I decided that I was really not feeling my best, and I left Helen and Freddy and headed back to the hotel. I was trying to decide when I would tell everyone about the recording contract, and I was playing the Schubert over and over again in my mind. I wanted to find all the sensation there could ever be in B flat.

I can remember that walk back, the long stretch of the rue de Rivoli before I reached the hotel, my decisions about the Schubert. What I cannot now remember is how or when I heard about the visit to the doctor, which we had all supposed that morning would be a routine business. My mother had had her hair done first thing that day: I do remember that. Then she had gone to the doctor. He had taken her along to the American hospital for a scan. What is unclear is just what I did and when. I can remember being in my room after the ice cream and socks, and standing at the enormous gilded mirror, studying my lower lip and trying to guess how long it would take for it to heal. And then I can remember what came later: my memory picks up around dinner that night. But I have no recollection at all of what came between looking at my lip and dinner, except that I can remember seeing the radiologist's report, which was in French. By the time I saw it, I had been told its gist. I can remember that the verb 'évoquer' was used; the scan, it seemed, could 'évoque une tumeur maligne.' Wildly, I told my parents – my French was better than theirs – that the verb 'évoquer' referred to the most remote possibility. I knew that there was some kind of mistake, and I wanted to protect my mother from it. This was, fortunately, not out of keeping with what the doctor had said; he thought it most unlikely that there was actually a cancer. 'One would feel better,' he had said, 'if one had a look inside to see. It is the most ordinary kind of surgery.' My mother would have to return to New York. It was Saturday, and the afternoon was gone. There was no point leaving before the early plane Monday morning, which would get her to New York at 8.30 a.m.

So we had thirty-six hours to spend all together, that first thirty-six hours of fear and sadness. How strange it is, though, that I can't recall the moment when my father (it would have been my father who would tell) actually said that my mother might have cancer. Was I alone with him? With him and my mother? Were Helen and Freddy back from their walk by then? Were we in my parents' suite? Some of the memories of those thirty-six hours are shaky; some are missing altogether; and some are too clear, so photographically clear that they seem not like memories but like the images that replace memories in the mind. Some moments from those thirty-six hours I have described so many times that I have no real hold on them at all, but there are others of which I have never spoken. That day my mother refused the offers Freddy and I made to go with her and my father. 'The surgery is very simple. There's no need for you to come home; you could all use a vacation. So long as it's not cancer, I'll be fine. But if this turns out to be cancer – then I'm going to need you by my side. If that happens, get on the first plane.' I remember like a series of snapshots our dinner that night at a modern restaurant that was just coming into fashion. It was August and so the usual favourites were all closed. I had heard of but never been to this one, and my mother had chosen it in part as a treat for me. I have never been there since. Someday, I may go back to bring to life the very memories that I now wish I could escape, but not this year, and not next year. That evening, the cut on my lip was so painful that I could hardly eat. I remember it all flat, all in two dimensions. I have no idea what we talked about.

I think I called Bernard that night when I got back to the hotel. He was his usual sensible self, and advised me not to worry. Like my father, Bernard was always sure things would be fine. Helen, though she dutifully said that these upsets were routine, clearly feared the worst. She and I lay in our separate beds in our large beautiful room; I hardly slept at all, and she seemed to toss and turn all night.

Sunday is as vivid in my mind as Saturday is confused. I can remember waking up to the fact of my mother's illness, and a strained room-service breakfast with Helen. That day my mother wore a shell-pink suit and a white blouse with a thousand little

flowers on it in shades of pale pink. The blouse looked like a
Monet painting. She wore shoes with small buckles. We had
a driver, one of those handsome young Ritz drivers, who told us
that he was really working in video production (though he gave
every appearance of really working as a driver for the hotel), and
we drew him out at some length on the subject of French video.
We were going to lunch at another lovely restaurant, another
landmark of my mother's Paris. It was a beautiful day, a day of
perfect Paris weather, the air warm, the breeze light, the sun clear.
We were meeting a Parisian friend of mine for lunch. My mother
was in a mood that being with my friends often brought out in
her, a philosophic mood of trenchant generalities.

'It's so hard to understand at your age,' she said to my friend, à
propos of nothing in particular. 'When you're in your twenties, so
many things seem exciting, or seem like fun, and then when you
try to hold onto them they fall apart. There are so few structures
that really last.'

This was the first in a series of remarks to other people that
were abstractly stirring in principle but that were in fact intended
to communicate to me my mother's discontent with my life with
Bernard and her belief that I was destroying all my chances of
future happiness. Her inkling that a disaster of her own was
impending seemed to make her more urgent in this communi-
cation than she had been previously; I wished that the portents
had distracted her from Bernard instead of making her focus on
him. I wanted to feel only affection for her in our moment of crisis,
and she was making it extremely difficult. She and Freddy had
somehow become closer as a result of his break-up with Melanie,
and I felt that she and I were drifting farther and farther apart. My
response to her conversation at lunch that day was a mix of
fondness for the particular mode employed, a mode I associated
with my mother at her wisest and most beguiling, and irritation (I
was not keyed up enough for rage) at her inability to accept that
all happiness for all people does not spring from a single maze of
roots.

'I think,' my mother said, with a tone of authority that made it
clear that what she thought was what other people of insight

would also think, 'that what you want early in life is different from what you want later, and that happiness comes of understanding early what you will want later, and finding it.' She ate a few bites of her salmon (my mother never liked fish much) and looked through the glass at the Bois de Boulogne. The meticulous waiters served the food on large plates. The vegetables were laid out in patterns as colourful and intricate as the plan du métro. I had duck. Freddy had lamb. Helen and my father both had monkfish. My Parisian friend had sweetbreads. I had been to this place for lunch with my mother on a dozen previous occasions, but I noticed as though for the first time how fresh the bunches of white roses and freesia on every table were, how enchanting the view of the Bois. I noticed the afternoon sun and the elegant cut of the waiters' uniforms. I took in what each of us was wearing, the way my mother's hair was brushed, how her hand lay on the table – I noticed then, though I was of course both nettled and frightened, how perfect it all was.

I can tell you in a sentence that my mother was dying, and in a way there is nothing more to be said about that. Or I can tell you every detail, and try to give you the quality of that lovely terrible Sunday and of the other days like it that were to become our way of life. To us they were vital days, their details immemorial. My father expected everyone to understand at once that my mother was more important than anyone else, that her suffering was more terrible. I didn't expect the doctors to understand that; I didn't expect headwaiters to defer to her on that basis; I didn't expect everyone who came to our parties to notice it. But at some useless level I was as much in the habit of believing it as he was. And in this we were fools. Illness is not the great equalizer, but it is a seven-league step in that direction.

When we finished lunch, we went for a stroll in the Bois. We made a little pilgrimage to admire my father's favourite copper beech (my father has favourite trees in parks across Europe). We talked, as always, about how over-trimmed French parks are, and my mother said how she always wanted to bring children into the Bois and send them running across all those prim lawns. We wondered at the well-behaved twins with a nurse walking ahead of us, stopping to admire the beds but never touching them.

My mother made plans for us for the rest of the afternoon. I had for some reason never been to Malmaison, so we had our driver take us there, and we sat in the little front garden. Freddy said he had not been to Versailles since his childhood. So we drove to Versailles, partly because of that, but also because my mother wanted to go and visit the Trianon, which she had always loved. Freddy and Helen and I walked across the lawn to look at the building from a distance, and when we reached an optimal vantage point, I turned around to see my parents standing in a measureless expanse of green beside a quick swirl of pink palace at the edge of the limitless woods of Versailles. My mother had put on a pair of large blue sunglasses and I was horribly struck by the picture of her, looking tiny and fragile, next to my father – in the perfect sunshine, with all the laughing thousands who had come to Versailles on a radiant Sunday. The pink of the Trianon is my mother's favourite colour; standing in front of that building, itself so pale and delicate, she looked like a shadow puppet made of paper. She waved; then she turned around and looked up at the folly. I thought of her careful memory focusing for a last view of something she had always visited on happy days. The shock of our situation had settled once over dinner that first night, and then it had withdrawn again. Now it settled once more. How could my mother have become so small so fast?

We drove back to the hotel in almost unbroken silence, and when we arrived we stopped at the Vendôme bar, where I had sat two days earlier with Helen and Freddy. Now, as we tried to get a waiter, I noticed how ridiculous the harpist was, and how ugly the brown velveteen on the walls. My mother sat holding her sunglasses. We discussed the logistics of her flight and of the visit Freddy and Helen and I would make to the south of France. My mother tried to tell us all the things she had planned to tell us bit by bit during the week, her private anecdotes of the Côte d'Azur. She described the hotel where she had stayed in Nice when she was twenty, and told a story about Picasso and a needlepoint pillow. Then Helen went up to the room for a minute, and Freddy and my father stopped by the front desk, and I was left alone in the bar with my mother. She said, 'In a real way, today may have been the last day of my life as I know it.' I dissembled, but she put a hand on my arm. Then she said, clearly and urgently, in the new voice she would make so entirely her own over the following months, 'Whatever happens to me, whatever this illness may do to me, however grumpy or difficult or unpleasant I become, I want you to promise that you and Freddy will always remember me as I have been until today.'

I had not noticed until then that our fixed emotions can perish as easily as new ones; nor had I noticed how changes can without warning violate what we love in ourselves. That request forced all the emotions one associates with an actual death: I instantly found myself searching for things to hold on to, trying to locate how I would remember her, snatching at the odd episodes that had stuck from early childhood. And I found, to my surprise and horror, that I had almost no memories at all, and that the ones I had were meaningless – memories of houses and hotels and restaurants, a few freeze-frames of her in conversation, a chance image of her waiting for me to come home from school or materializing for a visit at summer camp – but none of my mother fully herself. I felt the most terrible emptiness, of having made too little effort, of having lost what should have been my mind's pictures.

I knew of course how much of my life (even Bernard, even the piano) had to do with acceptance and rejection of what she represented to me – and I realized that to lose her would be to lose my reasons for most of what I did. When I looked for concrete memories, though, I came up with paper-thin images just of how pleasant our lives had been, of nothing more than the pleasantness; and I knew that our lives were something other than that, something at once more and less than that. 'Promise you will always remember me as I have been until today,' she said, as though there were one way she had always been, a simple way, a snapshot thing to remember – and my mind was cluttered with bits of long-vanished clothing and songs we had sung when I was six. Then suddenly I thought that if she died I would also have to die, that I would not know how to stay alive without her. I thought that I could no more readily conjure token memories of her than I could such token images of myself. By the time my father came back from the front desk with the confirmed tickets, it was he, and not my mother, who seemed like a visitor from some distant corner of memory.

Later on Sunday the world settled back into place. In my parents' suite we ordered an odd hodgepodge of dinner from room service, a mix of breakfast food and lunch food and dinner food. Sleek and efficient, the waiters brought it all in on a rolling table, pulled out the table's leaves, arranged the cerise-and-white floral china, and pulled over chairs. Each time one of the glasses touched another, a perfect note would sound, which the waiters would quickly arrest with their long fingers, as though in mystic regard for silence. We sat on the other side of the room while this was going on, pretending not to notice, and talked vaguely about the weather.

When the waiters had gone out, we all sat down, and for a moment there was the bustling sound of napkins being unfolded and glasses of wine being poured and people asking for the salt and all those slight room-service negotiations about whose glass of water was whose and whether the bread would fit between Freddy and me and whether we really needed to have the teacups on the table at the same time as the salad. My mother commented on how pretty it all looked. 'Wouldn't it be wonderful to have someone at home who could wheel in a table like this, flowers and all, at fifteen minutes' notice?' she said. 'Someone who would then come back and wheel it out when you got through, and you wouldn't have to think about any of the food or the dishes again?'

'Nice flowers,' I said. 'Nice plates. Nice silverware.'

My mother looked for a moment and then held up a fork. 'Do you like the silver?' she asked. 'I think it's heavy-looking. Hotel silver. It doesn't smile at you.'

'Does our silver at home smile at you?' my father asked.

'Of course, Leonard,' she said. 'It smiles at you and says, "Pick me up." Haven't you ever noticed?'

'Does Grandma's silver say, "Pick me up?" ' I asked. I had inherited my grandmother's silver two years earlier.

'Grandma's silver says it, but very quietly,' said my mother.

And somehow from then on we flew, telling each other all the stories that the plates and glasses and forks and knives had confided to us over the years, and my father repeated the anecdote that one of the red glass plates had told him about my Great Aunt Elizabeth, and the evening wove itself into fantasy and hilarity, so that in the end we left behind the terror of the day. Freddy took the part of the dish that ran away with the spoon, and I was a champagne flute, and my father was the blue teapot, and my mother was the two silver candlesticks with the curving feet that had stood in the middle of the dining room table all my life. Helen played along effortlessly. In this state, one short of dreaming, my family passed an evening as bright as any we had ever had together. With Helen half participant and half audience, we felt once more unassailable, and the mortality lingering over our heads seemed as remote as mortality had always seemed.

Though it embarrasses me to admit it, I was distracted throughout by the cut on my lower lip, which was so immediately and maddeningly and constantly painful that I could not really focus much on anyone else's complaints. These defences are conveniently on hand in the face of tragedy, and they countermand it, allowing us to stay in the comfortable world of detail, safe as room service. I also felt that I had my news about the recording contract, and that there might not be another appropriate moment for it, and I kept wondering whether I should interject it somewhere. The Schubert and the Rachmaninoff. But I didn't say a word.

Monday morning, like all mornings, is a blur. My parents caught their plane. I hugged my mother. We all agreed that she would certainly be all right. And then came the dream-trip for Freddy and Helen and me, another two days of Paris and then the south of France. You must understand how my mother planned our family trips. Everything was always laid out in painstaking detail, every restaurant reservation made, every route worked out. 'What shall we do today?' Freddy would say over breakfast in Saint Paul. 'I want to swim.'

I was guardian of the order. 'It'll have to be the pool,' I would say. 'The ocean's not on today. Today we're seeing the Matisses, and then in the afternoon we're going to see Cocteau's house, with the big murals and the garden. I want to take a look at the church there where they do concerts; I might come back and play here next summer. The car's due at 10.00, and lunch is being packed; there's supposed to be a lovely place where we can stop for a picnic just past the valley. And at some point I've got to practice for a couple of hours. Maybe at the end of the afternoon? You two could swim then.'

Freddy would glower, and Helen would make peace. Each day fell into a sort of inner coherence on the basis of the arrangements. Wednesday was clearly the day to go down to the sea: a boat had been arranged to take us to a particularly charming and inaccessible cove, and we could have lunch at a café in a nearby village. In the afternoon, there was time to swim at the beach. Dinner was to be at the hotel since the schedule was rather an exhausting one. Thursday we needed to go to a particular museum because we had a lunch reservation near it, and the lunch reservation was for 1.00 because the museum was open in the mornings from 10.00 to 12.30. In the evenings, to prove our independence, we sometimes did other things: once we drove to a local theatre and saw an American police film, with a lot of exploding vehicles, dubbed into French.

My practising time, like everything else, seemed to have been scheduled, and there was not enough of it. I could not get up and play at night, as was my wont, because I would have woken the other hotel guests. If the french doors to our room were open, I felt that people were stopping to listen to me, and this was somewhat frustrating; I tended to get exhibitionist, and did not work on the new pieces I needed to master. If the doors were closed, the room became suffocating. Helen had nowhere to go but Freddy's room while I was playing, and she sometimes got peevish. 'That

Schubert's lovely,' she said to me. 'But if I have to listen to the first movement again this week, I'm going to go stark raving mad.' I had still not told her about the recording contract, and could not explain why the Schubert was so urgent.

There was no way that we could transform the holiday into the sort that Freddy, Helen and I might have worked out for ourselves, because it was not that sort of holiday in any of its most fundamental components, and it was not subject to our regulation. We were staying in a château outside Saint Paul de Vence, one of those places striking for its irreproachable lack of ostentation. We had rooms painted very white, almost monastic in their simplicity, except that they were always full of flowers, and our rooms shared a private lawn, which commanded a view across the valley and the town of Saint Paul and on toward the sea. It was on this lawn that we had breakfast every morning, surrounded by the discreet sumptuousness that my mother loved so much.

We called home each day, and with each new test that was performed it seemed more and more likely that my mother was going to be fine. The suspense all led up to Thursday, when they would do the surgery. We spent Thursday at the scheduled museum, and then ate the scheduled lunch. It was one of those days when the weather was unduly heavy, like a tarpaulin over one's senses, and I remember feeling exhausted and numb and anxious. Then too, I was overwhelmed by that belief, which so often sets in at a moment of crisis, in one's own ability to influence fate by dint of the pettiest of actions. So I ritualized every footstep, every bite of food, every breath, every remark, every passing image of desire. We ate lunch on the terrace of the restaurant, with the playing fountains, and wondered whether the rain would come. Then we drove back to the hotel, where a problem on the telephone lines made it very difficult to get through to America. Perhaps half an hour went by while we got recordings in French and recordings in English, and then finally we reached my father.

Only after he said that it was cancer did I realize how fundamentally I had persuaded myself that it would not be. My mother had a cancerous cyst in her abdomen, and the disease had spread into certain internal membranes. The tumor had been removed, along with various expendable bits of anatomy, but it was not possible to remove enough of my mother, and so chemotherapy was prescribed as the only way to deal with the spread of the disease, a spreading not of what is fittingly called gross tumor, but of tiny pinpoints of malignancy. We did not know how high the chances were that the cancer would be entirely eliminated. We were all stuck on the word 'cancer', as though its consonants and vowels were the razor spikes of a barbed-wire fence that ran between us and how we had been. It was a word too full of obvious drama, like a bad TV movie, like a modern version of grand opera – and my mother, musical though she was in general, hated grand opera. 'All those maudlin women shrieking endlessly before they die,' she used to say. 'So implausible and so tedious.' The chemotherapy was scheduled to occupy nine months, and we were told that it would make my mother very sick for a week or so each month when it was administered. We also learned that it would make her lose her hair.

There is a fine line between tension and emotion; an excess of one can eliminate the capacity for the other. I had been so anxious for so long about the result of that test that I could feel only a sense of sorrow, not so much sorrow about the specific fact of cancer as sorrow that the irresolution was going to continue. It was like tumbling into something open and endless. For at least an hour Freddy and Helen and I all sat still in our hotel room, stiff on our chairs, staring at the ceiling and having nothing very much to say to one another, because there is nothing much to say about disease. After that, we booked our tickets to go home as quickly as possible – there were no flights until the morning – and packed our bags. Then we found ourselves once more in our rooms, and I did not want to play the piano, and it struck me as altogether intolerable to sit for another minute staring at those walls.

I had always wanted to go to Monte Carlo. It comes up in conversation a lot, and you always feel that you should have been there, if only so that you too can dismiss it rather casually. Also, I have a sort of mental checklist of European countries. I have yet to visit Belgium, Luxembourg, Finland or Norway. Or Andorra. I don't know why these should be the gaps, except Andorra, which

I think most people visit only if they keep mental checklists of this kind. To come so close to ticking off Monaco and miss it would have been a shame. It was a destination that offered itself, and the night was too long in front of us, and so we went. We had promised my mother, who feared the roads, that we would not drive to Monaco after dark – how odd it was to betray her at that moment.

It was the strangest of night journeys, driving out on the lowest Corniche and back on the middle Corniche. There is a geography that holds us forever in our places, that makes us feel clearly the size and scale of human life itself, and the views of that drive – the land and the sea and the sky in geometric monochrome balance – seemed to sharpen all our senses and to remind us of ourselves. On the way to Monte Carlo Freddy drove and I navigated and Helen was in the back seat; on the return trip, Helen drove and I navigated and Freddy dozed uneasily. It was a clear night, and mostly we could see only the sea stretching away from us. By night, Monte Carlo looks like an opera set, up against the water, spotlessly clean, busy with all-too-worldly figures rushing through lives of what the imaginative tourist suspects to be sordid extravagance. In fact, it seems also as pleasantly middle-class as a suburb. We parked the car and went to the casino, where everything had been gilded and carved and brocaded to the point of shapelessness. We walked through, the three of us, passing judgment: on the overly spectacular interior, on the over-dressed gamblers, on the over-tired croupiers. Afterwards, we went to an overcrowded café with an apricot-coloured post-modernist canopy covering the tables, and watched a light rain falling through the fairy-tale lights of the casino and the fountain in front of it.

We all felt guilty for being out in a city of lights and fashions, but though we talked without a break about my mother, and though I found myself lapsing horribly into the past tense as I spoke about her, we also felt reassured somehow by the palpable evidence around us that the world goes on. We adduced that we too would go on; we proved to ourselves that this was not the end. It was not the eternal ocean that told us that; it was the bright lights, the absurd clothes, and the chocolate ice cream in the café.

The next day, Friday, Freddy and I caught the morning plane, and headed for home.

Is the picture I have started here entirely accurate? Perhaps I was angrier that week than I remember, but I think in fact that when I first saw that my mother might be sick, my anger got put away somewhere, and my mother became as glorious to me as she had been in my childhood. Though I had gone to France to sever ties, I knew that I could not squander what might be a limited time on undermining a perishable intimacy. In fact, my mother was not always exactly as she would have wanted – even her control did not run so far – but she was always striving to be as she would have wanted, and it is really too late to take her to task for her occasional lapses from grace. In the first weeks of her illness, my mother was to reveal more clearly her terrible brutality. She could be harsh, and she was demanding, and she could be selfish. I will tell you about these things, because my mother's love, like any love, came at a price – but that is not to say that it was a compromised love.

Her world rose and fell by me: for I was as vast to my mother as she was to me. My mother wanted me to have a perfect life, more perfect even than hers, because she sincerely believed that the surest way to be happy was to be perfect. That is why she was so embattled about Bernard before she got sick: he was, to her mind, an imperfection in human form. Though I often disappointed my mother with my irregularities, she believed that I had what it would take to be perfect, and pushed me toward it. God knows the agenda is an absurd one; the battle for perfection that occupied so much of my energy and of my mother's is obviously a losing one. But I would not know how to give it up – or, at least, I would not have known then.

II

Home Again

I should tell you, for the sake of honesty, that I believed from the start that my mother would die of her cancer, though I held off that belief so vigorously that some of the time it seemed to recede, almost to vanish. I think that she too believed, most of the time, that she would die. How did we get back to New York from France? How indeed? How did we get from my mother's straight-forward life to the world as it is now? The processes that the mind cannot conceive before their time often prove to be as simple and as gradual as the summer twilight that unfolded outside my mother's hospital room every day of that first hospital week.

I knew as a child that my father would live forever: he is made of the stuff of tree trunks and of great lakes, of the things that last. And my father was never in a rush. I don't mean that he wasn't occasionally eager to get to the office, or hasty getting dressed to go out for dinner; I can say without hesitation that he from time to time looked forward to the weekend or to a holiday. But at some more fundamental level, he always had his leisure, world enough to do whatever he was doing; he made me feel that time itself was an ordinary thing, as eternally replaceable as the food we ate and took for granted. My mother, however, for all her strength of will, was as fragile as a new leaf, as indeterminate as a flame; it always seemed to me that she could no more linger in the world than a soap bubble can stay on the air. Many the hour she would devote to her long baths, many the quiet day, many the leisured walk on a spring afternoon; she scheduled her time well enough so that she was never late for an appointment, never hurrying (as I am always hurrying) to meet someone or to get somewhere. She did not (as I do) oversleep and then dress in a haste, did not underestimate the number of hours needed for transportation, did not make more plans than she could manage. But she lived life with the particular, careful, slow hunger with which you might approach the last dessert on earth. She held onto every moment as though it were the final one; she did not race through any given day, but, unlike my father, she rushed to have all the experiences of her life before it was too late.

'You've got to keep up with life,' she said to me more than once. 'It runs away from you.'

'Well, I guess so,' I said, 'but sometimes you've got to stop and enjoy whatever you've done.'

'That's part of life, part of what you're keeping up with,' said my mother. 'But what you can't do is to sit back and get distracted and let the world pass you by. There's not enough time for that. Stop long enough to make your experiences your own, but don't get so lost among them that you miss everything else. And don't end up having them alone.'

Freddy and I flew from Nice through London, and Bernard came to Heathrow with a suitcase he had packed for me. Though I felt already that he was a stranger, I held him tighter for that. I didn't know when or how I would see him again; I didn't know what place he held in this new world order to which I, too, was a stranger. When the fixed centre of your life comes under siege, you scurry around collecting all the other love there is, hoping that in some great balance the fragmentary affections will add up to more than the monolith one. It doesn't work; Bernard had never been a great love, and in the vacuum of my mother's illness he was altogether weightless.

But he and I stood at the airport like two overgrown boys, and Freddy looked at once jealous and embarrassed. 'We'd better go or we'll be late for the plane,' Freddy said nervously.

Bernard held my chin in his hand for a moment. 'It's all going to be fine,' he said. I might have preferred it if he had said, 'I love you,' but though Bernard had said that in the past, it was not a remark that he produced under pressure.

'How fine can it be?' I asked, and Bernard shrugged helplessly. He would have liked to reassure me.

'I'm sorry, but we're going to be late,' Freddy said, and pulled on my sleeve.

'I'll come back as soon as I can,' I promised Bernard.

'I'll be here,' he said. 'Call me when you land.' And he kissed me very gently on the forehead.

Then Freddy and I headed off through passport control, and in the dim grey light we set off for New York. It was in the same dim grey light that we arrived in New York. My father had sent Robert with the car. My indecisive luggage (how long was I staying? what would I need? what seasons might pass before I found myself back in London, able to pack again?) was piled in the trunk along with Freddy's two bags, and we set off toward Manhattan.

We stopped at home, at my parents' apartment, to drop off our things before settling in at the hospital. When we came in, Molly started barking; she greeted Freddy first, and then me, nearly knocking us over in her enthusiasm. Janet was dusting the chest in the front hall. 'Your mother's in the hospital,' Janet said in a half-whisper, as though we might not have known. We kissed her hello; Freddy started to haul the luggage back to the bedrooms.

'I'm so worried about her,' Janet said to me. 'I just hope she's OK. I keep on thinking about her and worrying and this house feels so strange without her here. I mean, she's gone on vacation before, but this is different.'

'We're all worried about her, Janet, but I think she's going to be OK,' I said. 'I certainly hope so.'

Janet stood and polished the top of the front hall chest, turning the cloth over and over. Then she turned around and dusted a Japanese bowl with a heron painted on it.

'She's expecting Freddy and me at the hospital,' I said. 'We're running, but I'll see you later, Janet, or maybe tomorrow – I guess we'll be there most of the day. Could you make sure there are fresh sheets in my room and Freddy's, and fresh towels?'

Molly, who had padded off toward the living room, chose this moment to rush at Janet's ankles, and the fate of the Japanese bowl was briefly endangered; but years of experience stood Janet in good stead.

'Even the dog is acting peculiar,' Janet said. 'The towels and all are there. As soon as your father said there was bad news and that you boys were coming home. Listen, tell your mother I want to come see her. Tell her I keep thinking about how she came to see me after my accident. You remember that?' I remembered. I could hear Freddy running water in his bathroom. There wasn't really time for a long conversation. 'There I was in that hospital the day *after* I fell,' Janet said, 'lying flat out, and I couldn't even get out of my bed. So I asked one of the other women to call your mother to tell her I wasn't going to be at work. And your mother, she got right in the car and came out to that place to see me. Right then, at eight o'clock in the morning. I'll never forget it, when she came into that room, and everyone turned around to stare at her, and she walked straight over to me. "Janet," she said. "How are you feeling?" '

'I remember, Janet,' I said.

'That day they gave me some different doctor and moved me to another room. And do you know your mother came to see me every single day the whole two weeks I was in there? She didn't stay too long, but she was there every single day, regular as clockwork, eleven o'clock in the morning. "You're looking a bit better today, Janet," she'd say. Always with some flowers or a piece of fresh fruit, and once with one of those chocolate chip cakes you all eat in the summer. And now she's in the hospital and your father told me not to go see her. But if she's there and so sick and all, it makes me feel terrible, not going.'

'She's under a lot of stress right now, but I'm sure she'd be very pleased if you came to visit in a day or two,' I said. 'She's very fond of you.' I remembered all that dragging to the hospital. 'You can't imagine,' my mother had said, 'how they take advantage of people like Janet in those places.' My father had shrugged. 'Still,' he had said. 'Every day.'

Janet's was the first of dozens of such monologues that were to come. Upon hearing about my mother's cancer, people would dig out tales of generosity, episodes, as often as not, that my mother herself had forgotten. It was a kind of automatic response built on authentic detail. Acquaintances, shop assistants, the doormen in our building, the man who sold vegetables at the store on Third Avenue, the woman who set her hair – everyone seemed to have an anecdote of benevolence. They recounted these partly to be polite, I suppose, but their stories were not fictive, and they were always moving to me. Within the family, and even among close friends, there were more complicated stories to tell, but in the hearts and minds of that world where she had busied herself from day to day, there seemed, at least in the face of her suffering, to be no end of noble recollections.

'All my friends,' Janet went on, 'are praying for your mother. In my church last week, we all prayed together for her. You know she's never yelled at me, not once in twenty-six years.' Janet put down the heron bowl and returned to the chest. 'Tell her I'm keeping everything just the way she likes it here. Tell her I've even been keeping some roses in that glass bowl by her bed, just the way she likes them. You tell her everything's just fine here, in case she's worrying.'

The phone rang, and I answered it. It was my mother, her voice as raw and ulcerated as though it too had been cut up with a scalpel. 'What are you doing there?' she screamed down the line. I tried to explain. 'Why are you fussing with the luggage? I thought you were coming straight to the hospital. I thought you would be here by now.' In my mind's eye she was not really in a hospital, and there was no bad news, and that urgent tone of voice was a little bit ridiculous. I persisted in imagining how I would tell her what a fright she had given us; in fact, in this past year, even, I have gone on sketching for myself how I would have narrated my anxiety at the false alarm. There is too much that is false in the world of illness, so much that is false that the less-than-watchful eye may never notice anything real at all. My mother was already angry at us for stopping at the apartment, but was it real anger? Was it at us? Later, I figured out just how angry she was.

I was born blond. I have thin, silky hair, straight on clear days and softly curling on damp days. I was born (so my mother used to say) with roses in my cheeks and blue eyes and the kind of hair not brown enough to make me brown-haired. As I grew up, my hair faded into dullness. And so I, to make my hair consistent with my personality and the rest of my colouring, used, when we were in someplace warm and sunny, to comb the juice of lemons through my hair to turn it gold. I was as full of wonder, in the face of this, as the king for whom Rumpelstiltskin had done his spinning, and I watched and studied my own hair with an obsessive fascination, seeking out new traces of the colours with which I had been born, and to which I believed myself to be entitled.

My mother was almost the only one who noticed these gradual changes, so slight they could hardly be credited to more than the sun itself. I never made it past the slightest hints of blond, but my mother hated it. She couldn't bear the idea of my vanity, though if someone had taught me this personal vanity it must have been my mother, who was forever discussing with me what clothes to wear and how to wear them, and how to get my hair cut, and how to stand up, and how to eat, and even how lucky I was to have eyes as blue as the royal navy. I do not believe it was the colour my hair turned that caused my mother so much dismay. Let us be quite honest: so far as my mother was concerned, my combing lemon juice through my hair was much the same as my sleeping with Bernard. One of these things implied the other, and, taken together, they were intolerable.

Freddy and I ran to the hospital. Or rather, we had Robert drive us to the hospital, and then we ran through its tentacular corridors straight to the room where my mother lay. We walked into the room with our love in our hands and found my mother the colour of typing paper, with her hair (it was almost the end for her hair) in slight disarray. My father was on a chair next to her bed, holding a hand as limp as if she were asleep. 'Boys!' she said, turning to us, and looking with an unflinching gaze of bewilderment. The harshness had been seeped out of her voice. So much of my hope was pinned on that moment; my father had said that my mother's misery was unyielding, but I imagined that I could break it down or penetrate it, that the very fact of me might somehow bring my mother back from the strange place where she had gone. She turned and looked out the window. 'Hello Freddy. Hello Harry,' she said. We went over to kiss her and she presented an unmoving and unresponsive face. 'Thank you for coming,' she said vaguely to Freddy, as though he were a dignitary on a state visit. She looked at me expressionlessly, and then her face suddenly darkened. 'Oh, Harry,' she said. 'Oh, Harry. What have you done to your hair?' I reached up to touch my hair, which I had encouraged with lemons just at bit in the château in Saint Paul. 'Oh, Harry,' said my mother. 'You promised me, promised me, promised me that you wouldn't do that to your hair.' And my mother began to weep, in a slow steady way, the tears seeming gradually to push one another out of her eyes. My mother turned her head so that she would not have to look, and though I tried to move into her line of sight to apologize, or to explain, or to say anything, she kept pivoting and would not speak to me.

'It's OK,' said Freddy.

'It's all going to be fine,' said my father.

And my mother looked back and forth between them and kept her gaze locked away from me.

I cannot quite remember how many of the flowers that were to arrive had shown up at that point. By the time my mother was ready to go home, there were more than a hundred arrangements in the room. Her private nurses, who had tended film stars and heads of state, said that never in their lives had they seen so many flowers. It was almost like being in a formal garden: the vases were crowded together, at first along the walls and the window-sill, and later in double and triple columns, so that you had to pick your way among them on narrow paths of linoleum. My mother, who had always adored flowers, said that the number of them, all cut, all about to die, was absolutely nauseating, and she kept having them cleared out and distributed to patients in other wards. 'The smell,' she said, though the rich perfume in fact was barely sufficient to kill the disinfectant rankness of that room. 'The smell of all those stems rotting in water is revolting.'

My mother was in the hospital, that time, for a week. She grew accustomed to my hair, but she was not nice about it. 'I came so far to see you,' I said, 'so far, so quickly. The least you could do is to look at me.' Or else I said, 'I love you. What difference does my hair make?'

And she said, 'If you loved me, you wouldn't have done that to yourself.' And then I would get angry, and my mother would stare out the window, as if it were all just too much for her.

'Would you like me to get some brown dye and dye my hair brown?' I asked, and then my mother looked at me dully and repeated, as though I were a slightly retarded child, 'Do not dye your hair. Men do not dye their hair. Just leave your hair alone.'

I do not remember at what stage my mother accused me of giving her cancer. The episode was not so long ago; this forgetfulness is not like my inability to remember events of my early childhood. It's more that what she said was so sharp and so petrifying that it has frozen itself into words to which there is no chronology. I can remember a dozen subsequent related conversations, complete with their time and place. I can remember how, later, she apologized. That first conversation, though, eludes me. If I'm to be honest, I think part of the reason I cannot remember my mother's first accusing me is that she accused me only of what I already suspected to be true.

I can remember thinking when I was still quite young, and the idea of desiring men had all the terrifying resonance of novelty to it, that I could do nothing more terrible to my mother than to experience and act on those desires. 'How could she have let you grow up thinking that?' asked Helen, later, but I don't know that my mother had chosen her horror any more than I had chosen my desires; and if her phobia was terrible for me, I accepted that it was probably no worse than my sexuality was for her. I can remember days when I had angered her, when she would complain at me in flushes of passionate rage – I can remember that this secret was my unacknowledged revenge on her. I would lie in the silence of my own room and imagine the pain I would later cause my mother, and I would exult in the appalling longings, in which, for all that I too hated them, there was power such as I had never before known. I believed at an early age that I could destroy her life; I had thought that I would use my desire someday to punish her. But I did not quite suppose that it could kill her. I thought of it as modern war-makers think of the most powerful weapons in their arsenals, as something too terrible to call forth, as something whose very existence could be the basis for an uneasy peace, as a device the precise effects of which were too complex and unspeakable to predict, too frightening even for secret tests on barren plains.

It was part of the love my mother and I had for each other to bruise each other, part of my love to plot injuries that, by and large, I did not inflict. But the most terrible injury of all, at the very prospect of which I had trembled, was one I could not help inflicting in the long run. By the time I talked about these matters to my mother, I wanted not to hurt her. I wanted somehow to take the unspeakable vengeance I had early recognized and make it sound like bliss, to show her a love as beguiling as my interpretations of Schubert. I wanted to be as perfect as one of my mother's holidays or parties, blighted by nothing more than the chance misfortunes of the weather, of a guest's cancelling at the last minute, of a slight argument among friends. If she could not see Bernard as an 'A' on a report card in a key subject, I thought she might be able to see such love as a 'B+,' something far away from her, not quite what one might have wanted, perhaps, but really perfectly all right in the midst of all those other high grades and music prizes.

I could not – for many reasons – explain to her how much more effort, how much more battle and agony, had gone into what she saw as my great failure than had gone into the many things she saw as my successes, how much harder it was for me to live with Bernard than for me to play Liszt. My relationship with Bernard was a triumph. What might my mother have said to other tales, to the real narratives of loneliness that lay between those angry afternoons when I was fourteen and my discovery of Bernard when I was twenty-four? If I had really wanted vengeance on my mother – but by then, that was the last thing I wanted – I would have told her all the insipid and hackneyed details of one-night stands in which affection was less of a consideration than disease and the grim prospect of attack. I would have narrated the anonymous encounters with strangers in which there was no correlation between pleasure and joy. I would have spoken of meeting men of every class and proclivity, sometimes four or five in a single day, in locations as dangerous and ugly as the Ritz was beautiful, of occasionally being hit, of occasionally hitting someone back. I would have described hiding from the police when their approach had interrupted a fitful spasm in the arms of some aging and mild-mannered sadist in a public park, trembling half-naked behind a scruffy shrub and trying to be as still as in a childhood game of hide-and-seek. I would have told her how unthinkingly and casually I gave myself into the hands of unknown men, how I, though I disliked sharing a glass with a friend, would open my mouth to the chapped lips of a nameless unshaven figure in faded jeans and a torn T-shirt, and give up that self my mother thought she knew to his immoderate hands.

There were whole embarrassing catalogues, spectacular lists of tedious and uninventive humiliation that I could have provided. I had descended to a level of banality that was so shocking in itself as almost to outweigh, in my mind, the pain of the experiences. If everything that has ever happened to me has happened in the same moment to my mother, then there can be no excuse for what I did to her in those years; the very thought of it all would have made her more violently sick than two years, than twenty years of chemotherapy.

But in fact, two things remained unsaid when she died, and this was one of them. Why should the tiresome matter of eros have been such an issue between us, when we were otherwise so linked? I blamed her for the ache of those sordid contacts that had stood in for adult love, as much as she blamed me for even imagining them. It ceased to be clear whose fault they were, even whose encounters they were. I have said that my mother never knew of them, but she knew me too well not to guess. I thought then and think now that she guessed everything. Since she thought my life was part of her life, my actions did not so much reflect badly on her as destroy the order she had selected and built for herself.

'And you're so unhappy yourself, Harry,' she would say to me.

'Because of you,' I protested. 'If I didn't have to think the whole time about how unhappy my life makes you, I could have a jolly old time of it myself.'

'There's no point blaming me,' my mother said. 'I'm sorry if I make things harder for you, Harry. I don't want to make things harder. I'm sorry that your life, as you now lead it, is not what I would prefer. But' – her voice took on an ironic tone – 'you're a big boy now, and you make your own happiness or unhappiness. You have to take a little responsibility for yourself. You can spend your whole life blaming me because you're unhappy; you can tell the whole story to a psychoanalyst someday, and say how your impossible mother ruined your life. But that's not going to make you happier. By then you're going to be talking about a ruined life. Believe me – I want to see you happy, more than anything.'

Bernard, whom I wanted so much to love, was caught in the middle of all this – he himself was in some ways of so little significance in my relation to him, except as a convenient line of demarcation, that it was often difficult, when I was in New York, for me to remember what he was like. I don't know how he put up with it.

The week my mother became ill, she said to me directly what had been implicit. She played the trump card that by some mutual agreement neither of us had ever played. She said, rationally enough, that her type of cancer was frequently brought on in women of her age by circumstances of stress. And she identified the primary source of stress in her life as my relationship with Bernard. And she finally said out and out what had always been hidden, what I had always feared might be true: that my desire was killing her and would kill her. For her to think as much was perhaps inevitable; we had set that up long before. But for her to say it was so terrible that I could not put it behind me, and will not.

While my mother was in for that first hospital visit, we set in place the rules that would hold for the next two years. Fortunately, I had cleared a long stretch of time without concerts for the holiday in France and for a short trip with Bernard that was to have come afterwards, so I could take a few weeks without worrying about work. My mother was never left alone in a hospital room except to sleep. My father would arrive at the hospital at seven o'clock every morning; visiting hours officially began later than that, but the morning guards assumed that seven o'clock visitors had come for some good reason and let him through. His face was marked with so much grief that they perhaps supposed he was already in the throes of bereavement, and were afraid to stop him. Freddy and I would drift over a few hours later. We would all stay until at least eight o'clock at night, often until ten or eleven. It never occurred to us to limit or eliminate this vigil; we went to lunch or to the telephone or to the bathroom in shifts, and none of us ever left the room for more than thirty minutes. My mother had always hated to be alone, and we did not leave her alone, ever, for even a moment; it was as though we, or she, were afraid that she might even disappear if she were in a room by herself.

We always had private nurses in the rooms as well. In general, therefore, anyone entering the room would find my mother, a nurse, Freddy, my father and me. There were never enough chairs in these rooms, and there was never enough space, and there was really not enough oxygen for all five of us. Except for the lunch shifts, we sat crowded together. My mother was usually too weak and too depressed and too medicated to come up with anything much like coherence, and the rest of us bit by bit ran out of news and insight to share, and so we would sit in semi-silence, reading books or working, our backs aching from the awkward angles we had been forced to adopt on the plastic chairs, our skin at once clammy and desiccated. We would spin conversation out of each doctor's visit, each rebarbative hospital meal, each new bowl of flowers, each telephone call. At first, my practising got squeezed into early mornings and late nights. Later, I brought an electric organ, a portable thing that could be reset to imitate a trumpet or bassoon. The keys were too oddly sprung to work out subtle questions of phrasing and I kept the miserable electric sound turned off, so I couldn't hear what I was doing. But I could at least drum through scales, negotiate fingering, and memorize new pieces. I sat with my silent music for hours at a time.

Friends of my parents' came, the women in attractive day clothes, the men in business suits. They were too animated to be quite believable, as though hospitals made them hilarious. 'Concerned,' said my father. 'Frightened,' said Freddy. Close family friends came to visit not only my mother, but also the rest of us: later, I would say of certain stretches not, 'My mother was in the hospital that week,' but, 'We were in the hospital that week.' They sat and joined us and gave us anecdotes, which were fodder for conversation after their departure. There were so many friends; people overlapped for long stretches, and my mother struggled for the energy to be comforted by each one of these many friends, all so eager to give their support; it would have worn out a lesser person to get pleasure from so many visitors. Even now, the thought exhausts me. 'You've got to be a good listener,' my mother used to say to me when I was little. 'It's more important to hear what other people are saying than it is to get across your own points.' So, now, very little of the conversation was about her cancer; it was about her friends, and their children, and their homes, and their marriages, and their dreams. My father and Freddy and I were struggling for empathy; we did everything but get cancer ourselves.

Some of the time my mother would drift off to sleep. 'What do you think?' Freddy said to me on the third day.

'She's suffering. She's really suffering. Is she just going to go on and on and on and on like this forever now until she maybe dies?' I asked. 'What are we going to do?'

'She's going to have her ups and her downs,' he said. Reasonable as ever, Freddy supplied information from his medical studies. He had called various professors and had got their expert opinions, and those professors were getting other expert opinions. Freddy had discovered a tone of balanced professionalism. 'We're all going to have our ups and downs. Don't you think, Dad?'

But my father was lost in reveries of his own; he had followed his mind backward to a happier moment that was buried somewhere deep inside it. When Freddy startled him, he shot us both a look of betrayal: he did not want to be with us in the present. 'We'll do,' he began and then looked at my mother for a long minute. 'We'll do everything,' he said. 'Anything.'

At night, that first week, I would leave the hospital gasping for air. I telephoned friends, and could not bear to come in from the late drinks I had with them, as though I too lived in fear that when

I was alone I might cease to exist. Helen would sometimes join us at the hospital, but the room got crowded; it was usually after visiting hours that I saw Helen. My mother and father were so changed in this period that I hardly knew them. Helen was the primary evidence that the world goes on. Not that she was insensitive to the developments, not that she was unsympathetic; it was only that she remained distinctly herself. Being in the hospital was like being forever on an airplane with no particular destination, breathing recycled air, hearing the persistent hum of white noise, eating pale approximations of food, feeling the life go out of your hair, your nails, your eyes, straining to read by the flat light of a weak bulb, or to work on the wobbling surface of a folding tray-table. Helen was like the one who waits just past baggage-claim and customs and runs up to you and hugs you and tells you how late your plane was and where the car is parked and who makes the interminable flight disappear into the here and now of being on the ground.

Helen and I would meet sometimes at midnight: she would see me through from tension to exhaustion. I did not think much about how Helen felt about my mother, though later on that would prove to be an important matter. I suppose I could see that Helen, though fond of my mother, had her reservations, and that is why I didn't tell her about the accusations or about my hair; I said, simply, that my mother was depressed and being difficult. Helen talked with insight born of no experience at all about how people respond to illness, and she spent a lot of time telling me how strong I was being. She reminded me that the constant vigil was something my family had elected, and not an obvious necessity. That was good: it made me feel noble instead of dutiful. There was something about the way she would look at me when I saw her, and ask, 'How was it today?' that would suddenly make the facts of the day melt away. When I could not love my mother, I could love Helen. She would sip a glass of white wine while I described every flower and every medical report and every detail, over and over. I would try to explain the quality of the fear that washed over me. Helen would hold her head on one side, and look into her wine, and stay so much herself that I was filled with the wonder of it.

Every day I spoke with Bernard. But the time difference was such that I could not call him late at night, when I was sufficiently awake to have full access to words, and so I would call in the groggy morning, or write letters, or phone from the hospital, or as soon as I got home. But unlike my relationship to Helen, my relationship to Bernard was changed. It was as though all these overwhelming emotions were a gate through which Bernard could not possibly pass. Since my love for him had been called into play as part of the reason for the whole terrible situation in which I found myself, that love of course became suspect and inaccessible. But beyond that, beyond all this explanation, we had nothing to say to each other. I think, I am pretty sure, that that was a change. Bernard told me about the plants in the window boxes and about the cat's new dish and about dinner with friends of his and about how the car had broken down (again) and about a new shirt he had bought. He described how the painter had redone the front hall and had got paint on the carpet, just around the edges. He told me that the local flower stall had wonderful delphiniums in, and that the gourmet shop had a new kind of very delicious yogurt. I in turn narrated to him the events of my days, and asked whether the plumber had been able to fix the washing machine, and about whether Jane was getting on better with her husband. His stories were as charming and as irrelevant as the books of my childhood, and I felt as though I were in my turn performing by rote; it was like playing piano exercises I had memorized for a long-vanished teacher. It wasn't even that I didn't want to tell him anything; it was that I had nothing to tell him.

Six months earlier, Bernard and I had taken advantage of chance clear weather and had gone off one Saturday afternoon for a walk in a suburban park that Bernard knew. We had taken a picnic. That day, Bernard's red-gold hair blew in the breeze like a mane, and the sunlight seemed to be caught in it, almost as though he were the source of the light itself. He had an easy, swinging gait that the uneven path could not frustrate. His voice was soft and relaxed, allegro ma non troppo, as Helen was later to say. 'Look,' he would say, 'just there,' and point, and I would spot a squirrel, still on the branches. Other visitors to the park smiled as they passed. There were some boys playing cricket and a group of teenagers with Frisbees and one young woman with frizzy hair and big kneepads who was trying unsuccessfully to rollerskate on the uneven ground. Many of the locals were drinking plastic pint cups of beer. Some of them had brought dogs. At last Bernard and I came to a quiet hilly end of things, and found a spot from which we could see no other people, and ate our sandwiches and fruit and drank, between the two of us, a bottle of white wine. Everything Bernard said that day seemed to me to be funny and intuitive, and we talked without thinking, the way I had talked to friends when I was a little boy. So we lay for half an afternoon, side by side, one of his legs crossed under one of mine, and watched the different faces of the park around us. It felt so slight: it didn't occur to me then that this might be love, though I knew that I had never liked anyone more. The day, like Bernard himself, could not have been less dramatic, less interested in calling attention to itself.

In the hospital, when none of my mother's friends was on hand, she would stare out the window for twenty minutes at a time. When she spoke, her voice was out of focus, its essential form familiar but its details obliterated. My father and Freddy and I spent long hours discussing what line of treatment she would pursue and at what hospital, but my mother, in the face of the crisis, became passive; she seemed not to care about these questions. She displayed a lack of interest in how the spots of cancerous flesh were to be eliminated – she, who a few days earlier had had energy to obsess about how a spot on one of my ties might be got out. 'What difference does it make which of these punishments you choose for me?' she would ask my father. 'You go ahead and decide which is the best way for them to kill me, how gradual to make it. It's all exactly the same.' And so it was my father who not only made the decisions but also took it upon himself to persuade my mother to move forward. He conveyed to her all the optimism he had extracted from the not-so-very optimistic remarks of the doctors. It was my father who wept at night, when my mother was sleeping a drugged sleep at the hospital, but it was my father who remained calmly wreathed in smiles for fourteen or sixteen hours every day in those hospital rooms. My father produced wonderful numbers: seventy per cent of women in my mother's situation were cured, and if she were chemotherapy-responsive this whole thing would soon pass from our lives like a cold winter. The hospital where we were sitting had statistics twice as good as any other hospital in the nation. Out of the air, my father produced thirty good friends of good friends, women who had had similar difficulties and were now in glowing health; they marched through the hospital room like members of a middle-aged cheerleading squad. My father would meet with the dourest members of the medical professions and come back newly encouraged, bubbling over with all the good news. And he selected a mode of treatment for my mother, a system to cure her, and pretended the decision was as logical as the choice of a car or an investment strategy.

On the day my mother went into the hospital, while Freddy and I were still in France, before anyone knew whether she had cancer, my father bought my mother an enormous bunch of perfect roses and scribbled on a white florist's card, 'Love, love, love. We will go on forever.' I kept that card when we left the hospital at the end of my mother's first surgery; I thought it was an amulet, and I could not imagine, any more than my father could, that it might prove not to be true. Of course the treatments were going to be terrible, but I had been brought up to believe that you recover from the woes of the body and of the spirit. Did I say that my mother was as fragile as a soap bubble, that I always knew she would die young? The touch of her hand on my arm, the way she would call out, 'Hello, Harry' – that sound of hello could not, after all, fade or decay; its continuation could hardly depend on something as technical and fussy as chemotherapy.

But that technical and fussy business, which could not begin until my mother had recovered from her surgery, was to prove darker than I could guess. I do not think she would have liked for me to tell you about the details of her surgeries or of her treatments. Forgive me, then, if I do not describe to you some things that I am trying, for my mother and for myself, to forget. Forgive me if I do not dwell on the acid white anonymity of those many hospital rooms, and on the ceaseless comedy of lumpy beds with elaborate control panels, which we never, or almost never, adjusted. Forgive me if I do not speak of how those needles were put into vein after vein, how one vein after the next collapsed, those tiny delicate veins of my mother's, more like filaments in the stems of flowers than like vessels to carry blood. Forgive me if I do not dwell on those sacs of poison, like giant spider glands, that were hung on a steel pole and then pumped into her arm or her abdomen as though she were a Strasbourg goose being prepared for the slaughter. Chemotherapy became as regular as a metronome, as tediously inevitable as days that give way to night. I will tell you until you are tired of hearing it how I lived from one test result to the next, but I will not tell you the complex, almost Masonic significance of those numbers, a system I learned so well that you could say twenty-eight to me and make me breathe easy, or say sixty-two and make me scream. I will not tell you too much of spread and containment, of bad cells we thought would wash away in the flood of sepia liquids, as if they were only markings in the sand on a tide-flooded beach. 'It's incredible to me,' my mother said one day, 'that I go into the hospital just as I'm beginning to feel better, and allow them to give me therapy that makes me feel terrible, that I go to the doctors, not when I'm in pain, but as soon as the pain abates.' What kind of faith is it that allows us to run so contrary to our own experience?

I will not teach you the vocabulary of disease, the thousand thousand terms I learned, until I could chat with the doctors and nurses and my father and Freddy in a language that, a year before, would have been far more strange than Greek to me, nor will I say much of how in my mind I translated those terms into words gentler than the bodily violations they in fact represented. I will speak as little as possible about the stream of medical staff for whom the quality of life was in the fact of living, and not in pleasure or the relief from pain. All there is not to tell about the modern way of death, the American way of death, the way of death we come upon when we suppose that all things may be cured with enough logic and enough pragmatism – I will not dwell on those ordinary indecencies, those bedpans and breathing games, one like a child's toy, a three-ball device in which your lung power is measured by whether you can keep all three balls at the tops of their vertical chambers. I have tried to forget the questions asked by interns in whose eyes my mother was an example of the grotesque, whose disease they battled as if it were an orange monster in a video game, and not as though it were something that consumed her very humanity. Forgive me for steering clear of the accompanied visits to the bathroom, of the days of guiding an IV pole around the hallways and calling the dull perambulation, from room 702 to room 740, by the ridiculous term of exercise.

'Of course he wants me to get well,' my mother said of one doctor, 'because it will give him a better statistical rate for this treatment.'

I will try to forget how we sought out every grain of kindness in those doctors, clinging to the scant evidence of feeling as though any emotion were a vein of platinum in a monolith of shale. I will not detail the complexities of blood tests, but I will tell you that they could have filled a swimming pool with the amount of blood that was taken from my mother during her two years of illness, that in my worst dreams I imagine all that blood floating like a tanker-spill over a sea far more than wine-dark. Perhaps you will laugh if I dwell on what they fed my mother after surgery and chemotherapy, when she could hardly have taken a boiled egg or a piece of toast, if I tell you about the thick leaden lumps of meatloaf, the pasty cream soups, the inexplicably slimy vegetables. I would like not to remember hospital arrivals and departures, installation and check-out, my brother and me collecting odds and ends as my father almost carried my mother (as light as a wilted spinach leaf on her weakest days) out to the car, only her anxiety bearing witness that she was still alive.

You will not know my mother better for learning what went on in those clean but dingy hospitals with their linoleum hallways and their greenish fluorescent lighting. Better to remember how my mother with tired patience transformed those rooms, as she used to change her suite at the Ritz, with flowers, with the plaid blanket on which I first learned to trace a square in my early childhood (its autumn orange and dark yellow and rich green, curiously not my mother's favourite colours, so immense in that dreary hospital). Surely it is better to remember the lace pillowcase, the little enamelled clock, the pink bedjacket, the half-glasses in their red case that somehow humanized the adjustable Formica table. Better to remember how the little suitcase in which her things were brought to the hospital lay in a corner of the room, and made it possible to pretend that the room was a destination of its own, found at the end of a pleasant flight.

So also I remember with precipitate clarity those moments when my mother would be animated by a passing fancy or a quick insight or a comic thought, and how she would suddenly become herself again. In those moments we would all become ourselves again, as though we were furniture in storage which had been abruptly liberated from sheets thick with dust. Our backs ceased to ache and the muscles of our faces became operative again and our eyes came back to us, so that we could see. The hospital smells faded away. My mother made all the agony – it was doubly hard for her because so much of it was her agony – seem small and remote and unimportant. Sometimes we would find ourselves convulsed with laughter ('I'm afraid this silverware doesn't manage a single kind word,' said my father, remembering the Ritz; 'You wouldn't either,' my mother replied, 'if you spent your life with this food. Poor abused forks, and these browbeaten innocent spoons.'), until the nurses and patients from other rooms would come and gaze wistfully in the door, baffled at our happiness. I would glimpse other visitors arriving to see other patients, and would think how they might envy me my mother, who could for a few minutes at a time be herself just because we were, all four of us, together. And in those moments I remembered (as I sometimes forgot) why we were keeping the vigil around her, what it was to be one of the four of us.

Sometimes, on those occasions, I would go to the end of the hall and phone Bernard, for whom I might have a sudden rush of affection. When my mother turned back into herself, it was as though my emotions had been given back to me, and I felt that I had love to spare. Bernard responded to what happened to my mother only insofar as it affected me. 'But how are *you*?' he would ask; and I was never, never able to get him to see how little meaning there was in that question, taken by itself. 'How are you?' he would ask, and I would say, 'My mother is in better spirits at the moment.' And when he would repeat his question, I would awkwardly manufacture moods of my own to fit his rhetoric of concern.

By the time my mother came home from her first surgery, we had become a new family. We were the afflicted, our pain a subject for public consumption. My mother, who had always required support and protection, was now to be buoyed up against all odds by every ounce of our energy, and by every ounce of energy we could solicit from her friends, our friends, from doctors, from the doormen in our building and the man who filled prescriptions at the local pharmacy and the shoemaker who had been resoling our shoes since before I was born and the headwaiters at her favourite restaurants. My mother had such broad systems of friendship that her friends seemed almost to compete for her notice, anxiously presenting their attention and their flowers (I associate my mother's entire illness with cut flowers), which we accepted as though they were sung ballads and tributes of gold.

We were transformed, but at the same time we were very much as we had always been. We were of course no longer bravely untroubled, but we were to compensate for that by having the perfect experience of illness. We would mention in a casual way the particular attentions paid by famous specialists whose names we had, two weeks earlier, never heard, as though these men and women were the medical equivalent of family silver. We noticed how much sympathy there was around us, so much sympathy that it became like part of the air, a supplement to oxygen and carbon dioxide. My mother had decided, for public purposes, to be brave and pessimistic. 'Leonard tells me I'm not dying, but I don't believe a word of it,' she would say lightly to a friend. And as we continued not to separate for more than an hour at a time, she would sometimes say, 'The boys are keeping a deathwatch over me. I keep telling them to go out, but they don't want to miss a minute of the fun.'

My mother had a succession of strange and powerful whims, like a child princess in a fairy tale or a pregnant woman in a myth: she would suddenly conceive a longing for the particular pasta she sometimes ordered at a restaurant we all knew, and so my father would go down and persuade the chefs to give him dinner to take home. She read books she would ordinarily not have read, and refused those she might under other circumstances have enjoyed. She arranged for a manicurist to come to the apartment and paid exquisite attention to her nails. A few days after she came home from the first surgery, she agreed to take walks around the block; it was the brink of autumn then, a favourite time of year, and the sun was pleasant, and my mother would wear loose clothes that did not constrain her and walk slowly, holding her head steady as if she had a book on it, and moving as though an abrupt gesture might dissever one of her limbs.

'I was your age when my father died,' she said to me one day. 'I remember so little about him. I hope you and Freddy will remember me. I'd like to be remembered.'

I told my mother that she was not going anywhere and that I would remember her for a good long time because she was going to go on reminding me of herself.

'You go on thinking that,' she said. 'Maybe it's true.'

I told her that I could never forget her anyway.

'I suppose you're going to be heading back to London soon,' she said. 'Remember me when you're in London.'

I did not tell her, for the moment, how my father had yelled at me that morning, and told me that it was selfish and wrong for me to go to London and abandon the family to suffering, right when Freddy had to return to medical school. 'Of course I will,' was all I said to her.

That was all in the afternoons. In the mornings, my mother was sad. She woke up weak and tearful and exhausted, unable to face the day. I woke up each morning afraid, and lived a strange blank minute before I remembered that there was some reason for what in the first moments seemed like irrational foreboding. In the mornings, my mother would sit in the kitchen and stare vaguely into a cup of chamomile tea so weak it was hardly more than hot water, and her face would sag, and her hands would shake, sometimes so badly that she spilled her tea, and she would seem like an old woman. My mother on those mornings frightened me; it took all my discipline to go into the kitchen. In the mornings, my mother's pain was fresh, like a wound picked open by the night. At the other end of the negotiable days, she would rail against fate; in the evenings she was furious. 'This is so unfair,' she would say, gritting her teeth until her jaw shook. 'What have I done to deserve this?' She was silently outraged at friends who could come and go as it might suit them, drinking the tea Janet seemed to be forever making, eating a cookie or two, going outside with an ennobling awareness of their own concern. She was furious at the days, furious at her own body, furious at the food she did not feel like eating. It was as though there were a big festival going on outside, to which everyone in the world but she had been invited. My father and Freddy and I stayed in to keep her company, but we could at any moment have gone out where they were dancing, and she was under lock and key. She hated us for that, too.

There were still occasional moments of life as it had been, which felt as though they had been cut out of a colourful magazine and glued onto our monochrome days. There were the snatched hours from each day that I spent practising. Sometimes my mother would come in and sit at the end of the piano bench and listen. This destroyed my concentration, but it was also a strangely intimate time, when neither of us thought of saying anything, and cancer did not intervene. She would stay for perhaps half an hour, and then we would lapse into conversation, and I would follow her back to the bedroom to talk.

Later in her illness, I was to incorporate the idea of her suffering, and had to make an effort to put it aside. At the beginning, however, I had to remind myself that my mother was really ill, or the strangeness and unreality of the situation would take over and I would dissociate myself from it entirely. If it was in the end hard to find the vestiges of our old lives, in the beginning it was in some ways difficult to be aware of the fresh changes. My mother and I could not talk about her or her plans without discussing the disease, but we could easily talk about me, and so with a kind of generous egotism (since my mother was also better off discussing something other than her own illness) I would drag the conversation to subjects of my own. This was, however, an imperfect solution, since too often my life braided its way back into hers. It was much safer to discuss friends; better yet to watch television in the evenings and analyze the people on the screen.

I have talked about my mother in Paris, dressed in couture, at her best and brightest, and about my mother in a hospital, at her lowest of all. What is hardest to describe is my mother as she was on the ordinary days of our ordinary lives. I have as strong a memory of my mother when I hear the theme tunes from certain television shows as when I sit in the bar at the Paris Ritz. Maybe the TV memories remain clearer, in fact, because I have celebrated them less often. Starting when I was eight or nine, and continuing until I was about fourteen, on Saturday nights when my parents did not go out, my father, after dinner, would sit in the living room and work, and my mother and I would watch television together. Sometimes Freddy joined us, but what we watched was not his kind of TV and he got bored; those evenings were mostly my mother's and mine. Over the years, the line-up varied, but the shows were all the same anyway, so the changes didn't really matter. We watched situation comedies about people bumbling through their lives, or their jobs, or their families. Later, my mother tended to dismiss that time; she referred to the shows as junk we had watched for lack of anything better to do. But in fact we loved them.

My mother and I would be in her bedroom, and she would sit up on her side of the bed, under the covers, doing needlepoint while we watched, and I would sit on the other side, cross-legged, in my pyjamas, and we would chat during the commercials. We talked a lot about the TV lives unfolding before us which, by intention or otherwise, were full of lessons to be learned. We talked about what various characters could do or should do or shouldn't do and we indulged in the sort of strong opinions that in real life need so often to be held in check. We would laugh and laugh and laugh: not so much at the funny lines, though some of those sent us into easy stitches, as at the absurdity of the relationships portrayed, or the clothes, or the unconsidered values. There was a letting go that went on on those TV Saturdays. So much of our life together was planned and complex – scheduled dinners, evenings at the theatre, weekends at our house in the country with visiting friends – and to have those evenings of just being, and of just being together, talking of nothing of great moment: it was palpable, something you could bask in. There was a sublimely effortless and undangerous quality to these TV people, to whom – since, after all, they were fictive – we did not have any obligation to be generous. When a series ended, we missed it: our affection encompassed all the people in the world and not in the world, and we breezily extended it to the characters who had amused us.

That world in the TV was a dream version of what was resolutely American and mainstream about our lives, about my life with my mother and father and Freddy. On reruns, the characters seem more than a little bit ridiculous. But those anti-heroes and -heroines were icons, as those evenings my mother and I shared were icons, for something solid and permanent, a kind of smiling middle-of-the-road way of life that nothing could change. The people were nice enough, some of them energetic, or funny, or resilient; underneath a very different exterior, my mother had some of their solid Americanness. Like them, she suffered disproportionately over the episodes of the moment, but in the end remained fairly certain that any real difficulties would be resolved into unimportance. Our lives seemed as ultimately safe as theirs. When my mother first got ill, and throughout the time of her illness, when she was tired, we would watch TV together, and I would remember how easy life was, and it was as though I were eleven, and everything could not help being all right in the end.

It was on one such evening that I finally told my mother about my recording contract. I had looked forward to the occasion for too long, and by the time it came around I had lost the sense of urgency with which I had carried the news to Paris. It was becoming absurd and inconvenient that she didn't know yet, and I made my announcement more to have it done with than because I longed to tell her. We were at a commercial break, and my mother said, 'I was just looking at the review you left me from Zürich. I like it.'

'He was unusually musical for a reviewer,' I said. 'I've never met him, but he's a friend of a friend of Bernard's, and I gather that he's charming and incredibly scholarly and very highly regarded in Switzerland.'

The programme was starting again, but I seized the moment. 'I wanted to tell you something,' I said.

My mother looked tense.

'I got a recording contract,' I said. 'I'm making a record. A cd. It'll go into distribution in about eighteen months.'

My mother looked almost blank. 'But that's incredible, Harry,' she said. 'When did you find out?'

'Just before Paris. But I was waiting for a good time to tell you,' I said. 'It's on the label I wanted, too. And they're going to let me do the Schubert, the sonata in B flat, and the Rachmaninoff, even though I had been worried about whether those pieces really go together.'

'Oh, Harry. How wonderful for you.' She looked back at the TV for a moment. 'That's more or less what you played in London, at that museum, when your father and I were there. I liked that programme.' She hit the mute button on the TV, then turned back to me, her face glowing, and she sat up on her side of the bed, and for a sudden moment it was as if her cancer were gone. 'Harry, how nice of you to save a piece of good news for me. I remember when you were a little boy, how you used to get up in the mornings and go play the piano. Your father and I would look at each other and I would say, well, it's probably time to get up anyway. And he used to joke that I had given birth to a genius, and that someday people would throng to hear you.'

'Genius is maybe a bit premature,' I said.

'It was more than a bit premature at the time. I once woke up in the country and told your father that the dishwater was jammed in the middle of the rinse cycle, and he told me that that was the Moonlight Sonata. It was the most God-awful noise I had ever heard. I don't know what you were doing to that piece of music.' The TV family flickered on. 'Sometimes other mothers used to tell me they thought you should be out playing football or swimming, and sometimes I worried that they were right. The predominant feeling when you were little was that you should try to help your children fit in with everyone else. But I thought I could try to push you to be good at football, which you clearly hated, or I could just encourage you at the things like music that you were so good at and that you loved. And I thought that the best way to help you be happy was to let you be exceptional where you could be exceptional, and not to try to make you uniform and monochrome and conventional, not to even everything out, not to try to fill in the gaps.'

'Here I am,' I said.

'Sometimes I think I went too far, or that we let you go too far. A little bit of conventional in some areas of life is not necessarily a bad thing.' She paused, pointedly. 'But – oh, Harry,' she said, and she smiled her big smile, which I hadn't seen since that first evening in Paris. 'I'm so proud of you. So proud. Enjoy this moment. You've worked hard for it.'

'Partly,' I said, 'it was just a matter of luck. If I hadn't done that funny recital in Budapest, that they called me in for at the last minute, and if the English press hadn't been in town for the reopening of that concert hall, then I don't think – '

My mother cut me off. 'We've been very lucky, all of us in this family, very lucky for the most part. But you make a lot of your own luck, Harry. It's one of your greatest gifts. You deserve every bit of luck you have; it may be luck in a way, but it's luck that you've struggled for.'

I laughed. 'So I've struggled,' I said.

'You have, though. Sometimes you don't even notice how much you're struggling. But I've seen it; you've had to struggle a lot not to be defeated by all the little defeats, to be one of the survivors. We should celebrate this,' she said. 'Have you told your father yet?'

I said that I hadn't.

My father was in the library, working. 'Leonard,' she shouted as loudly as she could. 'He's getting as deaf as a post,' she said.

I went into the hall outside the bedroom. 'Dad,' I called. 'I want to tell you something.' I walked to the end of the hall, and heard the sound of my father shuffling back in his bedroom slippers.

'It should have been such a lovely week in France,' I heard my mother say, later, to my father.

When my mother had been home for ten days, she went to see a wig-maker. She had investigated wig-makers as she would have investigated florists or caterers, as my father had investigated doctors, and she had found the names – so she believed – of the two best wig-makers in New York. She went to see them so she could order the wigs and have them in hand before her hair began to go. For my mother, the prospect of baldness was the worst of the punishments of chemotherapy. Internal suffering she could bear with equanimity, telling just what she chose to just whom she chose, willing herself to be brave in the face of it. But the external symptoms that could not be hidden were, to her, intolerable and humiliating. She was not so much shamed by the revolt of her body from within as by the damage that showed without. My mother was accustomed to the kinds of deference that her beauty had always won for her, and to have to give these up at the same moment that she confronted death seemed too unfair. To be a hair-less woman was, for her, to be freakish and grotesque. My mother's hair was heavy and soft and taffy-coloured with occasional flashes of gold. It was always neat and clean and orderly; my mother did not ever have hair that curled where it should not have curled, or that frizzed, or that got tangled. I can remember sitting with her as a child and talking when we had just come in or were just about to go out, when she would run a brush over her hair. I remember how any hint of chaos gave way at once to her disciplined and regular strokes. I can remember too the rain through which we did not walk, the taxi windows we did not open, the windy paths we circumvented for the sake of my mother's hair.

My mother had her hair done (it was her first time out of the house, after that first hospital visit), and then went directly to the wig-makers and ordered three wigs from each of them, so that they could copy exactly the appearance of her hair when it was freshly coiffed. My mother did not show any interest in getting a fun wig; she did not want to try new possibilities. My mother had spent some years negotiating the hair style that suited her; she had changed it when and as her age had demanded that she do so; and she was not going to change it again now. For the few weeks that her own hair was to last, she kept reaching up and touching it, patting it into place as though to memorize her own gestures and their effect for an unspecified future period. She arranged with her hairdresser to keep free her 9.30 appointment on Mondays and Thursdays, so that she could take it up again when her hair came back, as all the doctors promised that it would. For the sake of my father and Freddy and me, my mother imagined such a time.

'This treatment may make you feel nauseated for a few weeks, and wholly exhausted, and may cause general malaise,' the doctors warned. But my mother could contain those difficulties. 'What about my hair?' she would ask. The loss of her hair was like the loss of herself; when she went to those wig-makers (those horrible depressing basement offices), it was as though she were getting the most meager protection for a war with the world. She was like a bleached zebra getting stripes put on with ink. If it was hard for her to think of herself as a woman with cancer, obliged to submit to chemical assault, then it was twice as difficult for her to think of herself as a woman without hair, reliant on petty artifice. There is nothing to be accomplished by focusing on your own cancer; you cannot change it by an act of will. Her hair distracted her: she attached herself to its changes to avoid thinking too relentlessly about the changes within her body. She suffered over the passing humiliation as a means to circumnavigate the prospect of death. I volunteered to come along with her to the wig-makers' studios, but my mother took only my father. She took him because she could not face these things alone, but she left Freddy and me behind because she could not bear for anyone else to see them. At the time, I was just as glad; the few hours I got alone were a welcome relief from the intense claustrophobia of the vigil, which I felt then might easily go on forever.

I never saw my mother without hair. During the entire period of her illness, she wore wigs outside, and turbans around the house. She hated those turbans; my father told her that she looked like Gloria Swanson, but though she laughed, she told him he was being ridiculous, and believed that to be so. My father too was kept away from her humiliation. She would close the bathroom door when she was changing from wig to wig or from wig to turban, and she slept in those turbans as well. 'I'd rather you not remember me bald,' she said, 'and once you saw it, you'd remember it.' How much she looked at herself without hair I was never to know, but for the rest of us her baldness was little more than a verbal construct. It influenced all of our lives, and she and my father were to develop elaborate routines around it. He would intercept coat-check girls lest they tip the wig forward; he would walk between my mother and the wind when they were outside; but he would also pretend not to know that my mother was in fact hairless, and if her turban ever slipped in the night, I think he contrived not to see it.

'You have to get back and start working on your recording,' my mother said one afternoon. 'You've already missed enough. You have to keep your engagements for next month.'

'I've cancelled a couple of performances,' I said. 'My agent has been negotiating for me. But if I let it go much longer, I'm going to get a reputation I can't afford. It's beginning to get tricky.'

'It's OK,' said my mother. 'I love having you here, but I'll be fine without you for a little while. I don't want my illness to take over your work.'

'I'm thinking about flights,' I said. Bernard and I had spoken every day about when I would return.

'Flights,' said my father. 'Always off on another plane. My son the jet-setter. It's not as though you were going to forget how to play the piano if you stayed here for a little while. You could pick up next month. There are pianists who could fill in for you, if you really wanted to arrange that.'

My mother put her hand on his arm. 'Let go, Leonard,' she said.

Helen came over to help me pack. 'You'll be glad to see Bernard,' she said as we counted socks.

'I'll be glad to get out of here,' I said. 'To get back to real life. I have to say I wish Bernard were a little more clued in. He's trying to be nice about all the stuff going on now, but as for understanding – ' I let the thought slide.

'Have you tried to explain it to him?' asked Helen.

I was a bit irritated by this. 'I think it should be obvious.' I put down the socks. 'You know. You've known from the start.'

'What has your mother actually done,' asked Helen, 'to warrant – ' her voice trailed off. 'To make you want to give up everything else? To freeze you this way.'

Helen was not the first to ask that question, and it was not the first time I had been stymied by it. What had my mother done? In the way of mothers, mine saw to it that I had food to eat, a roof over my head, clothes to wear. She sat at the foot of my bed when I was ill, and gave me soup to comfort me. She was there every day when I came home from school; we would sit in the kitchen and talk for hours, and then over dinner, which she made almost every night, and then over breakfast, which she made without fail every morning. She was obsessively dependable, and was never, in my life experience of her, late for an appointment; she never changed or rearranged or rescheduled or cancelled a plan, and she never failed to do anything she had promised. She remembered what I told her better than I did, listened when I wanted to talk, and talked when I was prepared to listen. When I played the piano, she heard every note. She organized trips and parties; she took the time to spin of life's boring events a thread as rare and fine as any emperor's silk.

What did she do? Her intelligence cast into perspective the terrors of the given moment; she made life into a meaningful progression, rather than a random splatter, and ordered childhood's terrible chaos. To love people by knowing them is the most difficult kind of love to sustain, since no one can hold up that level of perfection we hope for, even demand, in the people we adore. My mother could only know people; she could not have preserved ignorance and distance had that been her fondest wish; and knowing me, she nevertheless loved me entirely and completely. It would be a gross inaccuracy to call my mother uncritical: she criticized my choice of ties, the objects in my home, the whole way I lived my life. But she did it all because she felt in the very core of her being so urgently and so clearly involved in my success or failure. In the face of any pleasure of mine, she evinced a quiet joy so intense and so poignant as to ennoble all my happiness. When something saddened me, she came and joined me in my pain, so that I was not alone there; she mitigated sorrow itself for me. You do not necessarily love people for what they do; nor does heroism lie always in action. Those single examples of valiant courage, those stories that sons might tell of their mothers rescuing them from the lions: my mother had never done anything of the kind. She would immediately have come running if the lions had roared in my direction; but we lived in New York, where the lions are gradual and evanescent, and where the defences against them are made of a slow accumulation of dialogue rather than of a sudden blade of steel. Such courage as she had does not lend itself to representative anecdotes.

I looked at Helen and shrugged. 'It's not anything she's done, or that she does,' I finally said. 'It's just the way she is.'

'That's what I thought you'd say,' said Helen.

'That's the most important thing,' I said. 'More than what she does.'

'Of course,' said Helen. 'But it's also the most inaccessible to other people. Including Bernard, I'm sure.'

'If he really listened to me, he'd get it,' I said.

Helen looked at me long and hard. 'The only way to explain that kind of love to someone who hasn't known it himself,' she replied, 'is to give it to him.'

To this piece of admirable advice I had no ready response, and so, with redoubled energy, Helen and I focused on the packing.

III

My London

The first year of my relationship with Bernard was the happiest year of my life. Being with Bernard was like being on a spa vacation. When I was with him I was calm, and balanced, and pure, and attractive, and wonderfully relaxed – I was everything but tan. I had sometimes longed for men who were all the dangerous things that I was not, for men who were rough and strong, for men who were casual and irresistibly male, with thick hands and coarse hair, men who didn't know what to do with words and music, and who grappled, instead, with bodies. But what I found was Bernard, who was tall and strawberry blond with chiselled features and attenuated limbs; he looked like an illustration of England. In surface ways, Bernard was a less self-conscious and less baroque version of me. He never frightened me, and at some profound level I suppose that he never fully satisfied me, but he made me very happy. No one had done that before.

The emotions that appear strongest are often the least, but I did not know that then. I had decided when I was growing up that I would occupy myself with emotions so powerful that they seemed almost to stand on their own, free of their objects. I engaged proudly with joy and tragedy, with the agony and the ecstasy. Before my mother's illness, and throughout its early stages, I indulged in the extravagance of this emotional range, and when I talked, I talked in a rhetoric of melodrama. What I was later to learn is that language is not necessarily transparent, and that free-standing emotions can stand far away from you. I realized eventually that memorable experience is not always ostentatious. I thought, when Bernard and I were together, that there was some virtue in my knowledge of joy to the exclusion of happiness, while he believed that happiness was the goal, and that most joy was contrived. Here more than elsewhere, compromise was too difficult, and neither of us considered it. It was not until much later that I wondered whether happiness and joy should not live beside each other, so that you could know them both, so that one could lead you into the other and back again. Only then did I think that some language is transparent, and some language not; that meaning can slide between the cracks or lie on the manifest surface; that both ostentation and understatement have their vitality. Then I realized that simplicity is often as much of a defensive affectation as melodrama, and that to be content is something, but not everything.

Bernard and I first met through mutual friends, two years before my mother got sick, and then chanced to run into each other in front of a neighborhood greengrocer some six months later. We made a plan for dinner, and within days I had moved into his flat – I kept my own house, but spent less and less time there, until I came to see it almost as storage space. My piano was of course there, but Bernard also had a piano, and though mine had a clearer sound, I eventually grew fond of the muted notes I made at his house. For the first month, the strangeness of being at last in a real proper living-together relationship kept me at bay, but then the easiness of it overwhelmed me. I put aside all the mannerisms of despair at which I had become so expert. I gave up, one by one, the elements of my life that had been about loneliness, and absorbed Bernard's affection as though I were a towel and he were a swimming pool. He cooked lovely things for breakfast, and he bought bunches of flowers, and he laughed at stories that were really only a smile's worth of funny, and he showed me that everything on earth was pleasant. He was of course no more in love with me than I was in love with him, but if I had not obstreperously blocked his love perhaps he would have been; it was part of his lovely English nature not to resist anything that would have been agreeable.

Bernard picked me up at Heathrow when I got back from that first hospital sojourn. During the year that followed, he was to pick me up at Heathrow an inconceivable number of times, driving monotonously back and forth, listening in his appreciative but impassive way to tapes of grand opera in one direction and to the confessions of my heart in the other. He came to seem almost as routine as the customs officers, as inevitable a part of transit as the porters; but the fact that he was always happy to see me was addictive, and I came to be more reliant on his smile than on the engines of the planes in which I flew. When I was in New York, Bernard seemed remote and insignificant, but when I came to London, I relaxed into Bernard and became myself again. In New York, I felt as though I were being peeled, and when I returned to London and saw Bernard my skin began to grow back.

The first time, I was in New York for a month. I can remember kissing Bernard in the carpark at Heathrow in the first minutes of getting back, driven not by passion or sexual longing so much as by the independence of the act. On the way into town, I asked him all about the recent events of his life, and found that the details which had seemed so tedious and so hollow on the phone in New York were strangely engrossing in London. I was delighted that Liz was getting married, and distressed by the continuing situation with Norman. I longed to see how the window boxes were doing, and was very pleased about the northern Italian restaurant near where that funny antique shop had been. I quite saw that it was inconvenient about Patrick's leaving, but suggested that in some ways one might do better than Patrick in the long run, and that this might later on seem a very good thing. We talked also about the concert I was to give later in the week. In New York, this had masqueraded as the primary reason for my trip, and I had invoked it almost as an excuse, but I had given the cold reality of it little thought. Now it glared at me. Bernard told me, in the car, how many of our friends were going to come, and I wished that they weren't.

When we got to the flat, Bernard produced a magnificent cold supper, and a bottle of the Australian wine we had discovered in July. There were new candles in the candlesticks. There were late cornflowers in the vase I had given him two months earlier. I had been so busy fussing over my mother for more than a month; we had all been so busy making her favourite things that I had forgotten what my own favourite things were. I looked at that food and those flowers and the pretty glasses and when Bernard went to wash his hands, I found myself at the brink of tears. Helen used to say that all tears were memories; I seemed at that moment to be remembering myself, whole and entire. But I pulled myself up short before Bernard came back. And aside from a sad moment while Bernard was in the kitchen making toast, I stayed wreathed in smiles all evening.

I had only ten days in London if I was to be back in New York in time for my mother's birthday. There were a thousand things to do, people to see, phone calls to make, bills to pay. I had some details of my contract to settle with my agent and with the recording studio where I would be working – which was not far from Bernard's flat – and we had to try to set up schedules of some kind, though I had apprised my agent of the situation with my mother and he was trying to make things as flexible as possible. 'You should be performing more,' he said. 'You should have a dense schedule this autumn.' But I insisted on a broken schedule with little clumps of engagements and larger clumps of free time.

Bernard had taken several days off during my absence to meet the plumber at my house to try to deal with the problem about the washing machine, but it was not really settled in any very satisfactory way, and I knew that in the end I was going to have to spend an afternoon with the plumber and the electrician if anything was to function again. I also had to decide whether what the plumber had said to Bernard about the basement wall made sense, and I had to decide what to do about that wall, which was not looking terrific. I had to get my favourite umbrella repaired so I could take it back to New York, and to get my hair cut, and to buy my mother a birthday present. Between all these other things, I had to practise the music I was to play for the concert. I had spent too little time at the piano in New York, even less time than I had thought.

After a month with nothing more sociable than the crush in my mother's hospital room or a late-night drink with Helen, I suddenly had parties to go to. What was happening in New York remained inexplicable, but it also turned into anecdote, so that I could speak of it with the same fluidity I brought to the continuing situation with Norman and the question about Patrick. At dinner at Claire and Michael's house, we discussed the nature of illness and the advantages and disadvantages of American hospitals and the National Health. At Frieda's drinks party, she introduced me to a woman called Elaine who had had exactly what my mother had about ten years earlier and who was now divorcing her second husband since the illness. Jane seated me at her house next to a friend of hers whose mother had recently died; we made polite but rather uncomfortable conversation. Everyone took me aside to tell me how anxious Bernard was. 'I've been talking to him every day,' Claire told me. 'He's keeping us all posted. And he's so worried for you. Michael's been absolutely worried about Bernard, being so worried,' I smiled and observed that this was very like Michael, and generally said how lucky I felt I was. And in fact, though I had spent the month mostly feeling cursed, I did feel that week that I was lucky.

My mother and I spoke regularly on the phone. Usually I called her, but the day before my concert it was she who called me, in the afternoon. 'How are you doing?' asked my mother.

'I'm fine,' I said. I was trying to practise and I was frustrated by the interruption. 'How are you?'

'Well, I have a new collection of revolting symptoms, but perhaps I'll wait and tell you about them some other time. Are you feeling ready for the concert tomorrow?'

I said that I had been practising constantly. 'It's not going to be a very difficult concert. It's all music I've played before. And it should be an easy audience. Tolerant subscription people and Mozart lovers.'

'You sound tired,' said my mother.

I was not aware of sounding tired. I was in fact not aware of being tired until she mentioned it. 'I had a strange dream last night,' I said. I had forgotten it until that moment. 'I was playing the Schubert at a very big concert in some kind of great arena, a sort of amphitheatre. I was playing it perfectly, better than I'd ever played it before, and then suddenly, in the middle of the andante, I realized that I couldn't remember which movement came next. And so I kept playing one phrase over and over again, hoping I

would remember, so I could go on, but I couldn't remember.
I woke up in a cold sweat.'

'So you're not feeling at all anxious about the concert tomorrow,' my mother said in a tone of light irony.

'No, I don't think it was about that. I'm not playing the Schubert tomorrow anyway,' I said. 'Funny, I'd forgotten it until this moment. I must have fallen asleep again a little while afterwards.'

'Do yourself a favour and go to bed early tonight,' said my mother. 'Don't keep getting out of bed to play little odds and ends over to make sure you have them right. Just go to sleep and stay asleep if you can.'

'I'll do my best,' I said. 'I don't usually get up in the middle of the night here because the piano wakes Bernard up. But with jet-lag and everything . . .'

'If you decide to stay asleep, you'll stay asleep,' my mother said. 'I'm spending the day at the hospital tomorrow, preparing for my first chemotherapy, so I don't know whether we'll be able to speak. If we don't, have a good concert. Call and let me know how it goes.'

'You let me know how it goes at the hospital,' I said. 'It can't be as bad as you think it's going to be.'

That night, I slept fitfully. Easy audience or not, Mozart or otherwise, I was nervous. It had been only six weeks since my last concert, but I felt as though I'd been on sabbatical forever. My fingers seemed tight and atrophied. I had included a divertimento that I didn't like very much because I had thought it would balance the other pieces, and I didn't feel like playing it. Bernard said I should announce a change to the programme, but that seemed theatrical to me. I kept working on the divertimento. I knew I was playing it too fast, but I couldn't seem to get it back under control. By the end of the afternoon, I was in a foul mood, and when the phone rang, I was tempted not to answer it.

'You're still tired,' said my mother.

'Jet-lag,' I said.

'Take a nap,' she said. 'You still have time.'

'I don't have time,' I said, 'and naps always leave me feeling bleary. You know that I never nap before a concert,' We were both silent for a moment while the line crackled. 'Weren't you supposed to be at the doctor's all day?' I asked.

'I'm between appointments. The man who checks my blood is finished with me, and I have half an hour until they do the scans. Your father has somehow managed to get me a private phone so I can call you while he runs out for sandwiches, which I have already told him I won't eat. You'd think, since they keep telling me to eat more, that they'd have scheduled in enough time to go and get lunch.'

'I wouldn't think so. I wouldn't think they'd think about it. Remember, I've been there and met them.' It was a bad connection with an echo. 'You sound tired. I know you're afraid,' I said, 'but I think the process today is pretty routine.'

My mother laughed. 'Breaking rocks in the noonday sun is routine for chain gangs,' she said. 'I didn't sleep well last night. Partly because I knew I had to come here today. I hate this place.'

'I know,' I said. 'I'm sorry.'

'And then I had your dream,' my mother said.

'You had what?' I asked.

'I had your dream,' she said. 'I had gone to one of your concerts, and I had seats in the middle of the hall. You were playing the Schubert, really beautifully. I love that piece. And then you began to get lost, in that low rumbly passage. And I knew what the notes were that you needed, and I kept trying to call up to you, but you couldn't hear me, and you kept playing that passage over and over again. You had the most terrible look on your face, a sort of lost, frightened look, a little boy look. And I felt so sad, so overwhelmingly sad, and all I could do was watch you.'

'I hope it doesn't happen that way tonight,' I said.

'I wouldn't worry about it,' said my mother. 'It'll be fine.'

'I'm not on good form,' I said.

'No,' said my mother. 'You sound grumpy. Think of it this way, Harry. At eleven o'clock tonight, one way or the other, it'll be over. It's not going to be a complete disaster with that music and that audience. If it's not the best concert you've ever played, then it's not the best concert you've ever played, and after eleven o'clock you don't ever have to think about it again. You don't really want to be thought of as a Mozartian anyway.'

That night, Bernard drove me to the concert hall, and then he came backstage and sat with me while I ran over some scales and tried to get the tempo for the divertimento. He retied my tie – he always retied my bowties – and then we waited together until we heard the crowd being let in.

It was not the best concert I had ever played, but it was perfectly all right, and the audience dutifully asked for an encore. I had planned to do more Mozart, but I suddenly remembered, as I sat down, what my mother had said the week before about the Moonlight Sonata sounding like the dishwasher jammed on the rinse cycle, and it made me laugh again, and I played a light early Beethoven prelude instead. All the time I was playing I thought about the dishwasher, that dishwasher we had had in the country, and the way the yellow china had looked against the dishwasher racks. I remembered when I *had* once jammed the dishwasher; my mother had been furious. Hot water and bubbles everywhere. 'If I had wanted to go wading,' my mother had said, 'we would have bought a house on the beach.'

That night, as we drove home, Bernard said to me, 'You're right about the Mozart. It was fine, but nothing more. But you were great on that Beethoven you did as an encore. It was just lovely. Maybe you should even think about trying to record it.'

I smiled and kissed him on the cheek. 'Maybe I should,' I said. I felt very tired, and I looked out of the window. I tried to imagine having one of his dreams, or his having one of mine.

The next day was Friday, and I had promised Bernard that I would meet him at lunchtime so that we could pick out a birthday present for his godson. We had looked briefly in a small toy store near the flat, but, not finding anything suitable, had decided to venture to central London. I was feeling relaxed. The concert was over; the weekend was at hand; the sun was out. Bernard was taking the afternoon off from work, and as I was fond of his godson I was pleased to be included in the choosing of a gift. It was a good kind of shopping day, which is no doubt why the store was busy when we got there – not so crowded that it was difficult to make purchases, but distinctly bustling.

We wandered around on the ground floor, looking at laminated furniture with Your Child's Name in balloon letters, and large plastic toys that could be fitted together into larger plastic toys, and an anatomically correct model of a racing car that was marked at some inconceivable price. There was a man in a clown suit blowing bubbles out of what appeared to be a chrome-plated saxophone, standing next to a pyramid of smaller saxophones. There were rows of plastic dolls in glittering sport clothes staring vacantly from a glass display case, and there were computerized video games of every description at which mobs of eleven-year-old boys stood transfixed. 'The things we want are upstairs, I think,' said Bernard.

And indeed they were. Upstairs, we found good, solid, wooden blocks in wonderful colours and shapes. We found big stuffed animals and little stuffed animals, most of them dressed better than the shoppers, all made by traditional British craftsmen in remote counties. We found building sets manufactured in Scandinavia, in which little dowels and motors and slate-like supports could be fitted together to form anything from a car to a fully functional model of Tower Bridge. 'This is rather good, don't you think,' Bernard said, as he lingered over a workbench with a dozen perfect miniature tools and a box of blunt-ended nails.

I agreed that it was good, that it was indeed a perfect gift for his godson, and waited while he went off to find a salesman. Standing by the workbench, I saw parents and children in every direction, contented-looking couples in their mid-thirties and early forties, mothers bending over eager little girls, fathers smiling as their sons held forth on the virtues of one set of model trains over another. Just before I had left New York, I had dropped Bernard's name in a conversation with my mother. She had put her hand on my arm for a minute. 'Harry,' she had said, 'I love your father. I love him more, maybe, than you can imagine. But what would I do now without you and Freddy?'

'You'd be fine,' I had replied.

'Don't get annoyed,' she had said to me, her voice taking on a saintly edge. 'Please don't. I wouldn't be fine. I didn't know when I was young and single how much it meant, or what a sense of purpose children bring. Maybe it's unfair that men can't have children with men, but it's the way of the world. I wish I could explain it to you somehow. What you do have with Bernard – I know you think you're being honest or true to yourself or something, but what you have with Bernard can't be greater than that combination of love and children that you could have with Helen or someone, no matter how wonderful he is. It's not just that I'm conventional – ' she had looked at me, then, and I had glowered at her. 'I know this only because I do love you so much, Harry, you and Freddy.' Her voice had sunk almost to a whisper. 'If you don't have children of your own, you'll never know.'

I had scoffed. 'I am who I am.'

'I think you could do anything, Harry, anything in the world if you wanted to,' my mother had said. 'I've always thought that about you.'

Now, standing in the toy store, I felt a sadness that was not just about children. If I was too idiosyncratic for convention, I was also too conventional to be blithely marginal, and among all these toys I felt as peripheral as though I had given up the rights even to my own childhood. I looked at the other adults in the toy store, and they seemed to me to be drifting already toward the relative contentment of middle age that I had seen in my parents. I knew that I did not really want to spend my life with Bernard; nor did I want to find myself older, a bit pinched and a bit faded, still looking for young pleasures. Male domesticity seemed suddenly fraudulent to me. I imagined what it would have felt like to come to this store with Helen, to be included, as Bernard and I clearly were not, in the approving smiles the other couples seemed to bestow on each other. I stood a little apart from Bernard, and hoped that we looked like old friends or like brothers; if I had come with Helen, I might have draped an arm loosely around her shoulders, and felt like part of how the world perpetuates itself. I believed that to do so would have been both a lie and a relief.

If I had said any of this to Bernard, he would have been outraged. 'You'll never be happy,' Bernard would have said angrily, 'if that's what you think.' He would not have forgiven me. And perhaps he would have been right. Bernard did not have such doubts and, not having them, was able to be happy in our life just as it was. I envied him that; I envied all the men who were unflinchingly happy with men (I knew any number of them) as much as I envied those familial groups in the toy store. The happiness of such men seemed infinitely remote to me, more remote even than the complacence of these parents looking at stuffed animals. Helen had told me I had to make sure I knew who I was, and then learn contentment. 'You just learn it,' she'd said. 'Like you learned to play the piano.' In subtle contrast, I heard my mother's voice saying, lightly, 'You're a big boy now, Harry. You make your own happiness or unhappiness.'

We paid for the workbench, and went back out to the street, and the mood passed. On the way home we talked about a workbench Bernard had had and loved as a child. I told him I'd get him the same one we'd just bought when his birthday rolled around. 'With two boxes of nails,' I said.

I had arranged for us to spend the weekend away. I felt that I owed Bernard, not least because I had been so vague to him on the phone from New York. I had a nasty feeling that I had often not sounded very pleased to hear from him, which was hardly fair. And I had an inkling that there were rough times ahead, that there was going to be a great deal of driving to airports and organizing suppers and dealing with my plumber. And besides – I wanted some time for us to be just the two of us. I wanted something romantic and intimate and relaxing, a weekend during which I could store up the ammunition of Bernard's affection like an arsenal against the onslaught of my mother's illness. I wanted a spa vacation.

So I booked us rooms in a country house hotel that had been recommended by our family travel agent. This was my first mistake; but no one I knew made a practice of going to stay in country house hotels, and I had insufficient time to phone around and do research and find out about various places. Bernard would have known of places, and would have revelled in the research, but I felt that to ask him to make the practical arrangements was like sending someone shopping for his own birthday present. I wanted to surprise him. And I wanted to do something with him that was my idea, instead of living with him in his flat and eating his food and driving in his car and all in all taking on rather too much of his life. I, after all, had a life, and had had a life since long before Bernard had entered the picture. It was really quite an interesting life, though the details were not so well negotiated; but I had been letting it slide, and I was afraid that it might wither from neglect.

I had a brochure from the hotel in which it looked charming, as such places generally do in their own brochures. The rolling lawns went on for miles, and the sun filtered through the branches of the glorious old trees and the gardens were as colourful as the land of Oz. The house itself was enormous and slightly Gothic and full of original furnishings of great beauty. The dining room looked as though it had sometimes held minor royalty and had delighted them. The bedrooms were grand and comfortable and full of inviting upholstery. It was possible to see, in several of the photos, Victorian-looking retainers in their pleasant and appropriate garb, imparting an air of period dignity to the many modern appointments which had been gracefully incorporated into the otherwise unaltered building.

What these photographs signally failed to show were the other guests, as dreary a lot of aging golfers as one could hope to find. And in fact the splendours of the place, so persuasive in the photographs, were in reality outlandish. The faithful retainers had been made to look just a bit too faithful, and were kitted up in outfits that I suspect were left over from TV productions of Evelyn Waugh. The superior panelling had been hyper-glossed and buffed; it was original, but it now bore an uncanny resemblance to the simulated wood used in cars. There was more upholstery than I had ever imagined in one place; you felt the whole time that you were sinking into the marshmallow kingdom. And everything was presented with a manner of British high seriousness that would have been fully credible (and perhaps somewhat more appropriate) at a coronation.

Bernard and I drove up to this place in his funny car, an elderly MG with faded green paint and bottle-green seats. We parked it among the many new Mercedes and Jaguars. I got out and went ahead to check in. Bernard was trying to get the parking brake to work – Bernard was always trying to get the parking brake to work – and so he did not follow immediately. 'Welcome,' said the man at the front desk when I had passed through the oak doors. 'We've been expecting you,' he said. 'We have a lovely room with a view of the gardens, as you requested.'

It was at this moment that Bernard walked in. He stood beside me and we both smiled benignly, and the man at the front desk looked down anxiously at his ledger. 'Lovely room, good view, large bath, double bed?' he said with subservient cordiality. I wondered whether he had had occasion to use this euphemistic line before.

'Yes, that's right,' I replied, to his evident dismay.

A man in starchy cutaways conducted us to one of the state chambers, in which there was a bed sufficiently large to support a full joint session of Parliament. The view from our window was rather wonderful, and apart from the curious stares of the three younger members of staff who soon brought up our two suitcases, we saw no reason to feel self-conscious. It was, after all, the modern and permissive era, and we felt that the novelty of our relationship could shock only just so far. We ordered a fantastically elaborate cream tea, and had a butler sort of fellow light a fire in the fireplace (it was a chilly day; we were in a chilly part of Britain) and then we roared with laughter. In a funny way, the setting became romantic because it so isolated us, and we pretended to each other that what was novel in the eyes of the locals was only the extent of our affection. I was never in love with Bernard, but I did love Bernard – and sitting in front of that fire with the cream tea looking inviting, I felt great waves of fondness.

Bernard and I chatted; we read books; we went for a brief stroll in the garden, but it was too cold and damp for that to be much fun, and after Bernard had identified various flowers (Bernard's horticultural knowledge never ceased to astonish me) we went back in and I took a long hot bath while Bernard paced up and down. I should explain that Bernard, for all his opiate effect, was not himself a relaxed person. I am also not a relaxed person, and relaxed people make me uneasy, as I always suspect them either of knowing something I do not or of being too stupid to see what is perfectly obvious. Bernard, however, was always apparently tense about things like the plumber and the flowers, and he was never tense about things like the essential singularity of human experience and the inadequacy of the spirit. Since I was in fact not particularly tense about the things that made Bernard tense, his tension always relaxed me. As I watched him pacing up and down, I felt in my heart of hearts that these problems were solvable, and I foolishly extrapolated that my own problems were also solvable, and I sank down deeper in the bath, and rested a foot on the spigot, and blew paths through the mounting bubbles, and felt that New York was as far away as Pluto. When I got out of the bath, I phoned my mother, as I had done every day in England, as I would do every day I spent abroad throughout her illness. The effect was as abrupt and disconcerting as a rocket flight to the outermost planet of our solar system.

I did not, originally, move to London to escape my parents; or, at any rate, I did not go there only to escape them. I went there because I had come to feel that I had no volition in the United States, that my life was the outcome of circumstances over which I could never gain control. And I went there to escape from myself and my nationality, having never been so keen on either one as I might have wished. I knew, of course that I could not really take on another nationality. What I failed to understand was that you can give up your own nationality only too easily, without knowing that you are doing it, without voting in a foreign election or joining another army or mutilating your passport. You cannot sell your sense of place, cannot exchange it for another sense or a sense of another place, but you can lose it as completely and irretrievably as a vodka tonic poured into the ocean.

Much of what I gained in England now seems trivial to me, but it was not so small at the time. Did I muster any kind of real independence? Helen was later to say to me, over one of those many glasses of white wine in New York: 'You put an ocean between yourself and your parents, and then you just watched them drink it.' She sounded almost angry when she said it. And it was true: I had thought I had crossed the Rubicon and settled on its far side, but by degrees and by wonders of telecommunication and in the end by the progress of symptoms, my parents reduced the Atlantic Ocean until it was smaller than the English Channel, smaller than the Hudson, until it was hardly a creek. These days, I think of that ocean mostly as an inconvenience.

Every one of our family trips to Europe, the trips that seem to demarcate my childhood, included England. When I was in my teens, I twice went with my father on week-long business trips to England, which fell in February, when Freddy did not have school vacation, so that he and my mother could not accompany us. My father and I would have breakfast and dinner together, and in between I would entertain myself, wandering the city, trying to imagine that I was a resident, striding manfully through the snow in Hyde Park or else drifting from museum to museum, from shop to shop, looking at concert halls where I dreamed of playing, or attending obscure recitals, as one does in foreign cities. I would sometimes have friends in London, and I would play at being my mother, sweeping them up into the glamour of smart restaurants to which my father encouraged me to invite them. I defined a life in London that was very much my own, long ago, before I went to live there. I never felt in London, as I did in Paris, that I was unequal to the city itself, to the scale my mother had brought to it.

Helen spent a year abroad in England when we were fifteen, and she and I spent a week of that year together. My father was having one of his business trips, and so I stayed with him at the hotel; Helen was living in Hampstead. It was one of our best weeks. It was February, but it was one of those spells of April weather that sometimes fall, in Britain, in the middle of winter, and on a bright Wednesday we woke to the essence of spring. We decided to go to Brighton, to see the pavilion. I had the hotel pack a picnic, and Helen came and met me in the lobby. The hall porter asked me where our car was, and when I explained that we were taking the train, he looked somewhat taken aback, and gestured at a porter with a picnic basket shaped like a straw suitcase, as heavy as the suitcase in which I had conveyed a week's worth of clothing to the UK, and wondered whether I would like to consider a car, which he could easily arrange. I said thank you, and that we were quite happy as we were, and took the basket from the porter.

We took the train, an 11.00 train that was almost empty, through the unseasonal sunshine, and we talked about Helen's year in England and about girls' schools and about my father and about Helen's crazy mother and about the prospect of going to college someday. When we arrived in Brighton we found a map, and we took turns carrying the enormous straw suitcase until we finally made it down to the beach. There were only about six people on the beach; one young man had taken off his shirt and was sitting with his bare chest propped towards the sun. Helen and I agreed that the British were incredible; it was a bizarrely warm day, but we were glad, with the wind coming off the sea, of our sweaters. We took out a large white tablecloth and then we unpacked lunch. We decided to eat immediately since neither of us wanted to go on carrying the food. There were different kinds of sandwiches and chicken legs and mineral water and champagne and a thermos of tea and the inevitable strawberries with cream and caster sugar and various sticky cakes and, because the insect kingdom is slow to respond to the eccentricities of British weather, there were no bugs of any kind, and Helen and I sat with the sun reflecting up at us and we ate until we thought we might burst. Then we sat, staring out at the water, and talked about poetry – we liked poetry – and felt as though we had discovered the very idea of picnics and could claim it for our own. The whole world seemed to belong to us, the stony beach and the glittering domes of the pavilion and the train that would go back to London. And Helen's hair blew around in the wind and her eyes caught the light, and she looked so very beautiful and knew so little of it – and indeed I too knew very little of it at the time.

We decided to go for a walk. But what on earth was one to do with the straw suitcase and all that cutlery, all those linens and all that blue-and-gold china? Helen was living in a school sort of way, in an uncomfortable and ill-equipped house, and such supplies seemed invaluable. It did not occur to us that the hotel might want them back. 'I shall have a springtime of picnics,' she announced. We soon grew tired of carrying the suitcase, and there did not seem to be a coatroom anywhere, and so Helen found a public convenience and hid the picnic suitcase in the ladies side, in a stall, and we went strolling along the beach. Later, we went to the pavilion, and Helen transferred the basket to another public convenience; then she left it at the train station while we took a final walk though town; and then we collected it and carried it back to London. If the hall porter wondered where its contents had gone, he was much too tactful to comment.

All these years later, I was with Bernard in a country house hotel. It was not what I had imagined for myself; it was the life into which I had tumbled readily and, in the end, easily. It was the path of least resistance (for all that it had looked difficult) that had dumped me with this strawberry-blond man among all this upholstery. Helen, who had tried to explain England to me when we were off on our picnic, ten years earlier, was back in America, and I was the one who had settled in Britain. I had arrived quite naturally at agonizing American self-consciousness at much the same time that I had given way to a lifestyle at which old school friends would have snickered, and did snicker.

I came out of the bath and settled myself on the bed.

'Feeling clean?' asked Bernard.

'Very clean,' I said, and stretched out my long clean limbs. 'It's a dream bathroom in there,' I said.

'You look like a little angel,' said Bernard, and came over to kiss me. But he had not yet had his bath, and was not as clean as I was, and for some reason I found him slightly ridiculous and a little off-putting. For just a split second, I hated the fact that he was a man. It seemed to me infinitely depressing.

'Go have a bath,' I said, with a light laugh. 'You've still got the drive all over you.'

My mother answered the phone on the first ring. As I spoke to her I could see Bernard's bath in the fireplace mirror. I do not know whether he realized that I could see him or not, but it would have been too much effort to look away, and so I continued to watch him abstractedly, as though I had intercepted his privacy in transit.

Bernard had in some way a very beautiful body, long and thin and supple, with none of the musculature of fashion, but with the strange and fascinating lines of a mannerist drawing. He faced the corner of the bathroom to undress, as though he didn't want the bidet to see his nakedness, and then walked slowly over to the tub. His movements were awkward without his usual mask of oversized clothing; it seemed that he had never had time to adjust to these attenuated limbs. He filled the tub with hot water, only hot, and watched the steam rise. He moved as if each of his gestures were commanded in some distant spot by some inexplicable intelligence; his hand, turning the spigots, was tortoise slow. When the tub was nearly full and the steam had taken over the whole bathroom, fogging the mirror and the window and moistening not only the towels, but also the walls, the fluffy chair in the corner, and the book he had placed on the floor by the tub, Bernard ran a hand over the water – over, like a hovercraft – and then, stunned, turned on the cold water and watched it gush into the tub. He lowered himself in slowly, as if he were afraid of the depths. First feet, and then hands; for a moment he was four-legged. Then bottom, and then, so agonizingly slowly, the rest of his body, until only his head floated on the water like a bubble. He took up his book and stared at the pages, but his eyes were motionless, and he did not turn the pages.

What was the meaning of all this stillness, while I talked on the phone in a voice too low to be heard across the steam? After ten minutes, Bernard put down his book (he had not once turned a page), pinched his nose, and allowed himself to slide underwater altogether. He curled up, as he had curled earlier on the chintz sofa, and he floated, in a little bundle; then he surfaced for air, and then he floated again. The book lay on a tiny ledge beside the spigots, but somehow it did not get splashed. Bernard shampooed his hair, and, to rinse it, he floated again, curled, tight, closed. Afterwards, he stood up, covered himself with a layer of lather, as though soap were a coat, and then went sliding as fast as he could through the water. He leaped out and let the tub drain, and stared at himself in a mirror steamed until it revealed only softness; wrapped in a long towel, he carried his clothes back to the bedroom, returned to my public eye, and retrieved the careful stance I knew so well.

While my eyes stayed fixed on Bernard in the sliver reflection through the partially open door, I talked to my mother. She was being brave; I hated it when she wept and made demands, but I also hated it when I felt she was not making demands, and as I tried to cheer her when she was sad, I tried to get through to her when she sounded more complacent than her circumstances justified. She told me about a long walk she had had with my father, and said that she was surprised how quickly she seemed to have recovered from the actual surgery. She mentioned friends who had come by that afternoon to see her. She told me that the wigs had arrived, and that she didn't think they looked too bad. She told me she'd had the piano tuner in. She told me that she was terrified of her chemotherapy, but that she had got used to the idea of it and was almost looking forward to the first treatment, or at least to having the first treatment over with. She told me about the dog's eye infection, for which she had been giving her drops, and about a novel she had just finished, and she told me that she had bought new sheets for the downstairs bedrooms in the country. And I told her all about the hotel, and made her laugh, and didn't mention Bernard, and hung up the telephone, and, knowing that the sheets downstairs in the country were in perfect condition, were only a year old and hardly used at all, I felt that Bernard and his bath and his windowboxes and dinner with Claire and Michael were full of unspoken sadness, and I looked around the room, our big luxurious room, and I disliked every detail of it. Then, as Bernard came out of the bathroom, I forced a smile, because I knew he would have wanted to comfort me if he had seen me looking sad, and I was much too tired for that.

Instead, we looked at neckties, and agreed that the yellow one that had been in my Christmas stocking the previous year looked terrific with my new shirt. Bernard wore the tie I had given him, with the pattern of knotted ropes, and a dark blue jacket, and a pair of slightly tweedy trousers. We looked so respectable, so eminently respectable. If we were not the couple I would have imagined for myself, the couple my mother would have imagined for me, we were, certainly, as bright and scrubbed and trim as Freddy and I might have been for dinner with the family.

We proceeded down the grand staircase to the grand dining room, and were seated at a table by the fireplace, and ordered drinks. Bernard had supposed we would be objects of curiosity in the eyes of the golfing couples, but in fact these couples were much too busy discussing golf and their children and their work and the weather and how hard it had been to get a line through to wherever they came from, and they could not have been less interested in Bernard and me. So we drank our drinks and looked at the large hunting scene over the fireplace and talked about the weather, and about our friends, and about how much we would miss each other when I went back to New York. I told him about the dog's eye infection and the drops, and he said that his cousin Gordon's dog had had a nasty sort of eye infection that had apparently been spreading among dogs in Britain, and that he had recently read a piece about this infection, and that one must be rather careful as it could cause complications. He pointed out that, since Molly was a terrier, she was very dependent on her eyes, not like a hound who could manage pretty well with just his nose; and I agreed that one could see how much Molly used her eyes, and said I hoped it would all be all right. Molly was getting very old. And of course Nora, Bernard's cat, was also getting old. So we talked about Molly and Nora and not about golf, and we looked at the menus, and we ordered some things that sounded rather appealing, and we felt that this was a safe and solid and secure sort of weekend to be having after all.

But when we sat down to dinner, I felt slightly queasy. At first I blamed the long ride and the tension, but then I began to recognize the symptoms: I was coming down with a twenty-four hour stomach virus. I am prone to twenty-four hour viruses. Dutifully,

I ordered the plainest and most boring items on the menu, and watched Bernard tuck into the dressed crab (dressed crab was a bit of a local speciality) and the rack of lamb. I drank ginger ale because it is settling to the stomach. I excused myself from the table at regular intervals to visit the stony loo and consider whether I was going to be sick or not. In the end I felt too ill to stay downstairs through dessert, and Bernard and I went back up to our room early. I lay down on my side of the bed, and Bernard said endless comforting things and remarked that twenty-four hour viruses did at least go away by the end of twenty-four hours.

I was not really made for spa vacations. Moderation had always been difficult for me, and with Bernard I felt I was playing a perpetual game of charades in which my immoderation was too often the winner. I was made for adventure holidays, or for glamourous tours, or for complicated business trips, or even for journeys home, but I was not made for spa vacations. I would like to be able to say simply that spa vacations bore me, but in fact they do not bore me. They absolutely fascinate me. The travel other people cannot carry off comes as readily to me as desire, but the vacations that other people find blissfully easy remain somehow inaccessible. I had thought in the beginning that Bernard might teach me how to live at a spa, but it didn't work; I always seemed to be turning the spa into an adventure, or at least a drama, and this too often defeated its whole purpose.

The next morning, I woke up feeling like half of myself, and not the better half. Bernard ate an impressive breakfast, the sight of which made me feel nauseated, and I sipped some weak tea. I then had a shower and got dressed and Bernard and I discussed what to do. It was raining out, and it was cold. We were not interested in golf anyway. So we got in the car and drove to a local town where Bernard had heard there were antiques, and we wandered through shops, half of which had broken furniture that was very old and not a bit attractive for extremely low prices, and half of which had beautiful antiques for the same out-of-the-question prices at which these items might have been purchased in London. We stopped for lunch at a restaurant furnished with the old broken furniture but priced for the people who came to shop in the out-of-the-question shops; Bernard had smoked salmon and I had some more tea. In the afternoon we went back to the hotel, and I slept and read while Bernard wandered through the garden identifying plants.

When we got upstairs that night, after dinner, Bernard was all for love, but I was still too queasy, and felt stretched to the limits by the physical exertion of brushing my teeth. How nice it would have been to find Bernard irresistible. Bernard was very good-looking, but we both had too many similar and incompatible bones that seemed to clank on each other. Under ordinary circumstances, I didn't mind about sex with Bernard; indeed in some sense it was very pleasant, in much the same way that repeating familiar stories to each other was pleasant. But as for love in the afternoon, love in the morning, love in the evening – it was just as well that I was in the last throes of my twenty-four-hour virus, and could only drift toward sleep.

By the time we got back to London I was feeling somewhat better. Bernard helped me to pack, and promised to collect my umbrella, which I had forgotten, and said that he was going to discuss the basic facts with Norman, which I felt strongly that he ought to do. We agreed to go on talking to each other every day. He was sure my mother was going to like her birthday present. He made a whole toasted breakfast for me in the morning, which I more or less managed to eat, and then we put my suitcase back into his faded green car and headed out through the newly arrived sunshine toward Heathrow. I walked up to check-in feeling much better than I had felt ten days earlier, despite the mild after-effects of my twenty-four hour virus. And it was not until I had hugged Bernard goodbye – what a long time it had been since I had hugged him in that same terminal building, on the way back from France with Freddy – that the reality hit me, and that I thought about the long trip home.

IV

Winter

It is not the case that all happy families are the same. I often think that there are no new sad stories; the ways in which my life has been sad are so much like the ways in which the lives of those I know and love have been sad. Perhaps that is just as well: on the analyst's couch or in the muted discourses of friendship, I learn that it is sadness that binds humanity, that the sadness I claim has been claimed, in some version or another, by everyone on earth. But my happiness, and the happiness of my family! There are thousands of happy families, but they are too private to earn the documentation tragedy claims as its due, and every one is so radically unlike every other, so frighteningly particular, that language itself shrinks from the task of describing them. Happiness is not too sentimental or too hackneyed to portray; it is too obscure, too personal, too strange to find a universal rhetoric. Sadness comes along well-worn paths and finds you, but since happiness is something you find yourself, it comes shaped in your own crazy image. The things that made my family happy were so much our own: no one else has ever touched them, nor will anyone touch them again. Our joy is forever ours, and its obscurity protects it; the unknowable is immune to decay. As for our sadness: it is only another version of the sadness that rings in everyone's lives every day, and with the clockwork monotony of the run from birth to death, it unfolds along a course as predestined as the last notes of a scale.

When I arrived in New York from England, the facts of our life were much as I had left them, but my relationship to those facts was changed. During my mother's first hospital visit, I had learned how things were to be, and it had been like learning Chinese. Never in my life had I confronted anything so alien, so bewildering, so different in its very structure from all previous experience. By the time I came back from England, I was conversational in this new language. The patterns of illness had become familiar, and though I did not like them and did not feel at ease in them, I was able to function in them. Absence does not so much make the heart grow fonder as give the heart time to integrate what it has not previously absorbed, time to make sense of what happened too quickly to have any meaning in the instant. This is always true. If it is in absence that people forget each other, it is also in the quiet pause of absence that, minds running in symmetry, people come to know each other; there is sometimes as much intimacy in the span of continents as in the shared hours before dawn. While I was in England, playing my concert and having my twenty-four-hour virus, I came to know anew both my mother and her illness, so that when I returned to town I greeted her ailments almost as comrades. In good faith, I started on the saddest period of my life. But we were a happy family, and so I also started, in some much more obscure way – obscure at that time even to me – to take possession of our happiness.

I came back to surprise my mother. I surprised my mother on her birthday over and over again, and every single time she was surprised, until at last I was as much amazed by her astonishment as she was surprised that I had come to surprise her. It never occurred to me not to go home for my mother's birthday in the first year of her illness, since it was from her that I had learned my own sense of occasion. It was my mother who taught me that you could never put too much faith into birthdays or Christmas or graduations, she who built these into feast days such as no jousting knight had ever dreamed. My mother never tired of these holidays: she built them out of spun sugar on a foundation of thin air, and nothing delighted her more than to see how Freddy and I spiralled upwards in her candied architecture.

My father simply assumed that I would come back, but then my father assumed that the clocks would have stopped in the face of my mother's disease had they known she wished it. My father's life was my mother; he no more wanted independence from her than he wanted independence from his arms or legs. He could not understand how Freddy and I could feel otherwise. He never saw what I wanted from England; it did not strike him as a sacrifice for me to return after a short ten days with my life and my lover and my own piano, without having recorded a single note. So far as he was concerned, it would have been odd and sad to stay in London when my mother was having a birthday in New York – when there was an opportunity to make her happy. I needed independence, a happiness of my own, and I was almost violent in my protests against the relentlessly depressing life into which we were all sucked in New York, the life around the hospital. I tried to close out this life. I believed in my career, and knew that my tenuous position as a musician would blow apart if left alone for too long. I argued with my father, then, because I did not want to admit to him that it would have seemed odd and sad to me too not to come home for my mother's birthday. I refused to admit to him that I could not have played a concert that night if the moon and the planets and the stars had planned to be in the audience.

Bernard put me on the plane to New York and Helen took me off. I felt like a shipment of glass. 'You look about a thousand times better,' said Helen when I cleared customs, and her voice sounded almost jealous. 'Good concert?'

'I've been having a virus,' I said.

'Couldn't you let your mother corner the market on medical dramas for a few weeks?' she asked. 'Watch your competitive streak, or it's going to get you into trouble.' She gave me a big hug. 'I think England suits you,' she told me. 'Don't stay in New York too long.'

We went back to Helen's apartment, where I was to spend the night, so that I could surprise my mother the following day. Helen lived in an old building with brown corridors that smelled like decaying cats, but her apartment was the more impressive for that. It had been painted in brilliant white, a white so sharp that it hurt your eyes. There were no rugs or carpets on the highly polished floors. There were funny old pieces of furniture that she had bought from the Salvation Army, which had been rubbed to an almost jewel-like lustre. There were several very large plants, and there were a few framed posters, and there was divine and terrifying order everywhere. On the dressing table, Helen's earrings were arranged in even rows. In the kitchen, the plates stood in perfect stacks, and the boxes of soap powder were graduated by size. Helen would have arranged her shoes in alphabetical order if she'd known how.

We ate Chinese food for dinner in a little take-out-eat-in joint around the corner. Helen did the ordering; the food was luke-warm, but it was not bad. I told her briefly about the concert, and she asked about my mother. But I was, for once, too tired to talk about myself; I sat with my head still full of the plane and listened to Helen plot the regulatory policies with which she hoped to make the world less of an unfair place. By the time we got back to the apartment I was worn out. Helen had set up a futon on the far side of her room, and had made it up with crisp white sheets and a large green quilt. I sank down to floor level and thought I would go at once to sleep. In fact, Helen slept first. I lay in the corner and listened to her breathing, and saw the way her arm dropped off the side of her bed, like Chatterton's. Helen had no curtains in her apartment, and the light of the city and the light of the moon came through her large window and lit her, and she looked like peace on earth. I got up and walked across the room to look at her more closely; I almost touched her hair, which had become luminous, but she turned slightly and alarmed me, and I lay down again. Then I too fell at last into a deep, exhausted sleep.

The next morning jet-lag woke me early. I showered in Helen's glitteringly white bathroom, turning the large, old, satisfying knobs that she had polished to a silver glow, and revelling in the bliss of American water pressure. Helen had to get to work, and when I shuffled into the kitchen, she was eating a croissant with some orange juice and a large cup of milky coffee. 'The jam's for you,' she said, pushing a jar of apricot preserve in my direction. 'And there's another croissant, and there's toast if you want it, and I got some yoghurt.' So I had the croissant with a great deal of apricot preserve – which I didn't particularly want – and I drank some orange juice, and I ate the yoghurt, and I made myself some tea. Bernard always said it was less painful to make breakfast for me than to watch me bump into things in my morning miasma; Helen seemed to think it was easier to let me fend for myself. I was in an expansive mood, but Helen was pressed for time. 'Lock the top lock, but don't try to lock the bottom lock because it gets stuck. Turn off the lights when you go, and please make sure you wash your dishes because there are bugs in this building.' Helen stopped for a second in front of the old gilded mirror in the hall and tightened one of her earrings, as though the mirror had shown it to be loose. 'I've got to run,' she said, and then she gave me a great hug. 'Sweetie, I hope it's a raving success tonight. Give your mother all my love,' she said. 'And call me.' And then she was out the door and gone.

I went back into the bedroom and turned on the TV to a channel that Helen's set – she didn't have cable – couldn't receive, so that a variable fuzzy noise filled the room. I dialled my parents' line, and made a point of pausing between sentences to reproduce the effect of a bad transatlantic connection. I sang 'Happy Birthday' as I had done on my mother's birthday morning every year. My mother told me that she was going to go out that evening for the first time since her hair had gone. 'Your father's made a reservation,' she said, and named a favourite restaurant as though it were the café at the gates of hell.

I remember once, when I was little, that my father came home without a cake for my mother's birthday. She sat through her birthday dinner with a set expression, and my father couldn't work out what was wrong; unsure whether there was really anything wrong at all, he preserved his sunny manner through two courses. At the end of the roast beef, he stood up to help clear the table. 'And what's for dessert?' he asked brightly.

'I didn't get anything for dessert,' said my mother, 'because I didn't think it would be necessary this evening.' I can still hear the injury in her voice. Of course my mother never ate cake, but she expected icing sugar and candles and she expected to be surprised. My father never failed again; cakes and champagne marked the passage of each of my mother's years. Now, it was my mother who, for my father, was going to have a festive evening, to open presents and seem glad. 'It's the first evening out for the wig,' she said, as though it were anyone's treat but her own.

I got to the restaurant half an hour early that evening, sat at our usual table, had a drink, and watched the other diners. I was calm in expectation of my mother's arrival; I knew the facial expressions with which she always registered her surprise, and I looked forward to them placidly. I had worked out in advance all the nice things I would say about the wig, which my optimistic father had said looked so like her own hair that only she could tell the difference. I felt certain that I would make the day as rich for her as any of her birthdays had ever been.

I will not forget the image of my mother entering the restaurant that evening. Our table is at the end of a long corridor of tables, commanding a view toward the door. I saw in the dim distance that my parents and Freddy had arrived, and I watched the rituals of coat-check, and then I saw the owner guiding my family toward the table. On other occasions, I had come to meet my parents, and had sat at that table, and had watched my mother walk down that aisle, maintaining her particular elegant composure and her social smile, asking the owner after his family and about how business was at the restaurant. That day my mother walked like someone newly blind. She was wearing a black-and-white wool suit that seemed to be too big for her, and her walk was almost loping. Her arms hung strangely and uselessly at her sides. It was not, as usual, that she did not pay attention to the other people at the restaurant; she did not see them. Her eyes were only partly open, and she blinked constantly, as though she were staring into a very bright light beyond which there were only indistinct shadows. As for the wig: if you had never before seen my mother, you would not have paid particular attention to that wig; it looked like hair, and it was not unbecoming. But it did not look like her hair. It hung down onto her shoulders like a dead weight. A few flyaway strands had blown over her face, and others were lying on the wrong side of her head. She was no longer herself, and she knew this.

My mother had never suggested to me that I come home for her birthday that year. My mother at that stage carried her illness outside of her, as though it were a bag of groceries she was never to be allowed to put down. She had found already that it was impossible to give the bag, or its contents, to anyone else. It took all her energy to keep holding it, and for the first time she had too little wherewithal even to appeal to the rest of us. My mother had stopped giving voice to her demands. She was so upset that she depended on us only in the wordless way that you depend on shelter. She needed for us to be at her beck and call, but she had nothing particular or specific or meaningful to ask of us. In other years, she had not asked me to come home for her birthday because she liked being surprised, and I had come most years, but not every year, because I wanted to be able to surprise her. But that year she had not asked me to come home because it had not occurred to her.

'Hello, Harry,' she said when she got to the table and saw me. 'I thought you were in London.' She sounded puzzled and neutral. 'I thought you had some meeting about your recording this week.'

'Surprise!' I said. There was a sort of terrible empty moment while she looked around the restaurant. Then she put her hand on my arm, and with an enormous effort of her conscious mind she opened her eyes all the way, and turned to face me. She did not laugh or clap her hands, and her face did not light up as it had when I had surprised her before. 'It's your birthday,' I added. 'Didn't you guess I might surprise you for your birthday?'

She looked through her open eyes to mine in silence for perhaps ten seconds. 'Thank you for being here,' she said at last, looking straight into me, and in that moment it was as though she could see everything – Bernard, her accusations, my love for her, Paris, how much I needed for her to get well, how frightened I was, how the appointment to see the recording studio had been rescheduled, how I too was learning this new Chinese, how I had left London after just ten days – all of it in the depths of my eyes. 'Thank you for being here, Harry,' she said again, simply, still holding me in that immense look; and when she said my name her voice went up, as though it were headed elsewhere.

Then, 'Good trip, Harry?' said Freddy, and my father said he had been worried all day about whether I would be at the restaurant on time, and we settled into birthday conversation.

'So what do you think of your mother in a wig?' my mother

asked in the light voice she had been using ever since her surgery, and I assured her that she had never looked better. 'Either you're becoming a very accomplished liar,' she rejoined, 'or your standards have been slipping in England.'

That winter I went back and forth every month. I was preparing for my recording, and had to be in England to go over details and talk to engineers. I also had a rigorous performance schedule, and had to get to various European and Asian destinations. At the time, I had no American engagements; I had been trying to make a foreign career first, so that I might burst on America already glorious. I accompanied a friend who sang lieder, worked on the Mozart, and learned everything Schubert had ever written for the piano. The Beethoven prelude became a standard encore piece for me, and I studied more early Beethoven. For a festival in Warsaw I polished up all the Chopin waltzes, and these were a great success. In Russia, I played Rachmaninoff's second piano concerto; when I finished, a stout woman came up to me in tears to tell me she had worked as a housekeeper for the great man. 'I think,' she said, 'that you are very sad, or you could not play so well this piece. For me, your sadness is very beautiful, and I think there will be more of it, for your whole life.' I thought this was a little grim, but Bernard assured me that the Russians are like that.

I seemed to be on a different piano every week, and my fingers never felt accustomed to anything any more. Notes came too fast, or they came too slowly; they were too loud or too soft. Everything felt disrupted and under-rehearsed. I dreamed of being one of those famous pianists who could insist on travelling with his Steinway and a trusty piano tuner. After every concert I would call New York; it always distracted my mother when I read my reviews aloud to her. 'That's so true,' she would say of someone's praise. 'Sometimes people just don't get it,' she would say of a disparagement, though once or twice she also asked, 'Were you feeling tired that night?' Once she said, 'Well, you haven't been practising Liszt for very long, and you don't really have a Liszt personality. I'm not sure you should be playing the Liszt in Paris next week.' It was good advice, though I did not always want it;

in any case, this subject seemed to draw her from the pondering of her own illness.

I wanted to be in London to be with Bernard and get on with my life, and I lied to my father in order to stay there. I pretended more concerts than I actually had, and said that I had to work with a teacher on the pieces I was to record. 'Don't keep rushing back here,' my mother used to say, but to my father I was one of the luxuries he could provide my mother, and he wanted me to be as full time as the hospital nurses. He paid uncomplainingly for every ticket, but resented the fact that they were always round trips. I did want to be in New York for my mother, and I came home at least once every three weeks, but I stayed for only a few days at a time. I was afraid my life in London would dissolve if I left it too long, that the gloom of our household would swallow me whole. In some sense, and to my surprise, my culture shock seemed to be getting worse and worse. I had somehow lost both the comfort of the familiar and the thrill of the novel; it was like altitude sickness every time, getting off the plane like a rude snatch back from the ecstasy of the deep and into the violence and shock of the appallingly familiar. Those were the heady airplane days. I could have papered the downstairs bathroom with my tickets. I had a favourite seat on each plane and a favourite seat in each departure lounge and a favourite desk at each passport control point and a favourite spot by each baggage-claim carousel. But I no longer had a favourite country. Wherever I was, I felt that I should be elsewhere; I thought of each place as a transit zone from which I would shortly migrate to some farther spot.

Bernard accepted the new shape of our relationship without protest; it was one of Bernard's great strengths to bow to the inevitable. You would have thought, to see me with Bernard, that everything was much as it had always been. Our jokes and routines were unaltered, and we were serious about those matters about which we had always been serious, and jokey about the things that had always amused us. This made me feel rooted and secure; it was impossible to believe, when I was with Bernard, that life was tragic. I would sit down to the cold suppers he made on my arrival nights – when winter began, he added soup and they became warmer meals – and he would fill me in on what had happened while I was away. In the way that people take care of other people's pets during a span of absence, Bernard took care of my life, so that when I came back I found it just where it would have been had I not gone to America. He called all my friends and paid my bills and dealt with the washing machine and bought me clothes I might under other circumstances have bought for myself; he spoke of me at dinners at which I would otherwise have been present, so that everyone I knew was always up to date on my various ups and downs.

'Don't worry,' Bernard would say to me.

I worried all the time.

'Don't worry,' he would say again, and when I was in England, some of the time, for his sake, I stopped worrying. Our relation-ship settled into a rhythm based on my nobility in the face of disaster and his kindness in the face of my nobility. It was what is known in the vernacular as an unequal struggle. I found that it was easier to let Bernard lead my life than to lead it myself; my time in England became more and more sedentary, and began to resemble time off.

I spent long hours practising the Schubert and the Rachmaninoff, and when I went to record, it was a complete disaster. I was terrified by the permanence of these sounds that would stay etched in metal forever, frozen by the thought of an eternal blun-der. In the recording studio I was so keen to avoid wrong notes that I played as if I were wearing wooden gloves. I went in every day for a week, knowing that there was no poetry coming out of me. My agent came over at the end of each afternoon. 'Well,' he would say dubiously, 'that sounds a little better than it did before.' But I knew that it didn't sound better. The joints of my fingers seemed to have gone out of my control. It was like trying to drive a car with a broken gear shift.

I attempted to explain all this to the engineers and the pro-ducers, and finally I played like a trump card the narrative of my mother's illness. My agent had some long discussions behind closed doors, and prevailed on them to let me redo the whole thing a few months later. 'Listen,' he said to me. 'This is not easy to arrange. You'd better get it together between now and then. Maybe you want to rent a real piano to take to this hospital in New York where your mother is, but you've got to do something.'

I practised more than ever. The Schubert was much trickier than I had expected. I played it accurately, and, at least in general, with feeling, but I seemed not to be able to get the magic of the first movement, and I knew that there was magic buried there.

'I've heard you play that first movement well,' my mother said one day on the phone. 'I think it's a matter of mood for you. Really I do. I just love that one phrase, that little melody we talked about last time you were home, which you play particularly well. It's all tone of voice, and carrying the feeling of that one phrase into the rest of the movement.'

'Tone of voice,' I said.

'Yes,' my mother said. 'Do you remember, after my third chemotherapy, I'd come home from the hospital and I was feeling so sick, and I thought I just couldn't eat anything. Your father was at the office and Freddy had gone back to school, and you and I and Janet were all alone in the house. You kept coming back to my room to cajole me with smoked salmon and poached eggs and that ghastly carrot bread you'd bought. Do you remember that day?'

'You were in bad shape,' I said. 'You kept saying how weak you felt, and I thought you should have something, or you'd really just collapse.'

'I felt as much like eating smoked salmon as I did like flying to the moon,' said my mother. 'Salty fish. On that stomach. But you kept telling me that the doctor wanted me to eat, and I finally said I would have some dry toast. You came back with that toast and a nectarine, and I sat there and ate the toast, because I knew that I had to have something. And then you waved that nectarine at me. And you said, "Oh, Mom, what about the nectarine?" And you sounded sad, and anxious, and forlorn. And so I ate that nectarine – which I will tell you now was mealy on top of everything else.'

'You ate two bites of the nectarine.'

'It's incredible that I ate any of that nectarine at all. Who buys nectarines in November, Harry? Ripened on a plane. Pretty to look at but inedible under the best of circumstances. Which those were not.'

'It had vitamin C in it,' I said.

'In the summer, Harry. Fresh nectarines in the summer. Anyway, I ate that nectarine, or part of that nectarine, because of your voice when you gave it to me.'

'Why are we talking about that nectarine?' I asked.

'That's the tone of voice you need in the first movement, Harry,' my mother said. 'The way you're playing it now is technically accomplished, but it should have a little bit of longing in it, something a little bit more urgent.'

New York was in too many ways the life I had outgrown. When I was there, I lived in my parents' apartment, back in the room of my childhood. I practised on the piano on which I had learned scales at the age of five. When Freddy came down from medical school, he was in his room next door. It was all set up as it had been when we were infants. He and I argued about whose turn it was to walk the dog and who should be doing the dishes. Janet did our ironing and in the end did most of the dishes and made the beds and smoothed the machinery between us as she had always done. 'It's OK,' she would say. 'You two go talk to your mother. I'll walk Molly.'

Then we would both be embarrassed.

'I've got some errands anyway,' Freddy would say. And he would shoot me an angry look and go to find the dog's leash.

Each day, morning and evening, at rising and at sleeping, I examined my state of mind. I measured its progress against the previous day and noted the details of its changes, as though it were something outside of me, a variation in air pollution or fluctuation of humidity. It is almost impossible to remember from one feeling to another: England disappeared as soon as I touched down on US soil. And whereas Bernard went on with my life on my behalf, my family life seemed to die when I went away and to die again when I returned; there was nothing to keep up with.

We lived in a strange and artificial world. The house was kept unbearably overheated in deference to my mother's lack of blood, and it was seen almost as a matter of poor form to comment on the temperature elsewhere. We all agreed with her that restaurants were icily cold; we all said that the winter was the worst in years; we all bundled into layers of sweaters and coats so as not to suggest that for us the days were bright and sunny and fine. And in time we came to feel how cold it was for my mother, who had always tended to feel the cold anyway, and our shivers became as authentic as hers. With time, we all found the days unbearable, because when we were with my mother and saw how her ever-delicate figure had become like some kind of exotic filigree work, as inexplicably fragile as inlay, we began to find our own flesh absurd, and we curled up within it as though to warm ourselves from the inside out.

In consideration of her illness, we ceased to get sick. My mother's immune system was so depressed that the slightest infection might have proved fatal to her; she could have used up her day's entire reserve of energy in five minutes of coughing. Even a touch of a cold would have delayed and extended her loathed chemotherapy. So we lived out her fragility. Sickness took on the status of a forbidden indulgence. To protect my mother, we all became untouchable. I longed for the old discomforts of a sore throat, cups of soup, valiance in the face of sneezes. It had been my habit, every winter, to contract some mild edition of the year's flu, and to go on in spite of it, to feel strong and brave and young because the illness did not stop me from practising and performing. In the face of a hacking cough, I had proved my heroism season after season. Now this occasion for dignity had been stripped away from me, and though I would, in previous times, have thought a winter without a single sneeze a great luxury, in this year it came to be another pressure. I refused to see friends who were feeling slightly off, and I never left the house with wet hair, and I made sure that I slept regularly and ate well – not out of concern for my own well-being, but out of concern for my mother's health. Much later, it would seem like the ultimate luxury to go out and feel that to risk a cold was to risk only my own cough and congestion. In the time of my mother's illness I took every possible precaution so as not to be the Typhoid Mary of the family; and so my own health became not my own, but a gift to her.

My mother herself became extravagantly untouched. You could not affect cancer with your own conduct, but you could control your chances of other diseases, and my mother, determined to control something, brought to bear a discipline extraordinary even for her. She would not kiss a friend hello. She would not use a public ladies' room. She would not sit in a public theatre, where someone might breathe down her neck, and she would visit only those restaurants where she could be guaranteed a corner table at some considerable distance from the other diners. She gave up public transport entirely; even a taxi might carry the germs of a stranger. So she stood unwillingly aloof from ordinary life. My mother hated solitude, but solitude was one of the prices this disease exacted from her, the solitude of a misery she could not authentically share, and then the added indignity of physical isolation from the people she loved, who loved her, who wanted to see her, and whose visits she was often obliged to prohibit. She placed as much physical distance between herself and the world as she could; she lived in a cocoon of privacy, with only her illness for an intimate.

During the period of my mother's illness, I became deeply superstitious. For two solid years, I avoided ladders, and handled mirrors like babies. I pulled my side of every wishbone as though it had come not from a boiled chicken, but from a phoenix. I was perpetually rapping on wood. I played – this was a private ritual – something in a major key first and last when I was practising, and played minor keys in between. I am not by nature a deeply superstitious person, but I had a voice of better-safe-than-sorry forever ringing in my ears; there was no precaution that could be overlooked. I thought it rash to tempt fate. I believed that you were more likely to get your wishes if they were unselfish, and so I sustained a struggle to be unselfish in every particular and at every level. After my mother got sick, I almost gave up on wishes for myself. With monotonous regularity I asked for my mother's health. Sometimes I wished to fall in love with a suitable girl, because I knew how happy that would make her. Sometimes I just wished for the sun to come out, because she so liked sunshine, or for the doctor to smile when she went to see him, or for her to enjoy her dinner for once, and not feel nauseated. Sometimes I wished for higher spirits for myself because they would have allowed me to sustain her better; I hoped to change my sorrow for happiness not so much because I longed to be happy as because I knew how my happiness would become a happiness for my mother.

Every morning when I was in New York, I would go into my mother's room and find her propped up in bed, post-breakfast, having a cup of chamomile tea. Calling upon reserves of energy – I am not naturally cheerful in the mornings – I would bounce in and smile broadly. 'How are you today?' I would ask.

'I feel terrible,' my mother would say. Often she would catalogue how terrible she felt.

One day I replied, in a harmless ironic tone, 'What ever happened to, "Fine, thank you, and how are you?" '

Her thinning eyebrows drew together. 'What ever happened to it? I have enough acquaintances who get, "Fine, thank you, and how are you." You're the family. You're supposed to be the ones to whom I can say just how terrible I feel. And when I tell you, you're supposed to comfort me and not criticize me.' Her tone of voice was deliberately grating.

'We all love you,' I said, 'but you've got to make some of the effort yourself. If I can try to be cheerful, you can try to be cheered. Why don't we try to make the best of things as they are?'

'I'm trying, Harry,' said my mother. 'Can't you see that? Can't you see how hard I'm trying?' Then tears began to roll down her face. 'I'm not trying to make your life miserable. You asked how I was feeling, and I thought it was because you really wanted to know. If you don't want to know, then go play your piano when you get up, and don't come in here. Or go back to London, where you can socialize with all your friends. Go work on your recording. I'm not making you come to New York, Harry. I've tried to tell you to keep doing other things, and I've tried to make it easier with your father, so he doesn't pressure you all the time. It doesn't help me to have you here resenting me. Believe me, I don't want to have all these problems myself.' As she worked herself up to a pitch she began to shake, as though a wind were blowing through her, and then, quite suddenly, she dropped her teacup. We both watched as it rolled the length of her quilt, fell off the bed, and smashed on the floor. It left a long pale stain behind it. For a second there was silence.

'I'll get the dustpan and brush,' I said.

'Go ask Janet to change the bed,' said my mother.

'I'm sorry,' I said. 'I really am. You know that I didn't mean it. I mean, I do want to know how you are when I ask you.'

'Harry, go get the dustpan and go get Janet before the stain sets,' my mother said.

A few minutes later, while I was sweeping up the pieces, she said, 'Do you think I would be like this if I had any choice?'

'No, I know,' I said. 'I'm sorry.'

'You'd better hope that if they don't cure me, I go fast, or there won't be anything in this house that isn't stained or chipped or broken,' she said.

Two months after my mother's birthday, they carried out the first serious tests to see whether the chemotherapy was working. My mother knew nothing of these tests in advance; my father wanted to protect her, and protect her he did. He made all the arrangements behind closed doors. 'You talk to the doctors,' my mother would say. 'Make me believe that you are telling the truth, because if I think you're lying to me, I'll go crazy. But tell me only what's important, in the way you think best. Don't drag me through what I don't need to know.' So far as my mother was concerned, they took extra blood that month to check her immune counts twice; they took so many tubes of blood every week that one more or less went unremarked. But my father and Freddy and I knew that they were performing the first meaningful tests, and we waited breathless for the results. If there was bad news, we would bear it ourselves and say nothing to my mother; she could not have taken it on. But if there was good news, we would bring it to her like a slice of heaven. The day the results were due, I was on a plane from Rome to London, and when I landed at Heathrow I made straight for a pay telephone. I called my mother, and not my father, knowing that if she were to say anything it meant there was hope, and that if she said nothing, it meant that she knew nothing, and that the hour for despair had come.

Every time I go through Terminal One at Heathrow I see the pay phone from which I made that call, next to baggage-claim carousel one. I remember how my hands shook when I dialled, and I remember how measured and flat my voice was when my mother answered the phone. 'You're back?' she asked when she answered the phone. 'How was your trip? Was the concert hall as acoustically bad as you'd feared?'

'It was OK,' I said. 'I got some good reviews.'

'How are you?' she asked.

'Fine. A good trip,' I said, making my responses as short as possible so that we could cut to the point we might or might not be cutting to. 'How are *you*?' I asked.

'Tired as usual,' she said. 'But we've had what your father seems to think is good news.' And it was at that moment as though I had got my life back from the place where I'd accidentally left it some months earlier. There it was, intact, just as I remembered it. No one had sullied it; no one had chipped it; no one had broken it. It was a bit dusty, but the dust could soon be blown off. And I loved it, loved life, as you love anything you thought you had lost that you find again.

'I'm so glad,' I said, and I must have said it eight times, and I felt gladness as I had never felt it before, as something that begins in the middle of your stomach and rises in shivering waves up your whole frame and into your mouth and your face and your mind, making the world shimmer in front of you, raising the pitch of every sound, concentrating your senses until it seems that everything around you exists five times. 'I'm so glad,' I chorused again and again, and told my mother about my trip, and then had to run because my bags had just appeared on baggage-claim carousel four. And so I claimed them, and cleared customs, and rushed into Bernard's arms. That night I ate the dinner he had made for me as though it were so many plates of triumph.

When I spoke to my father, he sounded transformed. 'These test results are not a hundred per cent conclusive,' he said cautiously. But he couldn't keep it up. 'According to the material I've reviewed, the chances are incredibly good. It's the most remote possibility that there's still anything there. It's better than we would have dared to hope.' My father explained the test results then, drawing in the Geneva study of ten years earlier and the Santa Fe clinical trials that had been completed shortly thereafter. I was speechless in the face of my father's unbounded information. While my mother had been worrying, he had been learning. 'In a secondary stage,' he began, and then explained the mechanisms of the cancerous cells themselves, as though they were some kind of fascinating new invention, a scientific fact and not an emotional one. He knew more than my doctor-to-be brother. 'You have to come home soon so we can all celebrate this together,' he said. 'And we have to work together to keep your mother's spirits up. I explained all this to her, but she's being skeptical.'

'I'm going to stick around in London for a little while,' I said to him.

'Don't do that,' he said. 'We need you here.'

I said I'd have to work out a schedule, and got off the phone, and put on a new shirt Bernard had bought me. We were going to dinner with Claire and Michael. We were going to celebrate quite satisfactorily.

When I spoke to Freddy, the next day, we laughed about it all. 'My professor told me we should be really thrilled about this. Seriously. So now it's back to full-time medical school,' he said. 'No more excuses for bad exam results. No more crazy trips to New York for dinner. We're free!'

If the following year seemed to go by in ten minutes, that first winter of chemotherapy lasted a decade. My mother's test results (there were results every two weeks) continued to point to her being cured, and I did not entertain the possibility that they were lying. We all felt sorry for my mother because of the discomfort of her therapy, but gave little weight to the fear of her disease. The knowing doctors told us that it was virtually certain that the cancer would not linger, and so death itself, to which we had begun to become accustomed, seemed to shrink and recede. At least it shrank away from me. Only my mother held onto the thought of her own death with what I took to be a morbid fixation. She operated at a low level of depression, like a cloud-swelled weather system. She hated her doctors, and she hated the hospital, and she hated her treatments, and she hated all the disciplined isolation. She hated the chemicals. 'You should see the stuff they're giving me now,' she said. 'It's the most hideous shade of orange, about the colour of those beach chairs we had when you were little. Remember? The ones that discoloured in the basement? You just watch it drip into your arm and wait to see whether you'll change colour yourself.'

I should say here that, since I did not have so much as a cold all winter, I forgot how unpleasant it is simply to be under the weather. Two years later, when I endured an upset stomach and general malaise and a slight sore throat for a few days – a seventy-two hour virus – I realized that I was experiencing some of the symptoms my mother had known during that long winter, and I tried to imagine what it would have been like to feel that way for an unrelenting nine months. Then I realized how hard it is to sustain any optimism when you are occupied with your own discomfort, and I saw that if my mother thought she was dying, this was in part because she had had too many sensations that were too much like death for far far too long. In the way that a slight skin irritation sustained over months becomes as bad as a deep flesh wound, so my mother's chemotherapy symptoms became terrible simply because they never went away. I tried to be a staunch support to her: I called every day when I was abroad, and came back to New York at least once a month. I went with her to have the wig fixed (in the end, she did have wigs that looked so much like her hair you would never have known they were anything else; but it required unholy care to make what was dead appear to be part of her living self). I did everything a perfect son would have done, but I did it in a spirit of largely unarticulated peevishness. I wanted credit all the time; I wanted a marching band to come to Kennedy airport each time I landed to sing out my praises on the tuba and the big bass drum. June sparkled on the horizon: in June they would do a final test, prove that my mother was fine, and abandon the chemotherapy. In June, we would be entirely free.

My mother apologized at least a thousand times that winter for the terrible accusation she had made in the first weeks of her illness. She had repeated that all she wanted was for me to be happy, that she accepted my decisions, and that she worried only about my having a lonely old age and living at the margins of society. I insisted that she had to meet Bernard when next she came to London, and she insisted that she wouldn't. I can remember sitting with her at tea one afternoon, telling her that if she loved me she had to include herself in the whole of my life.

'You cannot love me but close out Bernard and our relationship,' I insisted, 'because that is now a part of me.'

She said, 'You want to make this all more real, and what I am trying to tell you is that I will accept it but that I don't want it to be more real. I don't want to have to see it. As long as it remains invisible it remains remote to my time with you.'

I can remember that at that time her chemotherapy had affected her ability to balance so much that she could not lift a teacup at all, and so our tea together consisted of her watching me eat and drink. It was hard to argue with my mother under these circumstances – hard but not impossible. When I told her that her time with me had always been riddled with artifice, her hands shook even more and the lines of exhaustion that had set in around her mouth seemed to sag. As she got thinner and thinner, her resistance wore down, and by the early spring, she had conceded that she would meet Bernard when she came to London. I looked forward at that time to years of my mother as she would be after the end of her chemotherapy; if I had taken advantage of her weakened condition, I had done so with a wise eye to the future.

The crisis seemed to have passed by the time I went back to the recording studio in London, for my second chance; but when I sat down, I felt myself starting to freeze again, and I heard more of those wooden notes from which I had sworn I would free myself. I panicked. At noon, I stopped playing and called home, and I talked to my mother on the phone for a few minutes. She was going in for another round of chemotherapy that day. 'Come on,' said my agent, interrupting the conversation. 'Talk to her on your own time, not on studio time. Are you playing this for your mother or for the world?' I carefully avoided answering him.

As I sat down to play, I thought about what the actual cd would look like, the flat disk of metal, neutral as a large coin. I began the Schubert. I thought about the nectarine, and about my mother, and about the orange chemical. And then I stopped playing, brought up short at the phrase that had appeared in my dream. Suddenly I felt all the sadness that I had tried to close out in England, that I had put aside after my mother's good test results had started. I had not been able to explain this sadness to Bernard, nor to admit it to my mother, nor to share it with Freddy or my father, nor, much of the time, to see it myself; but it came washing out all over the piano that day. The Schubert is not exactly a sad piece of music, but it has enough sadness in it so that it could lead me to my own sadness in that sad season. It was the most incredible release, to play that piece, to say at last all the things I had not been saying. I played it from beginning to end without pausing, and when I stopped, I found tears on my face. I wiped them off quickly, before anyone else could see them.

'Well,' said my agent, delighted and ironic. 'I see we're finally getting someplace. Where the hell did that come from?'

'I've been practising,' I said helplessly.

'You keep practising,' he said to me.

It was on a clear day in May, when I was having dinner with Bernard and some friends in his dining room – Bernard had made the first of the season's lamb – that Freddy called. My father had not been able to bring himself to do it. It was Freddy who said that there had been aberrant test results, and that they would be doing surgery on my mother in five days, to make sure that she really was OK. 'It's all very unclear,' said Freddy. 'They seem to think she'll be fine, but they're a little vague. I guess we just can't tell what's going on until they get inside her and look.' His voice had that same upbeat tone that we had all used to protect my mother in the first months of her illness. I did not need to challenge him on it. I hung up the telephone, and ran down the hallway, past the dining room and all the people in it, and I locked myself in the bathroom. I lay on the floor and curled myself into a tight bundle and clutched my knees under my chin and closed my eyes and tried to remember the complacence in which I had been living for the better part of that long winter. After some time, Bernard came and knocked on the bathroom door and asked whether I was all right, but I was unable to answer him. I stayed curled on the ugly yellowed carpeting of his bathroom and made no sounds at all, because if I had opened my mouth a wail would have poured out of me that would not have stopped.

A minute later I went back to the table, but I seemed to have lost my ability to speak. I smiled vaguely at everyone, but I couldn't follow the conversation, and within a minute or two, everyone stood up to leave. I could hear a voice in my mind that said that we had company over, and that I was making a scene, and that I should just say something ordinary, but I couldn't do it. After the guests were gone, Bernard came back to the dining room and sat beside me and, with that infinite gentleness of his, stroked my hair. Then he picked me up and carried me to our bedroom and put me down on the bed. 'Come on,' he said softly, and he unfolded me and helped take off my clothes and put me under the covers. He lay down beside me and stroked my hair and held onto me until I did finally fall into that oddly peaceful slumber that comes when sleep can hold nothing more terrible than your waking dreams. I slept until noon; when I woke up I found a long note from Bernard, and a lovely breakfast standing in the dining room. I wanted to telephone him, but I was still unable to make a sound. In three days, it would be Bernard's birthday, and we were to have a party. I had planned that beautiful party endlessly, to be a fitting tribute to his measureless patience. I had poured all my affection for Bernard into it; it was to be the public evidence of a love in some ways so private I feared Bernard himself might not always have known it was there. In the silence of that morning my happy plans blew apart. I ate the breakfast, and then I hailed a cab to Heathrow. I quietly boarded another plane, leaving the party, like an orphan child, to take care of itself.

V

Valse Brillante

The morning of my mother's second surgery broke brilliantly clear. It was the kind of June day my mother had always loved, when the sun casts blithe shadows on the sidewalks and the air is bright and your skin feels blissfully soft. By the time of my mother's second surgery, my father had become a benefactor of the hospital where she was being treated, and she had therefore been given a room unlike any other hospital room on earth, the size of a small recital hall, with windows on three sides looking out at the stately East River. There were, as usual, flowers. The room seemed too good for bad news. We arrived at dawn on the day of my mother's second surgery, and gave her all our sunrise assurances, and half an hour later watched as they wheeled her away down the long corridor.

And then we sat down to wait. The time of my mother's illness was in some sense entirely a time of waiting. For two years, there was not a single day when we were not waiting for a test result, waiting for the end of a course of therapy, waiting for good health again, even waiting for my mother to die. The day of her second surgery, we had arrived in the hospital earlier than early, and we waited for them to take her up to the operating room, and then we waited for them to bring her back down, and every one of the many seconds that passed in such waiting was like a little death of its own, so that by the time noon struck we all felt as though we had died a thousand times without being once reborn. And yet the idea of ceasing to wait was also intolerable. I had in my mind a cartoon image of characters trying to stop short of some precipice and finding themselves unable, skidding along on their heels while the dirt churns up around them: we lived in eager dread that our waiting would end. On the day of my mother's second surgery, we tried at first to keep up conversation, then lapsed into the books we had brought for distraction. I drummed meaningless chord progressions on my silent keyboard. In the end, we gave up and let ourselves stare fixedly into our three kinds of middle distance, unable to connect by any stretch of our collective imagination. My father and Freddy and I were lost in a neighbourhood of pause, and it seemed to me that we remained stranded there forever.

Then there was a lull in the waiting. The doctor came down to tell us that the news was good, and as he spoke the sun poured in like butterscotch. He came to tell us that my mother's cancer had almost entirely disappeared. He came to tell us that only a rigorous search on his part had located the few resistant cells. He came to tell us that there was no tumour mass, that you could not be closer to being healthy without being in perfect health. He came to tell us that what was left would wash away with a little bit more chemotherapy, the tiniest bit of chemotherapy, minor, easy, nearly unnoticeable chemotherapy. How can I describe the glowing enthusiastic optimistic vocabulary that doctor used when he came into the enormous bright hospital room with its roses all in bloom and told us that my mother was still dying? Because this much was clear to us all: if some of the cancer was left after that agonizing nine-month treatment, then all the good predictions that had been made over those months were wrong. If so much as a shadow of the cancer had survived those traumatizing attacks, then we had been living in false hope. 'What's left will wash away in no time,' said the doctor, and we all remembered hearing him say those words after the first surgery. We knew how often first-line chemotherapy works, and how seldom second-line chemotherapy works. The upbeat tone the doctor had used was not far from the tone that someone in an older profession could have used to say that souls in heaven are happier than those on earth. All I know for sure is that the slow minutes that had seemed like prisons until that moment seemed now to be inside of us instead of out, to be pressing from the centre, like a sustained and ripping explosion, like some multiplication of our own flesh, like cancer itself.

For an hour, my father and Freddy and I held council on what to say, how to tell my mother, and in the end we came up with nothing much better than that radiant vocabulary the butterscotch doctor had spread around his news. Freddy called one of his medical school professors and discussed statistics, but none of us cared about statistics much; we had just fallen by the wayside of a tiny statistic, and were in that undreamed of two per cent that gives foil to a treatment with a ninety-eight per cent success rate. Each of us tried to believe the doctor's tone for the sake of the others, and so we repeated in apologetic litany that things might have been much much worse. And then the orderlies appeared with my mother on a rolling bed. My father, my poor father, was the only one who could tell her the news, her news, our news, and now she opened her eyes and stared groggily for a moment. 'Well?' she asked with all the fervid effort of anaesthetized concentration. 'It's good news and it's bad news,' my father said. Lines of anger etched themselves into my mother's face and her teeth set. 'It's not over,' she said, and closed her anaesthesia eyes before my father could progress into his efforts at cheer. On that day, the day we all understood that my mother would probably die, there was an expression on her face like nothing I had ever seen, a concentrate of the final rage that lies beyond despair. And my father, when he saw that she had locked herself back in unconsciousness turned to my brother and me, and said, 'What are they going to do to her now?' And then he paused and murmured, 'And she looks so beautiful.'

Freddy put a hand on his arm. 'Dad, she doesn't look so beautiful right now,' he said. My father turned to see again, as though he were afraid that it was the wrong body they had brought in, as though to make sure that it really was my mother who lay on the hospital bed. He looked at her pale distorted face, and at her almost hairless head – an eighth of an inch had grown in since the chemotherapy had ended – and at the emptiness where her eyebrows should have been; he looked at her features puffed from surgery, her teeth clenched tight enough to fix girders. He stared for a long moment as though he were trying to see clearly. And then he shrugged. 'To me, she's beautiful,' he said.

During the week of that second surgery, I watched my mother die. For two days after the surgery she remained in what looked like a trance. She did not open her eyes or move her face; when the nurses woke her up for blood tests or to make her bed she seemed not to know who they were, and she moved in their arms like a dead body. She did not see us. The IV drip continued to flow into her arm, and from time to time she would shudder, but she did not move or turn or speak. He face remained set in that expression of rage. When I was a child, I could make my mother completely happy, but I could also make her desperately angry, and I had seen her face when she was in a fury that touched on violence. Never, though, had I seen an expression like the one on her face those days, her lips pressed so tightly into their frown that the blood went out of them. To my father, my mother might be beautiful, but to me, my mother, who had always been so beautiful, was appalling.

At first, we didn't understand what was happening. It was not until the end of the second day that my father asked one of the nurses why my mother was recovering so slowly from her anaesthesia. The nurse – a kind, clean, efficient woman who had been helping my mother since she first got sick – shook her head and said, 'The anaesthesia is long gone. She's depressed. It's a natural response to this kind of news; she's been so disciplined all year, and she should have been well. She'll come out, but it'll take time.'

I suppose that these were really just instructions to wait some more, but how much more could we go on waiting while this inert figure lay in the bed looking like a badly drawn copy of my mother? My mother had been depressed many times that winter, and we knew what her depression was like: she was morose and sentimental and touchy and afraid. This frozen anger was like nothing any of us had ever met. My mother had a thousand different moods, and this was not one of them.

That night, my father and Freddy and I went out to dinner, as we had done at the end of every hospital day. Freddy and I were manic, making absurd jokes, laughing hysterically, until my father's reserve of calm ran out and his strained sense of humour disappeared, and he pounded on the table with his fist. Everyone else in the restaurant stopped what he was doing and turned and stared. 'Would you two stop carrying on!' my father thundered. Neither Freddy nor I could respond. We ended that meal in the same white heat of silence in which we had spent the day.

That night I called Helen, and she and I went sneaking out for one of our late drinks and I tried to explain. But my voice went running away from me; after all that silence, my voice wouldn't stop. 'It's just not livable any more,' I said to her. 'Last year, when my mother got sick, it was shocking, but I still had all my energy then, and now my energy is just about used up, and I just can't deal with it. I can't go back to that enormous hospital room tomorrow and spend another day talking to my mother while she lies on the bed like something out of a horror movie and I go on telling my father and Freddy that it's all going to be fine. I can't do it, Helen. I'm going to go crazy. In fact, I am going crazy, and so is my father, and so is Freddy.'

Helen reached out to touch me, but I was beyond touching by then and I jumped at her hand as though it were going to burn me. 'It's just for now,' said Helen, and she swirled her white wine around in its big glass. 'You said the prognosis isn't so bad, and your mother will have to get out of her depression, and then your father will be all right. You've pulled through all this so far, and you'll pull through today.'

I nearly hit Helen. 'I can't believe', I said, my voice rising, 'that my mother just doesn't care that she's killing all of us. What about the rest of us? Remember how the rest of us used to matter too? I keep expecting her to look at my life and say, I'm sorry. No. More than that. I keep expecting her to look deep into my life and *be* sorry. I've lost so much, Helen. We've all lost so much. We used to be joyful people, all four of us. She's killing us with her, and she just couldn't care less. If she loves me so much and depends on me so much then how the hell does she get off caring so little? If she's going to die, I wish she'd just do it already. I wish she would just die tonight, that we could get back to that hospital tomorrow and find out it was over and have a funeral and just go on from there. Because this can't go on this way, it just can't, and I can't, I can't any more, I just can't.'

I stopped for breath and Helen, in a single swift movement, got up from her chair and moved behind me and held me from the back, pinning my arms to my seat, in a cross between an embrace and the Heimlich manoeuvre. When she spoke, her voice had the softness of insight behind it, but it was sharp as a drill bit. 'Harry,' she said. 'Your mother is going to be in that hospital for another week at the outside, and then she'll be at home. You are in this country for another two weeks and then you're going back to see Bernard and get on with your life in London and then play at that Beethoven festival in Bavaria that you've been grumbling about. If you don't want to stay in the hospital room all day every day, then don't stay there. Your father hasn't tied you to a chair. Make a plan with someone and go out to lunch. Go home and practise for an hour. Keep a grip on yourself. You have not destroyed your life to help your mother. If you're mad, then go home and smash a mixing bowl or something. If you're sad, then cry. If you need to distract yourself, then watch TV or call friends or have a party or do whatever you have to do to get through this, Harry. But stop being hysterical. It's not helping anyone at all.' The hard, rational, moral, just side of Helen, the side that would change the world with legislative codes and make it a better place – that side of her came to the surface as she spoke. It was a rationality that was not incommensurate with kindness. When she finished, she let go of me, very slowly. I did not move, and she sat down again. Her face was calm, and my hysteria was gone, at least for the moment.

I reached out to touch her hair, which was hanging forward, because she looked, all at once, so very beautiful. 'We're all drawn to the romance of being slaves to love,' she said quietly. 'It happens in fairy tales and it happens in movies and it's a compelling principle. Lamb, in the real world that can't be the whole story. With your mother – you have to make yourself free. If you're a slave, it's not to love. It's to something else. Your mother is a remarkable woman, Harry, and God knows she loves you. That's not the question.'

'Then what is it?' I asked. Helen seemed terribly serious. I felt we were wandering toward a big subject I had not planned to visit, then or later.

'It's just what I said,' she answered. 'Love should set you free, the way your love for the piano does. Maybe Bernard does, at least a little? Even now, even if she's dying, your mother's love should do that. You should let it do that.'

I thought again about my mother saying, in her most honest voice, 'I think you could do anything, Harry, anything in the world if you wanted to.' It seemed to me that it was she who had made that true. Her powerful, unrelenting belief: who would I have been without it? Life, love – it did not strike me as a free business. But to be tactful, I told Helen that her friendship was a very freeing thing indeed.

'I'll walk you home,' she said after a second, and she did walk me home, and then came up to the apartment, and waited while I put on my pyjamas – I still wore pyjamas in my parents' home – and that night she stayed with me until I went to sleep.

On the third day, my father and Freddy and I took turns sitting on the end of the bed and talking to my mother. Periodically she would move, and once or twice she opened her eyes, but she seemed not to understand what we were saying. My father sat beside her and repeated and repeated her name, as though he were trying to call her back. 'It's going to be all right,' he said lamely. 'It's going to be all right.' The nurse became more forceful that day. 'You have to get out of that bed for a little while,' she said to my mother. 'You have to stand up today and walk at least across the room.' And with her sleek efficiency she pushed the buttons and made the bed sit up and propped my mother out and escorted her to a chair. We gathered around my mother then; her eyes were open and she was staring, but she continued not to say anything. 'Mom,' said Freddy, and passed his hands in front of her face. 'Oh, Mom!' he said, his tone like a joke, an echo of the previous night's mania. 'Are you there? Earth to Mom!' And my mother turned slightly in her chair, but that was all. Then the nurse came over and helped my mother to stand up and walked with her back to the bed.

Later in the afternoon, I sat for a long two hours on the side of the bed and held my mother's hand and looked at her. And she for a long time lay in her stony silence with that expression still fixed on her face. 'Please look at me,' I said. 'Please say something. You're taking this too hard, and you're making it even worse for yourself than it is. Life isn't over. You have less cancer than you had in the fall and you're going to have these few treatments and then that's going to be it. This is just taking a little longer than we thought it was going to take. It's going to be fine. It really is. It's going to be just fine.' And suddenly I saw that my mother had started to cry. Her expression was still the same, but there were tears running down her face, and she was looking up at me. And finally – we had begun to fear she had lost her voice forever – she began to speak.

'Let go, Harry,' she said. 'Just let go of me. I was sick, and everyone told me what I had to do, and I did it, and it didn't work. And this is also not going to work. You and Freddy and your father need to let go of me. You have to let me die.'

When my mother started talking, Freddy and my father came at once to the bedside. 'You're not dying,' my father said. 'We don't have to let you die. We have to help you to live. Because we love you.'

My mother looked up at him, and the tears continued to flow in an endless stream down her face. 'I'm not really here any more,' she said. 'What's here for you to love?'

'Oh, Mom,' said Freddy.

It was terrible how much I loved my mother. It was the most terrible thing in the world.

My mother looked at our three faces, and the hardness left her voice for an instant. 'Can't you see', she said hoarsely, 'that the person you loved is already dead?' And then she closed her eyes again, and lay on the bed with tears coming from under her eyelids. We stood around the bed, but she didn't look at us again, and after a few minutes the nurse came, and told us to go back to the chairs and sit down.

'She's very tired,' said the nurse. 'Don't push her too hard today.'

The rest of the afternoon lapsed in silence. I drummed away at my silent electric keyboard. I learned a Chopin nocturne by heart. I didn't have any plan to play it in concert, but it was satisfying to know I had it on hand should an occasion offer itself in the future. I felt I had come up with a musical interpretation, even though I had heard no sounds. I considered turning on the sound, but I knew it would bother my mother's sleep, and that it would sound awful. I thought about deaf Beethoven composing, and looked forward to trying the Chopin on the piano at home.

At eight o'clock that night, the three of us had a brisk conversation and chose a restaurant, and headed for the door. I felt like I was being let out of a cage. My father stopped by the bed and bent over it and kissed my mother. 'We're leaving now,' he said. 'We'll be back in the morning.'

Freddy and I were right behind him. 'Have some happy dreams,' I said.

And then my mother sat up for the first time and her voice seemed to rise suddenly out of the middle of her. 'I won't do it,' she said. 'I won't do another round of chemotherapy. I won't follow through with this. I've done as much as I have to do and I'm ready to die. Leonard, you have to help me. This is a hospital. Get me some pills or some morphine. They have enough poison to pump into your system for therapy, so they must have enough to kill me. I'm ready to die and I want to do it now.'

'You know I can't arrange – ' my father began, but my mother would have none of it.

'If you don't help me, I'll find a way to do it myself,' she said. 'There you all are setting off for dinner somewhere, and you get on with your lives, and why do you want to have more days sitting in this stifling, miserable room and watching me lie in bed? It's what we all need. It's time now. It's time for me to die.'

My father tried to calm her with his old reassuring voice, which he produced from the air like a magician's rabbit. 'You're being ridiculous,' he assured her. 'You're fabricating something. You're going to be here in the hospital for a few more days, and then you're going to come home.'

'No,' my mother screamed. 'No,' and her voice seemed to grow beyond her proportions.

It was after ten o'clock when we left that room that night. We ate dinner as quickly as we could. My father kept starting to cry, and Freddy and I just looked the other way; we had nothing to say to him. At home there were dozens of messages from friends who wanted to come to the hospital to visit my mother. 'There's nothing to lose,' I said to my father. 'At least they'll add a little variety to the day.' So I called them, and woke many of them up, and said that if they wanted to stop by sometime over the next few days, my mother, though weak, would be able to receive them.

Then I called Bernard and woke him up and tried to explain what was going on. 'You must just behave as you always have,' he said. It was four o'clock in the morning in London. 'I'm sure that it's all rather dreadful right now, but in a few days she'll probably be fine.' I tried to paint for him how awful it really was, but he seemed not to get it. Or perhaps he did get it; perhaps he thought that there is nothing to say about the parts of life that are that awful, that you can only look away from them. Perhaps he did not want to tell me that he thought I was being foolish, looking into it and into it and into it. 'The lobelias are blossoming,' Bernard volunteered. 'Blue as your eyes,' he said. 'I took Nora into the vet, because she isn't really eating properly,' he went on, 'but the vet says she's just getting old.' I sent my love to Nora. 'Come back soon,' he said, and I wanted to tell him that when I came back I would not be the person he remembered; I wanted to tell him that my eyes were no longer anything like the lobelias. But all I said was that I missed him.

I was of course responsible for starting the continental drift between Bernard and me. It was not so much that I had skipped town before the party, leaving him to throw it by himself. That morning when I woke up to find the breakfast he had made me, I should have called him and thanked him and told him that I was going to New York. I should not have left the house in silence and hailed a cab and flown home. I should have told him what I planned to do. Bernard made so few demands: he didn't want my sorrows, but he did at least want to be consulted about my actual activities. If I had called him that day and asked whether he thought I should go to New York, he would have told me by all means to go; he would probably have driven me to Heathrow; and I might still be living in the world of the lobelias and Nora and the vet.

After we hung up, I sat down at the piano and, in a sudden panic, practised the Chopin until nearly dawn.

On the fourth day, my mother was mostly silent. Periodically, she would sit up part way, and tears would pour down her face. When any of us tried to talk to her, she went into her litany about pills. 'If you won't help me to kill myself here and now,' she said, 'then I'll kill myself when I get home, and it will be worse and messier for all of us.'

At three o'clock that afternoon, a friend of my mother's arrived. The effect was absolutely astonishing. My mother sat up, and asked for her pink bedjacket, and made unremarkable conversation. The tears and the expression of rage – which none of us had been able to penetrate – seemed to evaporate.

'I hear the prognosis is pretty good,' said the friend.

'Still dying,' said my mother. 'They're planning a whole variety of new tortures for me.' A few minutes later, another friend of my mother's came in, and then another, and by 4.30 there were more than thirty people there, all the close friends in succession. My mother was sitting up in her bed; her remarks were occasional and negative, but she was still the focus of the room. It was like some kind of bizarre cocktail party. Everyone talked about the room. 'What I wouldn't give to have views like this at home,' one friend remarked. The flowers also attracted a lot of notice. 'Which are mine?' more than one friend asked. My father and Freddy and I were doing full-time duty as hosts, trying to circulate.

'This is too weird,' Freddy said to me at one point.

'It's more fun than yesterday!' I replied.

'What do you suppose Mom is thinking?' he asked.

But I got carried off by another friend who wanted to know what had been happening. 'How's her mood been?' people kept asking.

'Not great,' I said, but I provided no further details.

'How've you been?' people asked my mother.

'Oh, up and down,' she said.

At about six o'clock, people started leaving. 'You must be tired,' they said as they paused by my mother's bed.

She smiled graciously to each one, and thanked each for coming. 'Stop by any time,' she laughed to the people she loved most. 'I'm not going anywhere in a hurry.' When the last of these friends had gone, I went over to my mother's bed and took her hand. She was limp with exhaustion, and she had started to cry again, her tears as unconscious as breathing.

'That wasn't so bad,' I said to her. 'Weren't you glad to see all those people? It was almost like a party.'

'Oh, Harry,' my mother said. 'Everyone always had such a good time at our house.'

The last nine days of my mother's second surgery stay in the hospital took on a pattern. In the mornings, my mother was sad but it was possible to comfort her. We talked about the next chemotherapy. 'Why should it work?' my mother would say, and I would say, 'The doctors seem to think that it will be fine.' I told her about friends of hers, and we talked about who had come to the hospital and who hadn't come and who had called and why. We even talked about Bernard once or twice. Helen came a couple of times in the morning, and my mother would always perk up for Helen. I loved to watch them speaking to each other. Helen could not afford enormous arrangements of the kind that filled the room, but she always brought a rose, or a stem of lilies, and my mother would put the flowers from Helen into a little glass vase and keep them on the nightstand next to her bed. 'What a lovely haircut,' she would say to Helen, or, 'Those earrings are wonderful on you.'

In the afternoons, friends of my mother's would come, and she would make desultory conversation with them. She was hungry for the news they could offer, and she chatted away. Many of them sought her advice on small matters, and she gave advice calmly, bringing order to other lives as she always had. While she talked to these friends, I would take my electric organ into the hallway and practise with the sound on low.

In the evenings, things would degenerate rapidly. We were almost always there for a full two hours after the end of visiting time. 'Leonard,' my mother said every night, 'I will go through with this only if you promise me that you will get me some pills so that I can end this when I decide to end it. I won't go through with it under any other circumstances.'

And my father would say, 'You would take those pills right now if you had them, and right now there's no reason to take them. Besides, how do you think I'm going to get you pills to take to kill yourself? Where do you think I have my secret connections?'

'You figure it out, Leonard. That's your problem.' And then she would weep and sometimes she would scream and in the end that enraged sadness would come flying out of her. To be in the room with it was like being splattered with blood. 'I can't live like this,' she would say. 'I can't go in this way. Why won't you let me die? It would be so much better for everyone. It's so selfish of you to keep me alive when all I want is to die. I hate this, I hate it, I hate it.'

Once I became furious myself. 'So go ahead and die,' I said. 'Go ahead and die. How many times do we have to have this scene?'

My mother looked at me then. 'Oh Harry. I know that you all love me. But no matter what you do, I am alone. All alone. It's so terrible to be trapped all alone in this body. I don't want to be such a misery. Harry, Leonard, Freddy – wouldn't it be better, really better, for you all to let go of me?'

By the time my mother came home, I had had my fill of New York. The prospect of London and Bernard filled me with joy. How sorry I felt for my father, who had no escape, who had no one to go to! In some very secret part of myself, I thought I might go to London and never come home again; when Helen told me that I was being extreme, I told her about concerts, which I had in fact scheduled thick and fast for the following month. I planned various programmes for forthcoming performances. I talked to my agent daily. The drift away from Bernard seemed to me to have been arrested, or even reversed, as I had spent more and more time thinking about him as a way not to think about my mother. If anyone had ever been ready for a spa vacation, I was ready for one at that moment. My mother was about to start her minor, easy, nearly unnoticeable chemotherapy. I wanted to get as far away as possible, to where I could continue to imagine that chemotherapy could be easy, to where things happening to my mother might be unnoticeable.

'That sounded lovely, Harry,' said my mother, drifting into the living room one evening when I was practising. She had given up that hospital tone of despair.

'It's a technical nightmare,' I said. 'I want to work on the melody but I can't do that until I get the fingering down better.'

'I don't want to interrupt you,' she said. 'Go on playing. I'll just listen.' She sat down on one of the yellow chairs.

'I'll play something else,' I said. 'This is no fun to listen to.'

'No, don't do that,' she said. 'Play what you were working on. It changes each time you play it.'

I did not entirely know it then, but my mother had that week given up on the hope of a cure. She had stopped treating each day of sickness as part of a temporary punishment, to be endured until a better time would come; she had accepted that she had only these days left, and that she should make the most of them. She was trying simply to live in the world and in the moment, something she had never done before; it had been her way to negotiate the present as though it were laid on for future memories. She sat that evening in one of the yellow chairs, listening, and I worked on fingering, and after the first fifteen minutes, the fact of her being there ceased to distract me. I played better than I had played in a long time. When she stood up an hour later, I had almost forgotten she was in the room with me. 'Well, you've solved that,' she said with satisfaction as she left.

When I got back to London, Bernard told me how everyone had missed me at his birthday party. In fact it had gone off much as it might have had I been in town for it. Norman – with whom Bernard had finally reached an adequate peace – had taken lots of photographs, and Bernard and I spent a long and happy evening looking over them. Jane had worn the most purple dress ever made, and if the photos were to be believed, Frieda had spent the entire evening grinning madly. Bernard did not know why. I thought Bernard's choice of the grey linen suit very successful, and wanted a blow-up of the photograph of him with Claire and Michael, which was really a great photo. The flowers were not quite as I had ordered them, but they looked acceptable, and I was very pleased with the lighting in the room. They had remembered about the candles' being ivory.

In the first weeks that I was back with Bernard, I was afraid of calling my mother, afraid of being depressed or angered, afraid that I would be spattered with blood again. But in fact when I called her we would laugh and tell each other stories until it was difficult for me to say goodbye. I felt that my mother knew what I was going to say before I said it, and that I knew what she was going to say, and I sometimes wondered why, if that was the case, it gave us both so much pleasure to say these already known things. But I could not stop, and neither could she. My mother was slowly turning into my fondest memories of her. She did not drop her ironies, but she took on a tender mildness that surprised me by telephone. Her essential softness had seemed to disappear during the first year of her illness; now it was back, closer to the surface than it had ever been.

My mother's unnoticeable chemotherapy clearly made her feel terrible; sometimes when I spoke to her I felt that she was expending the most enormous effort to exchange the day's pleasantries, that to say what she had always said without thinking now required an intense concentration of hypnotic energy. The new chemotherapy did not affect her hair, and she told me by phone that she had given up the wig. 'I look like I've been shorn for the army,' she reported. 'But at least it's been trimmed and styled. Wait till you see your mother with a crewcut.'

My parents had planned a trip to Italy to celebrate the end of the chemotherapy, and in the hospital we had all assumed that it would be cancelled; indeed, in the hospital we had thought it unlikely that my mother would ever again travel as far as Madison Avenue. But her new softness was built upon an unfathomable strength, and she was all for going on this trip. 'We can come back through London,' she said. 'I can meet Bernard, and see what you've done with your house.' My father worried that she would tire herself, but she shrugged this off. 'It will be a good, relaxing trip. All of us could stand to get away for a little while.' Once or twice she let slide a little phrase of melancholy. 'I think this will probably be our last family trip,' she said. 'I want to enjoy it, and I want you and Freddy to enjoy it. I want you to have as many happy memories as you possibly can.'

Then I withdrew back into Bernard and London. 'It's not our last trip,' I said defiantly. 'And we already have plenty of happy memories.'

It was not to be our last trip, but it was to be our last trip to Europe, our last grand tour, our last journey in our own high tradition. We met in Paris, at the Ritz, on a clear August day, almost exactly a year after that fateful weekend when my mother had asked me to remember her only as she had been until then. She seemed to be free without her wig; she had new jewellery, heavy earrings and a cuff bracelet with rubies that my father had bought her, which went with her new look. 'Very modern,' she said as she ran her hand along her hairline. Sometimes she talked about how we were on our last trip, but she mostly tried not to do that. 'I might keep my hair short,' she said. 'Not this short. But I might not grow it down to my shoulders again.'

We were in Paris for just a few days, time to do some shopping and eat a few meals, time to shake the ghosts of the previous summer. It was as though my mother wanted to give us back the Paris we had always known through her. She wanted to give memories to Freddy and to me, but she also wanted to have the full pleasure of her own memories, and she pulled them all out, one after the next, as though they were the flowers of a hundred summers. Much has been made of the pathos of men whose strong exteriors mask breakable souls, of the ones who, beneath their cowboy hats and rough skin and murderous ways, are riddled with insecurities and anxieties. Too little has been said of the drama of those whose surfaces are fragile and mutable, who have all the mannerisms of delicacy, but who keep hidden at their

centre a devastating strength. You cannot live in this brutal world
with the fragility of sensibility that my mother had unless you
have concentrated much of your force in some hidden place. As
my mother's core became stronger that month, her discourse with
the world became more and more delicate, until it was virtually
transparent.

After Paris, we headed for Italy. From time to time throughout
my childhood my parents would go off for a week to Lake Como,
and it was the one spot to which Freddy and I were never invited.
'Someday, when you're older,' my mother would say when we
were little, 'you'll have a girl to take to Lake Como. It's not a
place for family holidays.' But by now we were past resisting the
romance of our own family, and at last we went, all four of us, to
Lake Como, to stay in a stuccoed pink villa hotel with rooms that
looked straight into the sunset. My mother had to conserve her
energy that week, and she spent most of her time sitting on the
terrace outside her room, reading books and doing her beloved
crossword puzzles. She always had a cup of chamomile tea or a
glass of mineral water at her side, sparkling water without ice and
without lime in a stem glass. She wore loose clothes that did not
press too much on the scars from her surgery. In the afternoons
she would take naps, sometimes also in the mornings, or just
before dinner; she saved up her energy so that when she was
awake and we were all together she could be free with it. Liberally,
almost squanderously, she gave us all that was best in her.

On an end table near my piano, where I can see them when I play,
I have three photographs of my parents together, in addition to
various photos of them separately, of my brother, of Helen, and of
other friends. One of the photos of my parents together is their
wedding photo; one is a picture that was taken by a magazine
photographer at a New York party just a couple of months before
my mother got sick; and one is a photo of my parents dancing in
that hotel room on Lake Como, when my mother's hair had
grown an inch and a half between rounds of chemotherapy, when
she had finally, however grudgingly, agreed to snapshots after a

year that, ostensibly because of the wigs, had gone undocumented.

The wedding photo sat on my bureau when I was a child. I remember that when I was about ten, my mother said that it was odd for me to have her wedding photo on my bureau, and she put it away; but how on earth but by her doing could it have come to be there in the first place? I took the photo back out, perhaps a year later, and after that it stayed always on my bureau. You can tell looking at that photo that it's had a rough time; the glass is cracked in one corner, and the support tab has separated from the black velvet panel at the back, so that the photo now has to sit up against a stack of sheet paper. The frame is of an unusual construction: the glass is at the front, and then the frame slopes like a false perspective toward the photo, which is some two inches behind the glass. The sloping part of the frame is silver, and it is covered with baroque engraved designs, swirls and eddies; at the corners are bas relief branches of oak leaves that must cover the joins of the sides. The photo has faded slightly. My father is wearing a morning coat and a double-breasted dove-grey waistcoat. He has what I now realize must be a spray of lily of the valley pinned to his lapel, what now seems, in fact, to be very legibly a spray of lily of the valley; but when I was little, I always thought that this blurred shape was a silver reindeer, which I took to be part of the traditional wedding garb, something one might easily don to complement the waistcoat. Even now, I cannot see only lilies; in my mind's eye, my father wore a silver reindeer on his lapel the day he was married.

My mother is wearing her wedding dress, yards of white satin and lace, and she has her veil pushed back from her head, held in place by a wreath of flowers, which looks, in its slight blurriness, like a crown of tiny diamonds. My mother is wearing a simple string of pearls. My father is staring straight out at the camera and smiling. My mother is holding a glass of what I think must be champagne, and she is also smiling, but she is looking just slightly off to the side, as though something restless in her draws her from the centre. In her right hand she is holding a bridal bouquet, most of which lies outside the space of the photograph; on her left hand, the hand holding the glass, her engagement ring is sparkling in the light.

When my parents were married, my grandfather's illness and death had eaten most of my mother's money, and my father had not yet taken over at the bank. The reception was just drinks, at the Plaza. It was in December. I have always imagined it like this: the ceremony ended, and my parents led all their friends and relations out into the crisp air of December. Everyone proceeded down Fifth Avenue in the light snow. The Plaza fountain would have been filled with small pines and lit with strings of Christmas lights.

This is what my mother once told me: on her wedding morning, she woke feeling tense and anxious. Her mother was busy getting dressed, and she also got dressed. Her mother came and corrected her hair, and corrected the way the dress hung, and then fussed about her own hair and her own dress. No one spoke to her about anything but her dress and her hair. And all the time she wondered whether she was making a terrible mistake. But when she got to her own wedding ceremony, and walked to the foot of the aisle, she saw my father look back at her. 'It was like a thousand lights had suddenly gone on,' she told me. 'He looked so happy, happier than I had ever seen anyone look, and all for me; and I stopped being afraid, and I knew that I wasn't making a mistake, that I was doing the best thing I'd ever done.' I can imagine the music – my father would have selected the music carefully – how its steady rhythms must have kept my mother walking down the aisle slowly and ceremonially, kept my father standing at the head of the aisle, kept them from doing anything more, for the moment, than look at each other. The photo in the silver frame, taken at the reception, is the aftermath of that look, and you can almost hear the music, a wedding march, romantic and precise, compelling them forward as only marches can.

The second photo was taken at the Metropolitan Club, just a month before my mother got sick. My mother was very fond of that photo, but I don't love it as much as the others. My father has a banker's contented smile, and my mother a doyenne's grace. This time they are both holding glasses of champagne. My father is in black tie, with what is very clearly a white carnation in his lapel; I can't think why he should have had a carnation on, but perhaps it has something to do with the function they were attending. My mother is wearing a black lace dress with a high neck, and she has on large diamond earrings, a diamond necklace, and a wide deco diamond bracelet. A great dark sapphire sparkles on one hand; on the other, her diamond engagement ring. My mother's smile in that photo is the smile of a woman who smiles out of habit, her smile for the photographer. She looks beautiful, but that is all she looks.

The third photo is the one Freddy took that week at Lake Como. My parents' suite overlooked the lake, which meant it also overlooked the small orchestra that played each night until midnight. We had come up from dinner, and my mother, who was tired, had put on a nightgown and a flowered silk dressing gown. In the photo, she is wearing no make-up, because the chemotherapy had by then made her allergic to everything; for some reason, she has not yet taken off her jewellery, and so she has on, with her dressing gown, a necklace of black pearls, earrings of gold and onyx, and a gold bracelet that belonged to my grandmother. My father has taken off his jacket, but he is still wearing his shirt and tie. I don't remember which tune it was that drifted up from the small orchestra by the side of the lake that evening, but it was some tune which for my parents had rich associations. I remember how my mother emerged from the bedroom, and stood for a minute in the door of the turquoise living room swaying in time, and how my father jumped up and went over to her; I think he may have been afraid that she would fall, because she had been suffering from dizziness.

But when my father drew closer, he must have seen that she was not so weak after all; he took her in his arms and they danced, laughing, around that room, to the sounds of the orchestra that floated through the half-drawn shutters. They danced that way for the length of the song, and it was a long song. In that photo my mother has the smile I know best. It is the smile of what-the-hell, the smile of the-world-is-full-of-possibilities, the smile of so-long-as-I'm-with-you-nothing-matters. She has on her brave smile, her reckless smile, her determined smile, the smile that was the reason for that whole trip. It is the smile of being afraid but knowing that there have been and may again be moments of not being afraid. She is looking straight at the camera, the camera from which her eyes somehow darted in the pleasure of the wedding photo; she seems to be looking beyond the camera at the time when the photo will have outlasted her. And my father has the nostalgic smile I have always known best on him. He is looking down and at my mother, apparently unaware of the camera. And you can see how this moment of happiness is recalling other moments of happiness, perhaps even that moment when my mother appeared at the end of the aisle in her white wedding dress; and you can see how happiness itself fills him with sorrow. So smiling and so sad he looks, with my mother's tiny, thin hand, a shadow even of the tiny, thin hands she had always had, clasped in his own.

Ten days later, my mother and Bernard finally met over dinner in London. How much weight I had placed on that moment! And like so many moments given too much weight in advance, it seemed extravagantly insignificant when it finally came. Bernard said only that my mother seemed tense and rather uncomfortable, which was perhaps understandable. My mother said that if a daughter of hers had brought Bernard home, she would have thought him a perfect son-in-law. 'He seems very nice, and very presentable, and I hope he makes you happy,' she said. There was a trace of the old brittleness in her voice, but she kept it to a trace. She even went so far as to invite Bernard to come to stay with us in New York.

'In our house?' I asked my mother afterwards.

'Why not, Harry? If it's what you want. Why not have Bernard to stay with us at home?' Sitting at dinner with the two of them – and Freddy and my father – I felt a profoundly hollow sense of triumph. So many years had gone into the abstract of effecting such a meeting as this, and when it finally happened, I felt only that all that energy might have been better used elsewhere. If I'd only spent it on Bernard himself, I thought, then perhaps I would really love him. That night, I lay by his side, and discovered again that he was a stranger. When I tossed and turned, he reached out to comfort me, and I could not tell him to leave me alone; nor could I say, as perhaps I should have, how sorry I was. That night was my last chance, and I failed to avail myself of it; I lay beside him in the tactful silence that had become the language of our sufficient affinity. In retrospect, I can see that I had loved him in the way of the Metropolitan Club, and that I never managed to do more than that. Nor, to be quite fair, did he manage much more than that for me. I understood, then, that he and I would never make it to Lake Como.

VI

October

Some days, I dream of a life without sequence, a life all mixed up like a crazy salad, in which, when you suddenly yearn for a week of childhood, you can have a week of childhood, in which, when you miss the quality of your grandmother's voice singing, you can find again your grandmother singing, in which, when you want a stretch of the calm maturity of middle age, you can settle into a stretch of it. I would love to move back and forth, to have days saved like summer flowers caught forever in winter ice, days that I knew were waiting for me. What use was it to try to spend every waking moment with my mother in the months of her worsening illness? I somehow had the idea that if I spent every moment with her, the accrued hours would fill in for all the time I might not be spending with her for the rest of my life. If only I could have held some of those days for the occasions later in my life when the need for my mother, that vivid longing that comes with the sharpness of a fever, seeks only the fact of her presence to answer – for what I wanted was not to be with my mother every second of every day (a programme well calculated to drive us both mad), but to be with my mother from time to time for the rest of my days.

Everything in life goes away or is taken from you before you are done with it. The present is always dark, since by having any moment you destroy the possibility of having it again. If death meant that you could see someone only once a decade for half an hour, and not that you could never see that person again, it would be a very different business. I have to be careful with my memories: they are like those pictures whose colours fade slowly in boxes or rapidly in the sun. I save certain memories and do not touch them, so that they will not get used up. I know that a time will come when the memories of my mother that I have traced as vividly as I can in these pages will seem as unreal as if they were someone else's memories. Then I will take out the other memories, the ones I do not allow myself to describe here, and I will lose myself in them. They will no doubt be brittle at that point, but they will still be real to me, and I will keep them by my side, and regret that life is not a crazy salad, that it operates in sequences and progressions, and that nothing that has happened ever happens again.

I suppose it is not surprising that Bernard and I were to break up within six weeks of that dinner with my parents. It is not surprising, but it was nonetheless shocking and horrifying to me. What you expect is perhaps somewhat easier than what you do not expect, but not much. Bernard and I had had an enormously peaceful relationship and a day-to-day life that functioned exquisitely, and though one cannot, perhaps, live for such things, they are in their way almost as beguiling as true love. Bernard and I were not – at least in relation to each other – very passionate people, and the demeanour of passion that we had partially sustained in the early months of our relationship had been allowed to fall away. Domesticity is passion spread very thin. Still, it has all passion's vulnerability. It is, whatever its shortcomings, a way of life, and to leave it behind is terrible. In the last weeks of our relationship, I found Bernard ridiculous and unimportant and inadequate, but when the end came I was more miserable than I had ever been before.

We started breaking up on a Thursday in late September. I had made plans to go to New York in October, and I had invited Bernard to stay with us for the two middle weeks of that month. 'I wish', I said to him, 'that you could come and stay with all of us the way we used to be.' Then we had gone on to talk about what the month would be like, and we had made plans for the time we would spend together in New York. Bernard and I loved making plans, and we were good at that. I had learned by then that my mother's condition was degenerating further, that her second chemotherapy was not so effective as had been hoped. 'Oh, Bernard,' I said. 'What to do?'

And Bernard, in his supportive way, said, 'You must just go back to New York and try to keep everything stable, and try to be the same with your mother as you've always been.'

I stopped him this time. 'No,' I said. 'It's not time for things to be the same any more; it's time for things to be different. I need to go back to New York and ask my mother all the things I've never asked her, tell her the secrets she's never known. We have to understand everything before it's too late, to find all the answers – so that, when she's gone, I will have no regrets, no uncertainty about who she is and what she feels; and so that when she dies she will know as an absolute certainty how much I love her.'

When Bernard looked at me pityingly, I wanted to strike him. Bernard was a master of sympathy, but he was unacquainted with empathy. The idea that my being sad might have made him sad was as odd to him as the idea that my being fat would make him fat. And so the idea that my mother's sadness had become my sadness was for him impossible to understand.

In the end, we argued about curtains. We had gone to stay in the country with Claire and Michael, and we had been given the upstairs bedroom at the end of the long hall, with the view out over the garden. We came up from dinner: Claire had made lamb, and pavlova for pudding. Some friends from down the road had come for the evening, people who were trying to bring art exhibitions to the county. We had had a fire, and talked about how the days were getting shorter. We'd dipped into claret that Michael had discovered the previous year, and of which he'd put up several cases. Michael's mother was also staying, and she had been in top form, telling her stories from the roaring '20s, including one about a performing bear in a striptease bar in Berlin; Michael had kept rolling his eyes toward the ceiling, but the rest of us had loved it.

And so it was quite late when Bernard and I finally went up to the bedroom at the end of the long hall to settle down for the night. We both climbed into bed, and Bernard read. 'I do think this is a pretty room,' I said.

'Mm,' said Bernard. 'Lovely mirror, isn't it. Regency.'

I looked at the mirror vaguely. 'Yes,' I said. 'And such beautiful curtains. I wonder who Claire got to do them?'

Bernard shifted in bed. 'Actually,' he said, 'I don't like the curtains.'

'No?' I said.

'It's those undercurtains,' he said. 'I think it's so much better just to have curtains, and pelmets, and not to have those fussy little gauzy undercurtains blowing around.'

I should explain that I was at the time in the midst of getting new curtains for my own house, and had just commissioned my curtain-maker to do linen undercurtains in every room. Bernard had told me that he thought they were not in good taste, but I thought they were convenient. Bernard's remark therefore seemed deliberately barbed. 'Any more veiled criticisms this evening?' I asked peevishly, fishing for an argument. 'If there are, I think it would be just as well to get them over with now.'

Bernard looked at me with an aggrieved expression. 'I don't think we were talking about your curtains, which we discussed, in any event, before you chose the design, and about which I made my views perfectly clear at the time. I think we were talking about Claire's curtains, which I do not care for, and which you apparently like.'

'Did it ever occur to you,' I asked, in a tone that I had been using more and more since the second surgery, 'that you could be fond of me and that your fondness could extend to the things about me and the way I live? Your flat is pretty dreary and depressing, with all that chipped furniture and faded, cat-clawed upholstery and stained carpeting. I don't care where the rugs came from or how significant the design of the furniture is or how original the upholstery may be.' Bernard made a gesture to remind me that Michael's mother was in the next room. I lowered my voice to a loud whisper. 'But I don't find it disgusting. I don't find it disgusting because it is part of you and who you are and how you live. I see all that stuff as an extension of you, and though I would never in a thousand years have all those chipped things in my house, I like being with them in your flat. I'm not always criticizing them and pulling them apart, and I've been living with them very happily for more than two years.'

Our conversation unfolded in whispers because we were much

too polite to wake up Michael's mother. We finished the night together in the same bed, because we were much too polite to trouble Claire and Michael about personal matters, and we were perfectly sunny to everyone all through Sunday lunch, because we were too polite to spoil the weekend, and then we continued to be sunny to each other in the car going back to London because we were much too polite to add to each other's burdens by being nasty. Indeed we were so polite to each other that Sunday that when we got back to London there was a sort of confused pause, because in our rage of politeness we were finally unsure as to whether we had broken up at all. Bernard drove to my house – which came before his on the way in from the country – and I didn't know whether I should ask him in. Reason had begun to penetrate, and I wasn't sure I could afford another trauma. I wondered whether it would be wise to swallow my pride, put this behind me, and go on with Bernard as I had always done.

'You're going to pack?' he asked.

'I guess so,' I said. 'The plane's first thing tomorrow morning.' There was a long pause.

'Do you need to pick anything up at the flat?' asked Bernard. I almost never slept at my house; we almost never slept there. None of my ordinary things was there.

'I think I've got everything I need here,' I replied.

'Well, I'm a bit tired,' said Bernard, after another pause. 'I'm going to go back to the flat and get to bed early. I didn't get much sleep last night,' he added.

'I hope you do better tonight,' I said. 'I must say I'm rather exhausted myself.' We stared at each other for a moment, then kissed each other goodbye much as we might have done if we had been planning to meet for drinks in an hour.

'I think it's best that I not come to New York just now,' said Bernard. 'But I'll see you soon. And I'll call.'

'You could still come if you wanted,' I said. It was a sentence that cost me impossibly much.

'Don't you think that would be a mistake?' he asked, and since I had already given him one opening, I said, 'Yes, I suppose it would,' and tried to sound cheerful. We were both much too polite to break up by anything other than mutual consent.

'I hope everything's all right with your mother,' he said, and we had another quick kiss goodbye, and then I went into my house and closed the door and gave in to the shock and relief and ghastly sadness. I lay down on the sofa and watched the silhouette, blurred through the soon-to-be-replaced undercurtains, of Bernard's car pulling out of its usual spot in front of my house.

It was on the plane that it occurred to me that I might as well move to New York. If Bernard was really over, then what was there to keep me in London? The recording was done, and I wanted to start performing more in America anyway. October had been left clear of concerts so that I could have a month in New York; the performances scheduled for the following months could all be negotiated with a bit of commuting. My agent had an American affiliate who seemed easier to deal with, and who had said years before that he would take me on if I wanted to base myself in the US. There were my London friends, but I had, of course, all my New York friends, many of whom I had known for much longer. And there was Helen. 'You can't make a new old friend,' my mother used to say. On the plane I lapsed into reverie, an absurdly happy reverie. A month in New York, unbroken, a month without any planes, without even having to go to the airport to pick up Bernard as planned! If I had never again had to pack a suitcase, it would have been too soon. I have always loved cumulative statistics: in the course of your lifetime, you will spend three years chewing; you will replace your skin completely a thousand times; you will drink as much water as is contained in Lake Huron. I felt that year that if I hooked up all my transatlantic flights I could have joined the voyagers on the Starship Enterprise, and I suddenly realized that I was being given the option of home leave. At that moment, it sounded better than a spa vacation.

I arrived in New York on the day of my mother's birthday. I had told my mother that Bernard and I were arriving together, a week later, because I wanted to surprise my mother on her birthday. 'If one only knew what was happening,' I had said to Helen. 'Then I could decide how much time to give my mother. If I knew that she had six weeks, I would stay by her every second. And if I knew that she had ten more years, I would ration my time a bit, because enough is enough.'

Helen said to me, 'Enough is enough; if you spend every minute with her, you'll go crazy. But don't be stingy about it either; whatever happens, the time you spend with her won't be time wasted.' And so I had decided to surprise my mother for her birthday again.

And again she was surprised. But this year, she was truly and unequivocally delighted. Now she seemed to see everyone's love so strongly and so clearly that she made it solid and coloured it in all her favourite shades. She had the whole time that smile she had had when she danced with my father in the hotel on Lake Como, that generous reckless smile she used to squeeze all the pleasure out of good days. She kept on reaching out, through dinner, to touch my arm; I can still feel the almost imperceptible weight of her thin hand on my sleeve. At her birthday a year earlier she had looked worse than I had ever seen her, with her terrible wig and her strange loping walk, and the sight of her had been unbearable; but on this birthday she was as beautiful as I could remember her ever being. It was as though the chemotherapy were purifying her: she had the transparent animated look of medieval saints in ecstasy. I told her about Bernard at dinner that night (though I'd told her a bit before by phone), and she said – not as though it were an insight, but as a matter of simple fact – how odd she found the idea of anyone's ceasing to love me. 'Just when I'd got used to the idea of him, too,' she said, and laughed sadly. 'Don't worry, Harry. The right person is there for you. It . . .' her voice trailed off. 'It takes time,' she said, and her inflection reminded me that time was the thing she no longer had.

A few days later, we went out to lunch. I can't remember how old I was when my mother and I started going out to lunch. When I was little, I remember that she and my father used to banter about whether he was taking her to lunch; they had dinner together every night of their married life, but lunch was a meal through which my father ordinarily worked. I can remember how my mother would get dressed up for the occasional lunches he afforded her; I can remember her leaving the house with the stinging smell of fresh perfume. Later, so confident in their love, they let lunch slide: my father worked during the day, and my mother had so many friends to see that it was perhaps easier all around for them to stick to dinner. At some stage, my mother and I took to going out to lunch together, and we would have one lunch out in every school vacation, maybe two or three in the summer. We would go to restaurants slightly less grand than the ones she visited with my father, and she would get slightly less dressed up, but they were still glamorous places and she still had that aura of perfume around her.

It was a beautiful autumn day, with the slightest nip in the air, and I was wearing a blazer and a new tie, and the breeze felt good. My mother was very weak by then, and had to wear a long fur coat, which she kept draped around her shoulders throughout lunch. Her very short hair was slightly less short than it had been during the summer, and it had been arranged into a boyish coif that seemed carefree, carefree as my mother had never been. I told her at lunch that I thought I might move back to New York. 'You don't have to move back here for me,' she said. 'You come and visit. That's enough, really, enough.'

But I told her that now that Bernard and I were broken up there wasn't any real reason to be in London. I told her that I had finally realized that, in moments of crisis, I myself reverted to American responses, and that it was easier to be in America. I told her about sympathy and empathy, the one so English, the other so American. I told her how alien Britain was, and I told her about the chill I'd had when Bernard had suggested that I go home and try to keep everything as normal as possible. I told her that I didn't think I'd like to grow old in that slightly-below-room-temperature society. I told her I was ready for an American career. And then I told her – because at that moment it seemed completely true – that when I was in London I felt so far away from her, and that I wanted to be on hand to help her get through this time of suffering.

'Before I met your father,' she said, 'I was in love with a man from Texas. And his family threatened to disinherit him if he married me, because I didn't come from their kind of family. And he gave in to them, and I cried and I cried and I cried, for months and months and months, and I thought nothing would ever work out again. And when I met your father, I knew that where I came from was where he came from, and that we would never have that argument, and that it made sense for me to be with him, in the world I knew. I thought I was being so practical.' And her voice took on a tone of wonder, as though, twenty-seven years later, she were still incredulous. 'It was the smartest thing I ever did, falling in love with your father,' she said. 'If it hadn't been for that boy's Texas family, it would never have happened, and I might have ended up as one of those displaced people in a world that was foreign to me. In Dallas.' And she paused again. 'Harry, I would love for you to be in New York. So long as you don't move back for me.'

There is a place, along the highway coming into New York from the airport, where they had to build a wall because the view was too beautiful and was causing accidents. In my logical mind, I know that the world offers more startling highway views – that there are mountains in nature before which the New York skyline pales. I like to imagine that it was not so much the sheer majesty of the architecture as the associative value of the New York skyline – which to New Yorkers carries a familiarity made only more meaningful by the likelihood that the streets below will have been transformed. That view is about the way New York changes and stays the same, the way it is always home to the people to whom it is home. I told my mother about this, and she smiled. Then she asked, 'Have they set a date for the release of your recording?'

'They have,' I said. 'Finally. It's going to come out in June. And they are going to include the Rachmaninoff.' There had been some talk of cutting the Rachmaninoff, and substituting early Beethoven. I had not been pleased by this idea.

'June,' said my mother. 'We should have a party to celebrate that. It's been so long that you've been working on it. Would you like to have a party?'

I always wanted to have a party. So we talked about the party, and I said I would start looking around for fittingly splendid places to have it, and my mother and I selected a date, and I said, 'You should be through your chemotherapy by then, shouldn't you? So we could celebrate that?'

And my mother said, 'Wouldn't that be nice,' and then the waiter brought her salad and my fish, and offered pepper, which she didn't take and I did, and for a moment we ate. The restaurant was enormous, an old warehouse space that had been converted, with great columns and enormous cloth lanterns. The food was delicious. We had tables near the great back windows, which looked out at a garden, and the last autumn flowers blew gently back and forth in the wind. The sun came in on the diagonal and lit up our food. 'Harry,' said my mother. 'I'm a little weak right now from the chemotherapy, but other than that I really feel very well.' She paused, and I nodded.

'You look terrific,' I said.

'You know that my second treatments haven't really worked. And that your father is discussing other options with the doctors, and that they'll probably start me on something new next month.'

'The cancer's not growing,' I said.

'The cancer's not receding,' she said. 'Please. I know that you have your routine that you go through, and I know you go through it to make me feel better, and I really appreciate that. But I'm not a fool, and I know what's happening, and you also know what's happening. It would be lovely if one of these things worked, and perhaps one of them will, and this time will all recede into memory. But it's not very likely. If the first therapy had worked, I might have been fine, and there was a chance with the second, but once you get to the third and the fourth rounds of treatment, the chances are almost nil. I don't mean that I don't have any time left, but I think it's limited.'

I could tell that there was something more coming, something terrible. My mother had that calm, rational, radiant quality she had had since Italy. Her blue eyes did not blink. 'I don't want you and Freddy to remember me as an emaciated wreck screaming in a hospital bed,' she said. 'I don't want that. And I don't want to go through all that pain myself. I hate physical pain; I've always hated it. I hate even discomfort. I'm telling you this now, while I'm feeling very well, because if I try to tell you later it will be more difficult, and you'll tell me I'm out of control and incoherent. Your father and I have talked and talked about this, and my decision is made. I will go on with treatments as long as the doctors say there is a chance of my getting well. But when they say that the battle is lost, that they can only extend my life for a month or two at a time, while I get more and more miserable, then I am not going to go on. I've thought about this, and I've made up my mind. It's the right decision, the right decision for me and for all of you. My friend Stella died screaming and contorted and it was horrible for her and it was horrible for her family. I've heard Philip say that he will never forget that last week in the hospital with the intravenous painkillers and the sedatives. That's not life, Harry.' My mother put down her fork and she put her hand on my hand, next to the bread basket. 'Harry, I have got the pills I will need to do it. I'm not going to do it now; I'm not going to do it until I have to, and I think when the moment comes we will all know it. But I wanted to explain this to you now, so that you won't be too shocked then. I am not going to see this disease through to the very bitter most miserable end.'

My father and Freddy and I had agreed a long time before that we would not cry with my mother, would not let her know that we too thought she might be dying; by and large we tried not to admit that even to each other. 'But you can't . . .' I began, without knowing the rest of the sentence.

'I can,' said my mother. If tears are memories, then there were memories streaming down my cheeks as my mother spoke, memories making my napkin thick and heavy, memories pouring out of me unstoppably and endlessly. We had been so joyful, a whole family almost wholly joyful. And there we were, she and I, in yet another beautiful place, watching the sunlight and the breeze stir the flowers, and my mother was so calm, so suffused with a light of her own, so beautiful herself in her dark blue suit with the high collar of her fur coat coming up around her face, and the easy words coming to her one after the next.

'And there's one other thing,' she said to me. 'You have to help take care of your father when I'm not here. I know how angry you get at him, and I know how difficult he can be. Of course I know that. But you will have to help him. And you have to encourage him to find someone and get married and get on with his own life. That will be better for you and for him. Whomever he finds – it won't be me, but it will be someone. He should live for a long time, and he shouldn't be alone. Try to be nice to her. Try to make her feel loved, and accepted. Try to help your father, Harry, even if you don't feel like it.' And then with a sudden voice of sorrow, she said across my steady tears, 'You are going to be all right. We are having a rough time, but you have a life ahead of you, and it's going to be a good life. You have to *make* it a good life. And you will do that, Harry. I know that you will.'

I was not sobbing or weeping; I just sat with tears running down my face, enough tears to fill the large glasses on the table, to water the garden outside, to make up for the rain that was not falling much that autumn. My mother took my hand in hers again, and squeezed it. 'I don't know how much time I have left,' she said. 'Maybe very little. Maybe not so little. But I want us, all of us, to have as good a stretch as we possibly can. I want to get all the joy there is left in my life, and I want to leave you with as many happy memories as I can. I'm sorry I had to tell you all this, right now, but now it's done. Don't cry yet, Harry. Wait and cry later, if you have to.' She paused and looked out. 'Look at that perfect yellow rose,' she said. 'A perfect rose, growing right here, in the middle of Manhattan.' And so I looked out the window at the rose, which was indeed perfect. 'And Harry,' said my mother, smiling. 'Can we please try not to fight, at least for a while? And would you try not to fight with your father and with Freddy? Would you try, at least, not to fight about nonsense?'

And so I finally laughed, as, in the end, I always laughed with my mother. 'OK,' I said. 'No fights. But you have to promise me that you'll try to get well, really try.'

My mother laughed too. 'I'll do my best,' she said. 'Now, how many people are you going to try to squeeze into this party in June? Could we manage something elegant that is not a mob scene? Could you restrict yourself to friends about whom you actually have some feeling?'

As we ate dessert, my mother described the terrible food at a wedding she'd attended the previous week, soup 'like library paste with small chunks of wood' and the meat 'which had been put in to roast the same week the invitations were printed' and the cake 'with icing you could have rollerskated on.' We began to spin out the plans for my party, and it became magnificent. We both laughed and laughed and everything we were imagining seemed so real to me that I could not hold onto the fact that my mother was planning to kill herself, and had just told me all about it.

I suppose that losing Bernard was my own doing, and I think I did it to practise for losing my mother. I spent the month of October loving my mother, and that love took on a purity because all my rage and hatred were taken out on Bernard. I wrote him a cruel letter about abandonment, and I plotted the terrible things I would do to him. I would go into his flat and smash the set of espresso cups his grandmother had left him. I would smash his Chinese vase. I would smash his Chinese vase over his head. I would find the keys to his windows and throw them away so that he couldn't get to his windowboxes. I would mutilate his cat. I would tell him that I had AIDS. I would go in in the middle of the night and smother him with his own pillow. I wrote him a letter carefully designed to make him fall in love with me, hopelessly in love, so that I could reject him brutally. I would cut the sleeves off all his favourite shirts. I would castrate him with a straight razor.

Helen was immeasurably patient with this catalogue of fantasies, but said very definitively that the most effective revenge was to be charming and blasé, so that he would regret having allowed the relationship to slide. I am not entirely persuaded that this was more effective than some of these schemes of violence would have been, but it was certainly more sensible; and, as Helen pointed out, it was something I would be unlikely to regret later on. It allowed me to keep some dignity, and was not illegal. For a while that October, Bernard phoned every day, but I did not answer my telephone and let him leave messages on my machine. I called his machine during the day, when I knew he would be out. At first, I told him what was happening, but finally I asked him not to phone me any more.

Helen and I went to find me an apartment, largely at my mother's suggestion. 'If you're living here with your father and me when I die,' she said, 'you'll have a hard time moving out. You've been living on your own for a long time. With you in this apartment full time – we'll end up arguing. Remember what you promised: no fights.' In fact, neither she nor my father wanted me to move out, but I think she knew that there was a great deal in my life that she would not care to see, and that it was easier, better, for me to be at some distance. And I think she knew that the illness that held her prisoner could hold the rest of us, and she did not want – at least for the moment – to trap me inside it, where she and my father were.

Helen kept saying that Jason had managed to locate the golden fleece with less high drama than I brought to finding an apartment. I suppose that I did fuss about where I was going and how I would live. I had decided to keep, at least for the time being, my house in London, and so I wanted to find someplace where I could be while I really decided about the US. I wanted it to feel completely different from London. Agents showed me places with scratched marble fireplaces and crumbling mouldings and I was absolutely belligerent. 'It's got to be someplace very New York,' I said to Helen.

'This *is* very New York,' she said. 'You're *in* New York. It's *all* very New York.' I told her that one apartment was too close to my parents, another too far away. I said I didn't feel comfortable with postmodernism. 'You know what?' she said at one point. 'This is a very uncomfortable period in your life. All the apartments we look at are going to seem very uncomfortable. Just find one you can make the best of.' My mother was too weak to come along on all these treks, and I was glad to have Helen's company. She would ask the agents all the tough-minded questions about whether the air conditioning really worked and what the neighbours were like and why the elevator inspection certificate had expired. After we'd looked at places, I would take Helen out for drinks and I would rant about Bernard. 'Let's talk hard sense,' said Helen. 'You never thought Bernard was the true love of your life. So you always knew you were going to have to break up sooner or later. So now you've done it and that's over with, and you can begin looking again, and maybe find someone who's really right for you. This is New York. The world's your oyster.'

Helen and I finally found an apartment for me. It was a loft space downtown, full of quirky architectural details and dramatic vistas. It had windows the size of front doors, and no doors at all, and it was big enough for the piano. It was not to my taste, nor was it to my mother's taste, and I don't think Helen liked it much either; but it was at least a far cry from anything in London. I moved my things in, with Helen's help, and the place gleamed with the supernal cleanliness of Helen's own apartment. I took very little from my parents' house, because I did not want to destroy the eternal space that I had occupied since childhood. I moved out of my parents' apartment on a Wednesday, and when I had put the last bag into the elevator, my mother looked at me and I thought for a second that she was going to cry. But in fact she laughed instead, and as the elevator door closed, I realized that I was the one who was sick with the sense of loss.

Everyone agreed that my new space downtown was spectacular, and I spoke of starting a new life, my new New York life. My mother came down the day after I'd moved in and brought me salt 'so that life would have flavour to it,' flour 'for growth and health,' sugar 'for the great sweetness of life,' and marmalade 'because I know you like it.'

My father had ceased to love me when my mother became ill. I cannot blame him for that; one man can manage only so much love, and my father had turned all his immense powers of affection toward my mother. Still, it was a disappointment, and I felt it to the core of my being. In fact, I thought that my father, who had always been able to deal with any situation, should have been able to make my mother well; and I think that he too thought that. He kept applying himself to her health, believing that enough money and enough willpower and enough intelligence and enough love could solve all the problems of the world.

He and I had lunch often, because Freddy and I were the only people with whom he could discuss my mother's terrible plan. He kept reworking the details, with me, then with Freddy, then with me again, then with Freddy again.

'I have a booklet,' he told me, 'with instructions in it. It's a booklet for people who want to end their own lives. It says when to take the pills and so on. I've been studying it.'

I said that I had not realized that these matters required much technical expertise.

'You have to do it right,' said my father. 'For legal and medical reasons. So it works.'

The booklet was only about thirty pages long. 'How much time have you spent studying that?' I asked. It looked dog-eared.

'I just want to make sure that I really know what we're doing,' my father said. 'You and Freddy should probably read this as well, so we can make a final plan.'

I told him I had no intention of reading it. 'I'll do whatever I have to do, and I'll play along with your plan, but I'm not getting any more involved than that.'

My father seemed not to hear me. 'I never imagined that I could find myself in such a situation,' he said. 'It's intolerable. It's unthinkable.'

I remembered that I had promised my mother that I would take care of him. I decided I should save such energies as I might have for the task until after she was dead. Unfairly, I began to hate my father. After so many years of confidence, he was lapsing into need, and all I did in the face of it was to hate him. I hated Bernard and I hated my father. This made it easier to love my mother.

Helen told me I was really hating myself. When she said that, I hated her.

I couldn't tell my father how I was growing to dislike him, and so I took it all out on Bernard, whom I was free to loathe from the core of my being, from the centre of my heart. I was afraid of my mother's death and miserable that Bernard had been able to leave me, but I was really most afraid of being left in a world in which I loved no one and nothing. That October, I began to imagine my own death. I imagined it as though it were a form of vengeance.

The third chemotherapy seemed to be working just then, but we had been through two success stories already, and we knew better than to feel too happy. More than I hated Bernard or my father, I began to hate time. I've never stopped. Time is still my enemy. I once said to my mother that I wished that I had a fast-forward button on my life, that I could skip over the darkest hours, and my mother shook her head and said, 'You'd just fast-forward your life away.'

Only later did I realize how much more complex my wish had been. I want a fast-forward button, and I want a rewind button and, perhaps most of all, I want a pause button, since I can see no evil in asking the fair moments to stay. I want these buttons for myself and for other people. It is a basic principle of traffic that if all the cars on the highway are moving at the speed limit, they cannot hit one another; only when one of them slows down or speeds up will an accident occur. We all know that our entire solar system is hurtling at some unimaginable speed across the galaxy, but since we're *all* moving at that speed, it feels as though we aren't moving at all. What is the point of time if it happens at the same rate to everyone? I want to be able to move and readjust and change in my relationship to other people and the world. I want to have some experiences over and over again until, like songs heard too frequently, they become tired and uninteresting. I want to skate through some kinds of pain and most kinds of indifference. I want to be born over and over and over, as though I were the world itself in all its changes.

VII

Three Loves

I will tell you about my last trip to London, the trip to collect my belongings, the January trip. I will tell you about a happiness so brief it did not have time to be fragile. It was in the dull period after the New Year, when the grey sky over London stayed close to the ground, as though to hold in the cold. I had come back to London to get away from the persistent misery of New York, and to sleep long nights, one after another. Each day I called home and spoke to my mother, and each day her voice, pale and thin and taut as the top notes of a piccolo, echoed off some satellite and across to me. I had come because in New York I was up too close to what was happening. And I had come to get the odds and ends, sweaters and books and sheaves of music, that had been left behind when I'd set off for New York that early October day.

I slept for days when I got back to London, slept as though I were practising for hibernation. My sleep followed the law of inertia: when I was asleep I tended to remain asleep, and when I was awake, I tended to remain awake. When I rose, the anaemic light by which it was possible to trace the passage of the sun behind the unbroken grey was already disappearing. I would go far enough to buy myself mineral water and drinkable yoghurt and chilled soups: the things I could consume without a kitchen and without cutlery and without any china but the bathroom cup that sometimes held my toothbrushes. It was too much effort to boil water. Then in the twilight I would practise, on until well after dark. I buried myself in music I knew well, but I did not learn anything new. And so days merged, with the regularly paced interruption of friends coming to inquire after my state of mind and my mother's health.

The precision of modern medicine is among its many punishments. You still have the nasty surprises of chance symptoms and unusual side effects, but you have also the knowledge that certain events will occur on certain dates: if the surgery is on such a day, the chemotherapy will begin on such a day, and you will have the first indication of its effectiveness (or ineffectiveness) on such a day. And so I spent my first week back in London with the image of a certain Thursday always ahead of me, as the next day for bad news. The news always came on Thursdays at about five o'clock New York time, and even now, years later, I have a sense of uneasy suspense attached to Thursday afternoons. It was like being a prisoner attending the electric chair and awaiting a pardon, counting the minutes in dread and intermittent hope, and feeling, by the time Thursday rolled around, that it was better to have bad news than to go on waiting in this agony of suspense.

Time grinds and polishes your expectations; the news we received would, through the murky hopeful lens of a year before, have been bad. But through the refined clarity of pain, it was good, good news for the first time since October, news of stability if not of improvement. Some part of some treatment (the fourth? the fifth?) seemed to be having some effect that might be sustained for some length of time. On that Thursday, a day that could have held the news of my mother's almost certain death, we had what I was determined to receive as good news. And armed with that, I began my holiday. I did not make new plans to travel: that too was part of the holiday. For me, there was no greater vacation than the calm of staying in a familiar place. Another test result was expected three weeks later; I said to my mother, and to my father, and to Freddy, that if we all managed three weeks of feeling light and easy and unconcerned, we could build up our depleted energy for the renewal of the battle. 'And if the battle need never be renewed,' I insisted, 'we will not have wasted this time by being happy.'

Sparkling that Thursday night, I chanced to pause on a corner to let the traffic pass, and on the opposite corner chanced to stand a broad man with unkempt blond hair and a skier's tan. I caught his eye, and he caught my eye, and I stood quite still as the traffic waned; and after a moment he crossed the road, and spoke to me in imperfect English with an indeterminate accent that seemed to live at the back of his throat. I broke with old rules, and with new rules, and I walked with him to his car, and drove with him to his home and slept with him in his bed. By the time we arrived at his door, I knew that we shared only a world of mutual surface; but I was fascinated by his face and his body and his movements, and by the gilded edge between eroticism and romance.

Our liaison lasted only a week. He told me that he was soon to go to Geneva; I knew that by the time he returned I would be in New York. I was never able to ask him whether he made it a habit to pick up young men on the busy streets, and he never asked me whether I was in the habit of behaving in this way; it would have spoiled that week to inquire too closely into the other weeks like it that might or might not have gone before. Once or twice our conversation drifted towards politics, and I was stunned at how little we agreed on, but I didn't mind it. He was, I was later to learn, a man of considerable influence in his country; perhaps I should have tried to steer him toward my notion of enlightenment, but to do so was then beyond my means. I was happy to speak instead of the weather, or about skiing, or to tell anecdotes of my childhood, or to hear from him about his childhood, which seemed to have unfolded in a land full of garden courtyards and fountains splashing under a crescent moon and the distant sound of children singing. I admired the renaissance pictures on the walls, the eighteenth-century furniture, the flowers that someone came and changed every day. He had a piano, and I played for him, sometimes before love, sometimes after; he had a sensualist's enthusiasm for music, as though it were another physical stimulus. Our nights together held pleasures I had never dreamed before, and though my skin and body emerged damaged by the extravagances of desire, I was lost in such rapture that these ravages were only souvenirs, marks to remind me, between our meetings, of the pleasures that had gone before and the pleasures that would follow.

That first night had the dangerous thrill of anonymity clinging to it. Much later, I learned that he and I knew many people in common – that we might, indeed, have met at a drinks party – but I was glad not to find that out during our week together. Did he kill Bernard for me, finally, once and for all? I never got to know him, and I never knew whether those nights carried for him such a burden of significance as they did for me. We never argued and never made up. I never asked anything of him but that he lie beside me and burn with desire, and he never asked more of me than that I look deep and straight into his dark blue eyes. But I felt with him what I had never known with Bernard; during that week I felt no desire at all for anyone else. I felt no anger. Bernard and I used to lie tossing separately and then drifting into sound and ordinary sleep. This man and I would hold one another all night, and when I was sure he was asleep he would suddenly stroke my hair or touch my leg or grasp me to him; and all night long we would linger uncertainly between sleep and wakefulness. Whereas in good photos Bernard can look like a model, this body had the more generous curves of too much pleasure. I would cling to that greater weight, as though bulk were an anchor to happiness. Sometimes, when he had curled around me, I would find that I was becoming unbearably cramped, or desperately hot, and I would take a steely pleasure in lying motionless for hours, until the cramping or heat had become the most hellish of tortures; it was the joy of knowing that through such wild efforts he was sleeping undisturbed behind me. Sometimes, I would find myself longing to climb out of that bed and stretch, or go to the bathroom; but I would restrain myself all night for the pleasure of remaining in unbroken contact with that noble body and those fond hands. Lying among my restraints in this way, I would feel my own happiness, the first happiness I had felt in almost a year, and I would cup my hands around it so that it would not be blown away. I knew I could hold that happiness for only a week, but in that week, I made up for months of indescribable agony. With the same restraint that kept me locked in a semi-fetal curl all night, I kept myself all day from talking about my depression or my mother; and when, one night, toward the end, I spoke about my mother, it was a Paris story I told, about the bar at the Ritz hotel. When he had to go to Geneva, we held each other in an unrelenting embrace. No one discussed driving to the airport. We made no plans to speak on the phone. We didn't even get each other's full names. We said goodbye in his bed, on those pure linen sheets, rumpled with our desire, and then I let him go, and felt that I had something to hold on to for whatever was to come.

Four days later, I found out (some intermediate test) that the therapy was not really helping my mother as much as had been hoped. I packed all my sheet music, and went back to New York.

My relationship to Bernard had been part of my appearance of a happy life and it had in fact made me happy. I found that I had begun, once I slept with someone else, to forget what it was like. I mean it literally; I couldn't remember what my two years with Bernard entailed, what we did day to day, how we made plans. I couldn't hold on to any of it, the way you find that you cannot remember a dream. I could still occasionally muster a deep, vengeful, passionate hatred for Bernard; I could still imagine taking the keys to his flat and going in and putting rat poison in his coffee, but I couldn't remember why. I called him and we had lunch the day I was leaving, which I thought would remind me; I expected to love him again, or to hate him, but in fact I was only a bit bored.

Moving to New York was like falling down an endless flight of stairs, gathering a momentum that blurred the pain of each new alarming contact with sharp angles and hard surfaces. It was like skiing down a sheet of bumpy ice, so fast that I simply sailed from panic to panic. If it was like dying in slow motion, in every other sense it was an event of desperate speed; and it was only when I wanted to calm myself that I thought how much slower all this was than the deaths of some young men through disease or disaster. Mostly, really, moving to New York was like falling down an endless flight of stairs, a flight of boys (thump) and the void of my mother's approaching death (thump, thump, thump); and serious work (thump) and physical discomfort (thump) and the exhaustion of my father (thump, thump); and more boys (thump), and parties (thump) and cold days and homeless people and all the sordidness of the rest of the world which, in London, somehow remained so much more hidden. I used to remember how Pooh Bear had come to hear a story of an evening, bumping his way down the stairs in Christopher Robin's hand, bump, bump, bump, and then, after the story, going up, bump, bump, bump, and then to bed. And some days I liked to imagine that there was someone pulling me down the stairs, someone who later on might pull me back up to a safe room in the almost-darkness where I could lie in the bliss of silence. Sometimes I tried to imagine that the boys and the void and the cold were all just part of the story someone was telling, and that soon it would all be light and air in the Hundred Acre Wood, and that I might dance forever in the last rays of sunshine of a golden afternoon. Moving to New York was like falling down an endless flight of stairs – but surely you set off on such a course from the love at the top of the stairs, and tumbled only as far as the love at the bottom? Yes: on good days, I would think (thump) that that was it – a bumpy ride from love to love. And then I lost myself only in wishing there had been some landings to make the intermediate days livable.

I had a double life in the city. At the top of the stairs sat my mother, making lots of demands. It was her last chance to make them, and it was my last chance to answer them. I took great pleasure in the easiness and familiarity of this. I would call my mother four or five times in the course of a morning. I would get up and work for a few hours, and then I would without thinking much of it cancel my various appointments and go up to my parents' apartment to sit with her. We would toast English muffins and eat them for lunch in the kitchen, or we would take short walks; the weather in New York was strangely mild for the time of year, and sometimes, since my mother tired easily, we would have Robert drive us just as far as Madison Avenue, so that we could stroll the few blocks she could stand, and look at the shops, and hypothesize about the shoppers. Sometimes I would play the piano, the old piano on which I had learned to play. My mother would come to listen, and she and I would talk about music. When my mother was very tired, we would sometimes watch TV together. Janet would bring us tea, and we would compare notes about the news. We talked about whether the dog was turning very grey, about whether Freddy would find a new girlfriend, about why certain of my father's business associates were not going to last. Or we would talk about the big things: our relationship to each other, her marriage to my father, the prospect of her death. We talked about my party; when my mother was most fragile or most depressed, I could draw her out by asking what she thought of a tablecloth fabric, or of putting the musicians in the same room as the buffet, or of having the salmon on skewers. These were the subjects on which she had an easy expertise that predated her illness, and they recalled the time before it, when we had had few greater concerns. I wished and dreamed and imagined that this time might last forever.

But when I was not uptown with my mother, I was at the bottom of the flight of stairs, looking for any and every kind of love. I went off deep into that search, as startled by the strength of my own new emotions as if I stood at the brink of sexual identity. I went out with new people, masses of new people, part of a New York whose existence I had not dared to imagine during my childhood. They were all the friends of friends of friends; I have heard that New York can be a lonely city, but it seemed then that there was an infinity of humankind waiting to meet me, that there was no reason not to have a thousand new friends every week. After all my time within the clean barriers of London society, I had been set free in a world in which nothing was clear. In this context, I pressed myself into new, alien confidence with men who were tougher than I was or than Bernard had ever been, and I pretended to myself and to them that what we had in common was greater than what stood between us. In the months of my deferred adolescence, I threw myself into perpetual loss as a way of feeling perpetual love, and hardly noticed how I was myself dwindling into the sum of my losses, as difficult to know or to love as the spaces between the stars.

I was afraid of this new and brutally male circle, but Helen laughed off my fear. 'You might find someone who's perfect for right now,' she said. 'Remember, not everyone provides everything. Not everyone is a supermarket. Some people are just butcher shops or vegetable stands or twenty-four-hour convenience stores, and those places can sometimes give you a few things that you really need.'

I must have looked unconvinced.

'You know, there are a lot of ways to find a perfect ten,' she said. 'You can find a perfect ten, or you can find four and four and two, or you can find seven and three, or six and four. You have good friends. If what you're looking for is adventure or romance – that's OK, lambchop.'

So I came to Nick, saw him often at parties, and eventually – it seemed a matter of chance – agreed to meet him, with some others, for a drink. I did not like Nick very much at that time; nor do I recall being particularly attracted to him. It could have been someone else with whom I made this plan to go out, but Nick was the one who mentioned drinks and the name of a bar; and I, game for anything that month, agreed at once. The place where we met had that singular combination of expensive lighting fixtures and deliberate shabbiness that I had come to associate with sexual freedom in New York, and it was full of young men who, apparently unacquainted with the February weather outside, were dressed as though cloth were too precious to be squandered on such insignificant extremities as arms and legs. The multitude of leather jackets seemed to be breathing animal smells at each other; their attar mixed with the smells of the men, and with the old wood of the floor, and the effect was surprisingly fresh, and reminded me of the wooden barns filled with livestock that I had visited as a child, some summers, in New England.

Nick had taken over a table in the corner (there were a few tables) and three other friends were there. Nick was drinking a martini, which had been served in a V-shaped glass. 'I'll get you a drink,' he said, and I asked for a martini too, because I wanted to touch such a glass, and could not bring myself to reach out for Nick's. I have always had a good head for liquor, but I have never much liked drinking. That night, with Nick and the others, I quietly drank six months' worth of alcohol. I can remember ordering the first martini, and I can remember deciding to have a second one, because I was tense, and I remember ordering a third one because it seemed unsociable not to, since everyone was having another round. What I cannot remember is how the third one led on to the others, when three seemed so sensible a final limit. So far as I can remember, I did not decide to go ahead and get drunk. So far as I can guess, I did not decide to relinquish control.

We were in that bar for a long time, until at some point the other friends left, and Nick and I were on our own. 'Whaddya want to do?' he said to me. 'You're a little drunk, y'know.' His voice went suddenly double bass. 'This place is getting too tired,' he said, weighing down the last word to make it more urgent.

We went to another bar, and then to another, and then to another. The cold air outside woke me up part way, but I had by then lost some part of myself or my mind. Someplace we went, where everyone was dancing, Nick bought drugs from a very fat man with a moth-eaten fur hat, and told me to take them. Without considering the matter, I took whatever Nick handed me, whatever came along to make my heart beat faster and my eyes move slower. It seemed to me that I woke from one dreamlike state and passed into another. I was at a gathering of the male young and beautiful, of men who spent the better part of their waking hours improving and polishing their bodies. I saw the most beautiful men I had even seen, pressing close against each other. The very number of these men overwhelmed and for a moment rather saddened me; how could I, I wondered at that moment, have passed so much of my life in cities populated with such trunks and torsos, and not have plunged myself into the experience of them?

'Where are we?' I asked Nick.

'You've never been here before?' he said, as though we were at a grocery store, and I amazed at the canned tomatoes.

It was hot, the heat of so many bodies' working themselves up to greater heat by constant motion, and Nick and I danced, with each other, then with others nearby, then with others less near, sliding along on the strength of other men's eyes. I sensed all around me the wild affirmation of crowds of people looking on, taking as much pleasure in my pleasure as I was taking in theirs. Partly I discovered an impulse of exhibitionism, but there was also a more simple relief in this enormous mutuality, the very real pleasure of feeling that I was as much a part of the fantasies of the other men in that room as they were of mine. You could not keep on all your clothes that night in that place, and so you began by taking off your shirt; and you went rolling through the mass of men, getting to a place on the floor where you wanted to dance and then shifting as the music and the other dancers shifted. I had in the past held on to the subtleties of Schubert and Rachmaninoff, but here repetitive sound held us in its grip, and I thought that this was the original reason for music. Everyone's bodies swirled into everyone else's bodies, and soon it became impossible to tell whose sweat was pouring down your body, or to count the number of men whose arms and chests and faces had rubbed the length of your own arms and chest and face. Perhaps the drugs made me want to touch everyone (though I might well have wanted that anyway), and everyone wanted also to touch me, and though it was in one way very erotic, in another way it transcended eros, the way that cold water transcends its slaking of your thirst on a hot day.

Male appetite usually builds to a pitch and then is satisfied, but this was just a slow and constant building and touching and rubbing, a never-ending progress from limb to limb and person to person in which the stimulation of your entire body seemed almost to dull the senses, in which your curiosity for other bodies was satisfied before it was formed, only to give way to more bodies, more entire satisfaction, more of the pleasure of the shapes of muscles and planes of the chest or buttocks that you could only half-associate with the unlit faces above them. If you wanted, you could drift from dancing to a rhythmic rubbing and pulsing that was still part of the music, and then, almost without noticing the stages of the development, on to sex itself, a sex validated and confused by the people around you, and by the people dancing below you. Late into the night, I let all my clothes go, and half in time to the music, whose ruthless beat was fixed in all of us by that time, half in time to my own pulse and the pulse of the strangers around me, I gave myself naked into the naked arms of a Hispanic construction worker and those of a seventeen-year-old go-go dancer, and I felt lucky to be pressed between them.

But still time did not give. All my senses were so strung out by then that I was simply lost in the event and the bodies around me, almost unaware of the cheering of the other men – it seemed like thousands – whom I would half-discover when I occasionally opened my eyes, men cheering me and one another and everyone else there; because as they were incorporated into my experience, I too became a part of their experience. I slipped then into other arms, felt other men above me, around me, within me, beside me; I occupied their bodies and they mine as though the physical boundaries of human flesh had fallen away. Pleasure ripped through me over and over again, until I found myself shaking and unable to stop. In a moment of clarity, I realized that music and my education had simply disappeared, taking with them kindness and whatever other daily virtues I had clung to with such pride. I was surrounded by people who lived in digital-clock time, where you cannot see what the moment before looked like, and you have no hint of what the next moment will look like, where you can see only the minute you're living. I had been, always, analogue as a grandfather clock.

In a final exhaustion, after this elation, I felt my body give out, entirely spent. I looked for Nick and saw him standing at the edge of the floor, grinning. He helped me to gather my clothes (my thick black belt, which I had loved, was lost, probably stolen; later, I'd buy a new one), and I got dressed. My body was sore, so that my shirt and my jeans hurt. When I was ready, Nick and I walked to the door. Outside, it was eleven o'clock in the morning. Ordinary people in daylight clothes rushed back and forth to their offices and to shops. Suddenly ashamed of my night-smeared body, of my drunkenness, of all of it, I hailed a cab. I was abruptly rigid with fear of my own experience. 'Sleep tight,' said Nick, as he closed the door for me. Then he pulled it open again. 'You're a sweet boy,' he said, slammed the door, and somehow I made it home.

It was a night of folly, the fulfilment of an unremarkable set of fantasies that would probably pall if they were too often fulfilled. But I had got so into the habit of living for the long term, of not running off with people I might not love forever; there was something glorious about living for the moment, the more glorious because I had until then controlled my life so well that I had forgotten that that was ever even an option. And the publicness of it became a real part of its pleasure. I had had my days of anonymous encounters in public parks, and those too, I suppose, were of the moment; but they were always cloaked in some shame, in secrecy, in everyone's knowledge that it might be necessary to hide or to run, in the understanding that what could be done quickly should not be dragged out over time. I cannot even remember the faces of my construction worker or my go-go dancer in any real detail, nor of the other men whose bodies I merged with my own; I remember the fact of them and the sensation of them, but their selves I never knew and have now lost entirely. I am sure I am even more lost to them.

Nick and I did not become lovers until ten days later. I cannot write of Nick without some terrible pinching at the middle of me: in the month that we spent together I travelled a range I have never known elsewhere. I can remember his feckless smile, and his crazy laugh, and his powerful body; I can remember the reflections of the world in the big gold hoop he wore in his left ear. Like a sunflower, Nick was always facing the light. I can remember his self-assured swagger, the way he would reach out when we were in my apartment and open my jeans as casually as if they were his jeans, on him. I can remember the weight of him on top of me when he threw me onto my bed, and the easy way that he had of pinning back my arms. I had never given myself altogether to Bernard, and I had never even told my full name to the blond skier I met that night in London, but I abandoned myself entirely to Nick, so that there was nothing left that was my own. I can see now that it was a way to deal with the prospect of my mother's death, falling deeply, deeply in love, with all the mad passionate conviction of my own exhaustion. I tumbled headlong into an ardour as immediate and incontrovertible as it was preposterous.

The day before I started seeing Nick, I had dinner with Helen. I had suggested we eat at one of the new spots I had found downtown, and when we got there Helen looked almost like a period illustration: the delicacy of her features seemed to clash with the style of the restaurant. She ordered a glass of white wine – as always – and told me that it was undrinkable, and insisted that I try it. 'It's not a white wine sort of place, Helen,' I said irritably. Helen and I made desultory conversation, but some of our usual comfortable intimacy seemed to be lost, and by the time we stood up to go, I was feeling bored, and restless.

As we walked toward the door, a voice called out, 'Hey! God, I don't believe it! Harry!' It was Nick, wearing jeans and somewhat less than two thirds of a tee-shirt. 'Hey, Harry,' he said, and kissed me. I could feel myself blushing a deep red, as I had never blushed when I saw Bernard. I stepped back gingerly.

'This is Helen,' I said. 'Helen, this is Nick.'

'Hiya, Helen,' said Nick. 'Great earrings.' Helen reached up to touch her earrings, perhaps to remember which earrings she was wearing.

'Great earring,' she said, eyeing his hoop. It annoyed me that Nick couldn't hear the irony in her tone. We exchanged a minute's pleasantries, and then Helen and I made our excuses and beat a hasty retreat.

On the street she said, 'Did you sleep with him?' I was hit by the vulgarity of the question. Helen was never vulgar, and though she knew almost everything about me, she knew it without resorting to direct questions.

'No, I didn't,' I said. 'I went out with him the other night, but that's all.'

Helen looked at me with an expression of frank mistrust. 'He's certainly very good-looking,' she said. 'Almost too good-looking. Archetypal,' she said, drawing out the word on the end of her tongue.

'Archetypally what?' I asked.

'Just archetypal,' said Helen, who was good at being difficult when it suited her.

The next day my mother called to tell me that the dog had gone to the vet. 'She's not doing very well,' said my mother. 'I think we're going to have to put her to sleep.'

I did not want to discuss with my mother the ramifications of putting the dog to sleep. 'Poor Molly,' I said.

'Freddy's going to come down from school,' my mother went on. 'He wanted to see her a last time. I think he'll be here tonight. If you want to come by for a little while, I think that would be nice.'

I rearranged my plans with Nick very grudgingly. He hardly noticed, since his life didn't really include plans. He said dinner at nine would be fine. I imagine dinner at three in the morning would also have been fine.

When I reached my parents' apartment, they were sitting in their bedroom with Freddy. Molly was lying on the rug in front of the fireplace. When she heard my footsteps, she hauled herself to her feet and came over to greet me. The vet had removed something from her paw, and she had on a bandage, and she trundled toward me with a lopsided, rolling walk. I looked around in a daze. My mind was with Nick. Through the air came the sad sound of my mother's voice. 'I loved that dog,' she said. 'It's fifteen years since we went up to the breeders and you boys picked her out among all the puppies.' She turned to my brother. 'Do you remember?' she asked. 'She nudged away from the rest of the litter, and you picked her up, and you held her in your hand, Freddy, and she squirmed around, and you said, "This is the one".'

'She was tiny,' said Freddy. 'And completely black, then. She did leave the litter to come over. She picked us out.'

I patted Molly on the head.

'Do we have to put her to sleep?' asked Freddy. 'I thought you said the vet could do surgery on that paw.'

'Her whole system is breaking down,' my mother said. 'It's a kindness at this point.' And then she sat down on the floor and rubbed Molly's coat. 'I'm going to miss you,' she said. 'I thought you'd outlast me, Molly. I'm going to miss you every day I have left.' She sighed. 'Fifteen years. It's been a good fifteen years, Molly, don't you think? A good fifteen years.'

'I've got to go back downtown,' I said. 'I'm sorry, but I've got some plans I couldn't change. Good luck with the vet tomorrow.' I bent down to give Molly a last pat, and she looked up at me with her big brown eyes, hazed over with cataracts. I almost ran out of the apartment.

The world is full of good-looking men, and no others have wedged their way into my soul as Nick did. How to explain him, when my desire has been formed so often by the difficulty of articulating it? He represented my opposite in many ways, though we had in common our gender and abiding curiosity and a certain measure of intelligence. Having found in Bernard and others a dilute version of myself, or an ideal I had but half-achieved, I now sought what I did *not* have, as, perhaps, men have often sought women. I found in Nick the ease of physical connection, a complete contentment in the fact of being a sexual being, an ability to reach out to the bodily fact of another. If Bernard was an experiment in domesticity, then Nick, I suppose, was an experiment in physicality. Nick lived for now, and did not tremble at the uncertainty of the future. I have supposed that the pain that came when Nick and I parted is not incommensurate with the pleasure our love might have brought; but perhaps I am wrong. Perhaps I found Nick because I needed to suffer, and knew that he would be a recipe for disaster. Perhaps his name was just another name for me to give to loss, and my grief for him just another excuse for loneliness. Perhaps the real potential for real joy would have terrified me, sent me running from the room like a crazy cat. At a certain rational level, I saw at once that Nick could not step out of himself enough to be with me, and that it was foolish and self-indulgent to imagine or hope otherwise. Perhaps it is only my own self-indulgence that keeps me from saying that dreams are always dreams, that a dream realized is in the end a dream forsaken, and that my dream of Nick was as cinematic and irrelevant as the ringing of bells at eventide. He never even heard me play the piano.

I try and try to remember what we actually did with each other and what we said: whereas the man with the skier's tan and I had

had nothing to say to each other, and did little but eat and drink and learn each other's bodies, Nick and I not only made love, but also talked through the days and nights, went places, saw things, made friends. In the month that we were together, I did not sleep at all. My mother, to whom I mentioned Nick only in passing, and who carefully showed neither disapprobation nor interest in meeting him, started to ask whether I was all right, because I had grown at once so manic and so worn from the very fact of him. I told her that I had never been better, and in some sense it was true: Nick almost crowded her out of my mind. Nick went with the architecture of my new apartment. He was part of the new life I was going to have in New York. My relationship to Bernard had been like a mineral crystal formed over years and based on obscure formulae so strange that only a few dedicated scientists could chart them; but my relationship to Nick was like an explosion, in which there is no logic of any kind at all. My concerts that month – I had two, both in Boston – were almost mad; I played fast, with technique I had never had before, but my interpretations, I knew, were eccentric to the point of brutality.

The first night I slept with Nick, we talked until dawn. He presented his past as though this were part of a monologue he had memorized long ago, acquitting himself admirably with tears where tears were required, or with laughter where it was appropriate to laugh. It was as though these were all things he had heard about someone else, and was now duly reporting, as though his own life were something he had observed, and not something he had lived. 'And where were *you*?' I wanted to ask more than once – but perhaps it would have been better to wonder, 'And where *are* you?' since to that question some immediate answer might more reasonably have been expected. He and I were the same age exactly, but he made me feel wizened. It was as though he had found, with his detachment, the secret of eternal youth – and though in my mind I was ahead of him at every turning, mistrusting his distance, I in fact envied him his innocence, an innocence not of the fruit of experience, but of experience itself, which left him full of restlessness. I gladly conflated his lust for me and his lust for life. I talked to him all night, night after night, and my own confessional monologues were given not so much from an urge to communicate anything (I seemed not to care about myself then), but from a hunger to draw him out, a belief that if you tell difficult things with strong emotion, you can extract their authentic equivalent. I wanted to give him the gift of his own sophistication.

Two weeks into my relationship with Nick, we had dinner with Helen. This had been her idea, and Nick had been very enthusiastic about it – since I had, sometimes, told him stories about Helen while the hours ticked by – and I was going along with it to accommodate the two of them. I thought Helen was trying to place herself within a relationship of which I knew she did not approve, and I thought that when Nick met her, he might see that I was from a world a million miles from the one where we were living. We went to that same restaurant where Helen and I had run into Nick the week of the party. Helen had worn her biggest earrings, with the obvious intention of extracting further comment. She and Nick laughed and talked their way through dinner, while I sat poking at my pasta primavera – the food there was repulsive – and watching Helen knock back the undrinkable wine. After dinner, Nick and I went back to his apartment, where he threw me onto the bed. 'So that's Helen,' he said as he traced the length of my neck with his mouth. 'She's amazing.'

'Amazing,' I sighed back, as I felt my clothes sliding off again. They came off so often that month that I sometimes wondered why I bothered to put them on at all.

'No, she's completely amazing.' Nick sat up and looked at me. 'She's like someone out of a movie or a book or something. I mean her mind just goes on and on. I'm not sure how much I could take of her, but she's completely amazing.'

'Helen's great,' I said.

'She's fucking gorgeous too. She got a boyfriend?'

I explained about Helen's breaking up with the man in films eighteen months earlier, and said that she had been single since then.

'Totally crazy,' said Nick. 'Totally crazy, the straight world.'

Helen and I talked on the phone the next day. 'How's the cd going?' she asked, as she always did. 'Are we going to get to hear it soon?'

'I've got to call London later,' I said. 'To check about some things. Basically, it's all on schedule.'

'And the party?'

'I've just arranged about the flowers,' I said. I made a mental note to arrange about the flowers.

'So now I've met the love of your life,' she said.

'Don't be snide, please.'

'He's very charming,' said Helen. But it was two weeks later, when Nick and I broke up, that she said in a tone of sudden passion, 'Harry, I don't know how you could. I don't understand it. He wasn't a person, Harry. He was like someone who was imitating a person. He was like someone who had seen a lot of people and who wanted to be a person but who didn't really know how to go about it. He had an idea of what people do, and so he did those things. When people would laugh, he laughed. When people could be loved for being sexy, he was sexy. When people asked questions, he would ask questions. But it was absolutely eerie how blank he was behind that. It was as though he hoped to be mistaken for a person, as though he were impersonating a person. And when he talked about you, it was as though he were trying to impersonate a lover, and not as though he had any love at all.'

'That's not true,' I said. 'He was a little bit afraid of intimacy. Like a lot of people.'

'Afraid of intimacy?' said Helen. 'It was more like the whole idea had never crossed his mind.'

But that was two weeks later. In the meanwhile, I believed that Nick was as profound as the earth, and that he needed only my excavating skills to locate his tremendous character.

Three days before we broke up, Nick and I went out and we took drugs (we always took drugs) and in the small hours of the morning, he hit me across the face. He had never shown any violence before, and I was too surprised to say anything. Then he hit me again, hard, and I bellowed. 'What the hell do you think you're doing?'

Nick began to laugh. 'So, Harry,' he said. 'You're vulnerable after all. You're a normal vulnerable guy just like the rest of us.' And he kissed me then. 'Sorry I hurt you,' he said, and his voice sounded like a caress. 'I just had to make sure.'

I looked at his big frame and his strong muscles and his face that was always creased with laughter or desire, and I looked at my own thin limbs and thought how much of the year I had spent at the brink of tears. I was the most vulnerable person in New York. But in my family, we learned long ago not to make a habit of wearing something so fragile as our own vulnerability on our sleeves. Nick had apparently not learned that those of us who carry our vulnerability wrapped in all the protections of insight and social polish have a vulnerability unequal to the changes of weather that anything worn on one's sleeve must be hardened to endure. He could not tell that it was the hidden and not the manifest vulnerability that bruises most readily and recovers most slowly.

I now see that the only thing that Nick and I really had in common was that we were both changing. During the month that we were together, I tried to tell him so much. I said to him that balance seems like the most boring thing in the world, and the absence of balance, a rainbow miracle of seduction. On the day I said that, we were lying side by side in my bed, beneath a downy duvet, on cotton sheets that had been ironed that morning, and that seemed to be yielding their smoothness to us. Nick's dark skin glowed against the whiteness. It was late at night, incredibly late, and I had curled myself up around Nick, my right ear just over his heart, my legs clutched around one of his powerful legs. I too, I said, hate the middle path, the road more taken. But balance is not always so tedious. Try to see (I begged Nick to see) the metaphor of balance as being not one of scales and blind justice, where tiny grains of sand are added to one or the other of two lumpen golden dishes until they hang, neither of them higher or lower, in dull ideal symmetry, but rather one of surfing, where imbalance leaves you floundering first on the far side, then on the near side, of waves so tall and so glorious that from their heights you might see the magnificent extent of the sea entire. Balance allows you to slide up instead of down: it is the only authentic extreme that there is. Oh Nick, I said, you have within you the discipline to stand at the centre of a piece of fibreglass and control the power of the ocean itself with the shifting of your weight and the turning of your ankles.

Nick's arm was heavy around me, and as I spoke he held my head down, pressing it into his chest. From time to time he would grunt an acknowledgement of something I was saying; mostly, though, he would respond to sentences by pulling me in tighter, by letting me go, by running his free hand through my hair, or by reaching down to hold the shape of my back. I kept talking; the sensation of Nick was no longer sufficient to quell my need for words. Love itself is, I told him, perhaps more than anything else, that state of delight in which each single moment becomes globed and complete, so that thought may linger beside it and within it; it takes place in the silence, in the moment's pause, in the expanse of yourself – and these are matters of balance.

And as I said this, Nick pulled me on top of him, and then he rolled over, so that I was beneath him. While I went on speaking, his mouth closed over one of my shoulders, and then it began its slow meander south. I felt that my whole body was disappearing into his mouth, that there was nothing left of me but my voice, the sound one short of music that I made for myself. I tried to move or to shift my weight, but he held me too strongly for that, and after a minute of helpless struggle, I gave up. He seemed to know better places for my limbs than I knew; he twisted my arms behind me and pulled apart my legs and pushed back my head as though he were getting rid of everything unnecessary about me.

I told Nick what Helen used to say to me (it was a quote from someone) – that the sublime is a matter of exchanging easier for more difficult pleasures. Helen and I once thought the truth was hidden in such aphorisms; but our attachment to that one outlasted many that had come before and quite a few that came afterwards. Sometimes it seems foolish to give up easier for more difficult pleasures: there is so much pleasure to easy pleasures, pleasure that is only squandered when we give up what is easy for something so deeply buried we are more than lucky if we ever find it at all. It seems foolish to give up easy pleasures, and sometimes it is foolish. But I don't think, in the end, that volition is at issue in this. We have to look forward to the surprising, difficult pleasures that come upon us when we least expect them, the strange rewards abruptly bestowed for opting against easy ways of living.

When he turned me over, then, so that my chest was down, my face was almost buried in the pillow. He pulled my head back by the hair, gently but firmly. 'So I can hear you,' he said, and did not let go.

Nick, I said. You cannot turn in the easier pleasures for the more difficult ones as though you were exchanging appliances at a department store, submitting the cheaper model with some cash and being given the fresh and better one to take home. You must give up those easy pleasures, and only some time later do you begin to achieve the more difficult ones. In between, there is a period as empty and void as despair: but it is not despair. Despair is a time without reason or redemption, and this time of void is so pregnant with reason (I felt that Nick must know this even when he did not feel it) that it is a time when you need only the infinite courage of patience (not, perhaps, Nick's rave favourite virtue). Nick, I said, if you fill that void with drugs and novel affairs and the poetics of an unfelt pride, with those successes of the mind and body that lie to the west of joy, you will lose not the emptiness, but the reason.

And still I went on talking, as his muscles contracted in a tempo as irrefutable as plainsong, rhythms I had that month learned by heart, that I held on as though they were my rhythms also. I contracted beneath him. I said: I have tried to create a life of relentless beauty, and have seen that by putting yourself in a position in which no one can betray you, you lose more of the world than you gain. The true nature of fulfilment, I told him, is to do with giving up each thing you strive for and achieve in the hope that there is something better and finer to strive for next, building the self, not undercutting it, giving things up, not giving up on things. The painful process of longing is all there is in life, the longing from one experience to the next, from one pleasure to the next, from one kind of loss to the next. Nick, I said: you are full of such longing; you scream longing from every surface. The longing from pleasure to pleasure, by way of voids often more sustained than the pleasures themselves, is not sad; in its own way, this is a credo of the utmost optimism. It describes a life without stasis, complacence, or stagnation. If you truly accept this, you will contain the voids, relieve the anger, mitigate the sadness, triumph over fear and panic, and become not a pale shadow of your dramatic self, but the self of which you are now a shadow.

By then, he had finished with me. He lay on his back again. I lay beside him: his arm was around me, but now it seemed to be holding me away, rather than pulling me to him. My body was covered with bruises, and if I moved I felt new ones. I did not know where each of them had come from, nor did I care; they made me feel that Nick had infiltrated my whole body and that his imprint was a part of me forever. Still I had not finished with him. In the heat of my emotion I told Nick: perhaps I am wrong in some or all of what I have said. But I believe that I see you with great clarity and great accuracy, and I want you to understand that this makes me love you not less, but more. I was drawn to you not by naïve fixation, but, I think, by seeing you as you are, and I liked you only the more for that, because you are someone not only of careless joys and fresh, enchanting enthusiasm, but also of great substance and nearly infinite depth, strange and rare and many-splendoured as this abruptly clear February night itself.

But by the time I had said all that, the night was pretty much over, and Nick was asleep. He was not what I imagined him to be, nor was he what Helen perceived him to be. After we broke up, I saw that it didn't matter that he'd fallen asleep before the end of my monologue, because of course I had been talking to myself all along.

The next morning Nick said, 'God, it's the *best* just listening to you talk. I completely love that.'

I said that I was glad to hear it. 'I like talking,' I told him wryly.

'And how,' he said. 'It's like it doesn't even matter what you're saying. I mean, it's like listening to the ocean or rain on the roof or something.'

'I think it kind of matters what I'm saying,' I said.

He gave me one of his long looks from half-closed eyes. 'Yeah, it does,' he laughed, and he kissed me. 'It *really* matters a *lot*,' he said, and he pushed me across the bed toward the wall. 'You're something, y'know? You're just totally unique.' And he kissed me again, and said, 'I just love this. You're the best.'

When Nick broke up with me, he did it in the cleanest possible way, by telling me that he had realized that he was not very attracted to me. 'You're the best, Harry,' he said. 'But you're a little physically unsure of yourself and – I've gotta be frank – you're not my sexual fantasy.' Nick lived in a world in which desire was so immediate, formed by type and by fantasy, that woe betide anyone who tried to interpose the reality of either flesh or character. Any unimagined scar, any odd formation of the muscles of the groin, could serve to betray the fact of your physical reality. So too the joy of a sad person, or the sorrow of a joyous one, could appear like a blemish or a welt in one who ought to have been as pure and smooth as the pupil-less eye of a classical sculpture.

It was a lot worse than when he'd hit me. For a moment I thought that if I showed a vulnerable side again, he might take me back, tell me he'd just been testing me. He had noted early on that my vulnerabilities were staunchly in the realm of the physical, so to pretend that his statement's honesty made it a kindness, that our relationship really was over because I was not his fantasy, was unduly cruel. That was the thing that took me aback, since Nick was not, whatever his other failings, cruel by nature.

I responded, just for a change, with words. While I was with Nick I was unable to stop talking; it was as though I thought I would disappear if I were silent. I told Nick that part of the pleasure of actual people is that they are not fantasy, and that part of the process of discovering someone is the discovery of his reality, which can, when you fully grasp and hold it, be more deeply eroticized than the dreams that make his hold on you unshakeable after two nights in bed. I told Nick that he was too intelligent to have so fixed a notion of type as to be unattracted to anyone who failed to conform to it, that though I did not fit with some model in his mind, I knew that I was not so far divergent from the outer reaches of his erotic sensibility as to be unknowable or unlovable. He had, after all, slept with me for a month with an abundant display of enthusiasm. I told Nick that it was not so hard for me to reach out to other minds and hearts as to reach out to other bodies. I told Nick that the physical is the area in which I unfold slowly, and painfully, and uncertainly, the area in which I need help to be myself, the area in which I can, as though by some law of nature, come into my own only with the passing of the weeks, and with the passing of my own fear. I do not lack imagination or energy, nor am I so far from physical sensitivity that I remain forever stranded on the high ground of my remove. But in the presence of someone else whom I hardly know (for all the variety of my love, how well did I know Nick?), I cannot – I told Nick – be even my own fantasy.

I could not stop remembering things that Nick had said. I recalled how I had once woken up in the middle of the night to find him looking at me, and how he had said, very slowly, in his tone of perpetual interest, 'You have such a beautiful face.' Then too I recalled the way he had asked once, in the middle of love, with that boyish grin, 'Do you like this?' and, before I could answer, had announced with another thrust, 'I like this.' I remembered equally well the various times when he had said, 'Not there,' or 'More gently,' or even 'Stop. Stop for a second.' Nick, I said in a voice that was broken, every life is made up of sequences and priorities and hierarchies, and where you place someone in the sequences and priorities and hierarchies of your life can form desire, rather than the other way around. And more. Nick, I said, do you remember about the sublime being the exchange of easier for more difficult pleasures? We were speaking of emotion, but sexually, too, there is such an exchange to be negotiated. I cannot provide you with the easier kind of sexual pleasure at which you arrive when you come across your fantasy in real life. I can suggest on faith that in the physical as much as in the emotional arena, it is sometimes worth the struggle to arrive at the particular pleasure that comes of time and profound openness, at which you cannot arrive when you work from a prototype – that pleasure which comes as the aftermath of fallen boundaries. I told Nick that it was in the sudden and unflinching radiance of feeling with and for each other that we had found each other. I told him I was worth the effort.

And when I finished telling him as much of this as I could, I told him I had loved him with a passion in many ways as inexplicable to me as it had been to him. I told him that I knew that this had sometimes been difficult and awkward for him, and I told him I was sorry for that. I said that these strong emotions were beyond my poise to control, and I acknowledged that when they did not seem like gifts, they could seem sad or even ridiculous. I said that my hopes had always been good hopes. And I remembered all those days and nights and afternoons as bit by bit I came to know Nick and to find in the very fact of his existence a joy such as I had seldom known before. I knew that I was losing Nick, and so I told him that in my tired eyes he had shone like the ten thousand lights of the night sky. Nick, I said, I have loved you as though you were my own past, and though that love has by and large left me feeling only more alone – you have seemed sometimes not to notice it, at other times not to like it – it has also, in a few bright moments, filled me with joy.

I actually said all of that to Nick. At the time I believed that by saying such things I could change the world. I even imagined that I could make someone love me. At that time the words poured out of me like tears. Breaking up with Nick was twice as bad as breaking up with Bernard, though Bernard was real to me and Nick was in many ways a fiction of my own creating. I had set out to find love and had become a collector of pain; in the long nights of that winter I would sit awake classing my sorrows as though they were rare objects destined for museum display, ranking them by scale and by type, marvelling at how one had surpassed or been surpassed. I hoped in this way to remove myself from them, to see them as objects external to me; but I discovered that to

study your sadness is to know it and to own it, and that to own it
is to cease to separate it from yourself. 'Here I am!' I wanted to say,
'With my bag of sorrows!' But in the end that was as impossible as
to say, 'Here I am! With my brain and my heart in tow!' as though
I might, under other circumstances, have left them at home.

When Nick had looked at me with his quirky grin, and told me
that he wanted us to be best friends *always*, and when he had left
and closed the door, I went uptown and saw my mother. I had not
been to see her as much as I ought to have been in the preceding
weeks, and when I had been with her, we had tended to argue.
My mother and I had been arguing a lot; I was constantly annoyed
at her – more so, for some reason, since Molly had been put to
sleep. I went uptown that day and saw my mother and I did not
feel angry. I could hardly speak. She sat with me for a long time,
and then she made English muffins with Swiss cheese, and sat
with me some more. 'I always love you, Harry,' she said. 'It's not
the same, I know. I'm just your mother. But it's always there.' I
looked at her, embarrassed. 'Harry, you have my love for the rest
of your life,' she said. 'I wish I could give you more than that.'
And she held out her hands to me, as though to show that this
was all that was in them.

I went into my old room, the one from which I had not taken all
my childhood things, and slept through the afternoon. Janet had
put winter blankets on the bed even though I hadn't slept there or
mentioned sleeping there since autumn. That night, I had dinner
with my parents in the kitchen. I told them that I had not been
practising enough lately, and that I wanted to spend whole days
at the piano, completely uninterrupted. My father asked me about
the party plans. He was very kind; I remembered, as though I
were waking from a dream, what a tremendously kind man he
was, although it would be several months before I had the wherewithal to love him again. My mother told me she thought grilled
scallops were probably a mistake as passed hors d'œuvres
('Greasy fingers – yuck'), and asked whether I'd arranged about
the flowers. I told her that I had, and made a mental note to do it
the following morning.

After dinner I went back to my apartment; but the emptiness of it filled me with horror. I called Helen and asked whether she wanted to get a late-night drink. 'Why don't you come up to my part of town?' she asked. 'I'm actually not in the mood for that dingy place on your corner. You must be getting tired of it yourself.' I put on an oxfordcloth shirt and a pair of corduroys and a big Shetland sweater, the kind of clothes I had worn all the years I had been going to school. I left at home the slightly ripped jeans and the leather jacket I had been wearing for a month. I turned off all the lights and took a taxi to Helen's house. I rolled down the window and felt the wind in my nose. That day, the bracing weather had arrived.

I rang the bell, and Helen came downstairs wearing a blue dress with tiny drawings of African animals on it. She stared at me for a minute. 'Harry,' she said. 'You look like hell.'

As I stood in the doorway, I felt as bad as I had ever felt, but I also felt as though some part of me that had been sleeping for too many seasons had come to life. 'It's been a rough day,' I said.

'Well, then let's not go out. Why don't you come upstairs and I'll warm some cider or something. I've got some leftover orange cake.' And so I followed Helen up to her glowing apartment, to the divine order and the polished furniture and the pleasant kitchen. Helen produced things to eat and to drink, and we sat and talked into the small hours of the morning. I told her a bit about Nick, and she said very little, but I felt that she understood everything that Nick had not understood, and this lulled me into a sense of safety that I had not had in many days. I was relieved to be drinking cider instead of taking drugs, to be in the easy company of Helen again. I hadn't been to her apartment in a long time. She had a few new plants, and a new dishrack, and she had re-covered (at last) the old chair her brother had given her.

'Oh, Helen,' I said to her at one point. 'Don't you think it's ever going to get better and easier?'

'No. I don't think it is,' she said. She looked at me for a minute. 'It's going to get better and harder. It just gets better and harder.'

It grew later and later, and I didn't want to leave. I didn't want to leave at all.

It might have been four o'clock in the morning when Helen went into the kitchen to wash out the pot she'd used to warm the cider. I went to help her, and paused in the doorway. Her hair was falling forward over her face as she rinsed, and her slender hands were turning the pot deftly. She threw back her hair to look at me, and she smiled. And suddenly Helen was the most beautiful thing I had ever seen. I had often wanted to touch Helen, and this time, almost in spite of myself, I walked over to her by the sink and ran a hand through her hair. She looked up at me, more curious than expectant, and it came to me in a flash that Helen was the answer to the questions I had posed to Bernard, and to the skier, and to Nick. I kissed her with an awkwardness made unimportant by our years of friendship.

I took the pot out of Helen's hands and turned off the water. I led her through to her bedroom; she looked at me with uncertain eyes, and at one point I thought she was going to laugh; but I had never felt more certain of anything in my life. I cannot describe to you how beautiful Helen's body was; nor can I describe to you how much its beauty, and my own pleasure in that beauty, surprised me. It was as though I were discovering someone entirely new, a Helen that my own and old Helen could hardly have imagined, could hardly have known. Had this other Helen been there the whole time, hidden under the wool or silk or cotton of the seasons? Of course Helen had always been beautiful, but there was suddenly a wholeness to her, lying there, unclothed, in the faint moon-like light of the streetlamps outside her apartment. When I was little, I went once to the Musée Rodin and bought a black-and-white postcard of a marble figure, naked, her head thrown forward; and this postcard made its way into a collage that stayed in our house. Helen, stretched beneath me in the night, reminded me of that Rodin, an image of beauty from the dim reaches of my past. That I could touch her, could claim this beauty after these years of male bodies pressing roughly against me: I was terrified, but I was also ecstatic, and I felt that I could never have enough of looking at and of touching that strange body. And I also felt ignorant, and I was startled by the oddity of a body formed so differently from my own. How could one ever know what sensations one produced in something so foreign? There are fewer kinds of mystery in the love of men for men. I had often indulged the luxury, in bed, of supposing someone else's body to be my body, and at such moments I would close my eyes as I performed some act that was also being performed on me, and imagine that I had reached a perfect solipsism, that what I did was solely responsible for what I felt. What peculiar bliss it was to take responsibility for sensations I could never know; what confidence there was to be drawn from that endlessly paradoxical territory of the unimaginable.

I felt that I did not want ever to leave Helen, then. I had always slept naked beside naked lovers, and I was startled that Helen put on a long pink nightgown. I loved the way the silk moved around, revealing by chance this or that part of her, but I disliked the sense that it was closing me out. I wanted never to let go of her. That feeling did not leave me. Sometimes, in the weeks that followed, I would lie in the dark with my hand across one of her breasts, astonished by its inviolate shape; but what I loved most was the entire delicate mass of her, the thin, supple limbs, the fineness of her torso, the softness of her breath. Being naked in front of a woman was vastly different from being naked in front of a man. It was like being five times as naked, as different anew as the naked-ness of the bedroom is from the nakedness of the locker room, as different as the whole truth is from the truth. The smoothness of the sexual act itself astonished me, the absence of pain, the fluidity of it. I felt none of the manic pleasure I had known with Nick, but I felt a joy that seemed to touch every inch of me, a high bliss, unnervingly quiet. Had I spoken to Nick about balance? With Helen, I found a balance that incorporated what we had in common and our differences. It was a balance – it seemed abun-dantly clear to me at that time – that I could never have achieved with Nick.

I suppose that I would not have ventured toward Helen if I had been fully happy with men. During the first week she and I were together, the image of Bernard at the toy store in London came back to haunt me more than once. That feeling in the toy store, of being marginal, of being excluded, had propelled me toward

Helen. My mother talking about children and telling me that I could do anything had made me try to prove to myself that we have choices in all things. What I could not have known or imagined then was the pleasure that I was to find with Helen. I see now that I had been drawn to her since we were in high school. It could well have been otherwise, I suppose: I could have led Helen from the kitchen and met with disaster. It could have been humiliating, or strange, or awkward, or fearful. When the moment came, it surprised and delighted me to find that I loved her as much with my body as with my mind, that desire formulated largely as an act of will had become so startlingly genuine and irrefutable.

I had always subscribed to the much-vaunted theory that everyone is bisexual, and that circumstance turns us toward one gender or the other. I had thought then that if one could triumph over circumstance, the difference between sex with a man and sex with a woman would be like the difference between sex with a short person and sex with a tall person. But for me, the two experiences proved so different that the use of one word to refer to them both seemed hilarious. The Eskimos cannot be more puzzled by the huge generality of the English word 'snow' than I was by the generality of the word 'sex'. To feel that one kind of sexuality should exclude the other saddened me, for I cannot pretend that I did not still long in some ways for Nick; even as I lay with Helen, images of men ran through my mind. It was not like choosing between apples and oranges so much as like choosing between the mountains and the sea, whose beauty is clearest in their contrast. That you cannot be monogamous and encompass both genders – this is one of life's gross cruelties. With men, I had felt something urgent and terrible that built up and then broke, suddenly and entirely, and then was over. With Helen, I felt something constant and slow and continuous and infinitely pleasurable, something that grew by slow degrees, that seemed to wane only to return again more strongly. Perhaps it was more profound; it may also be the case that there was less of me in it.

It was as though I had been practising all my life to love Helen. If my mother had not developed cancer, I might have gone on practising and practising and never got to the thing itself, to the fact that I loved Helen with more of my self than I had known I had. But I don't think so. It would certainly have taken longer, but I think I would sooner or later have realized that Helen was, at the very least, a shadow of the love I had been seeking all of my life. I learned so much in the course of loving my mother and being loved by her; and though Helen was a different matter entirely, the quality of that love between my mother and me was relevant to my relations with Helen as it had never been relevant to what I had with Bernard. My mother showed me how love is the business of life. She made a singular and perfect world out of her love for my father, and his love for her, and her love for me became a part of that. My mother showed me a love made of bricks, rather than of straw or sticks, a love powerful and inviolable enough to withstand every one of the disasters of which any life is made. My mother showed me how to live in love. But Bernard was the one who showed me how to live outside love, how to move through it and around it; he put windows into that strong house of bricks. It was with Bernard that I learned that what you touch does not automatically become your own; it was from Bernard that I learned the nature of love's strange and wondrous equalities.

Helen and I took things slowly and privately: I had been able to pull my relationship with Nick to psychological bits, turn it into phrases and rhetoric, and so contain it, but my relationship to Helen did not allow for such analysis. There were two things I never told my mother: one was the lonely narrative of my life before Bernard, and the other was the amazing fact of my love for Helen. I couldn't tell my mother about my life before Bernard because it would have horrified her too much; and I couldn't tell her about Helen because it would have made her too happy, and I needed at that point to have a secret, something that was entirely mine. If I had once confided in my mother, I would not have been able to tell what was her delight and what was mine, and I needed, for as long as possible, to preserve my happiness, this happiness, as my own.

I thought there would be time to tell my mother later on. Also, I had fought so hard to get her far enough to understand my anguish over Nick, and I wasn't sure that there would never be a Nick again, and I didn't want to lose that sympathy. It was too late for my loving Helen to make my mother well, and so I loved Helen for myself alone. When I held Helen in my arms, I came back to life. Nick had left me for dead. Helen saved me, or my love for Helen saved me, from despair. When I was with Helen, I believed, as I had not before, that I could do anything. I felt strong where Nick had made me feel weak.

'What would have happened if I'd been a boy?' Helen asked me one night. We were lying on my white sheets, and I was cupped around her body; her head was beside mine, but she was not facing me when she spoke. I touched her face, to get its expression.

'You're not a boy,' I said. 'That's become extremely clear to me this week.' And I pulled her tighter, as though to remember her female body.

Helen laughed. 'But if I had been,' she said. 'Would we have become lovers years ago, or this week, or not at all?'

'If you'd been a boy,' I started, but then I stopped. Helen as Helen. Helen as a woman. Helen as the one in my life while my mother was getting sicker. I couldn't separate it all.

'Would you love me more if I were a boy?' she asked.

'I couldn't love you more,' I told her confidently. 'I've never loved anyone more.' This was automatic, and true. Then I said, thinking, 'Well, it would have been easier.' It was too much for me to explain to her. 'It just would have been different, Helen. It would also have been different if you were a sixteenth-century Spanish courtesan and I were a pirate of the high seas.'

'But not easier, I think,' she said. She sounded almost coy. 'Shame, isn't it, that you never get to know what would have happened.' And I reflected that this had never seemed like much of a shame to Nick, and, to fill in the silence, I turned her over and stretched my body on top of hers.

I suppose that my mother and I may have stopped being in a rage with each other before I started seeing Helen, though it seems to me that I noticed how we were no longer angry only in the weeks after I started seeing Helen. It was, so far as I am concerned, one of the great miracles of modern times that my mother lived long enough for us to make peace. For though I had loved my mother entirely for my whole life, though our flashes of intense hatred had never really undermined our adoration of each other – still, there was no ease between us until that moment when I finally held Helen in my arms. Bernard had been a pawn between my mother and me, but Helen – Helen knew me. She was as kind as Bernard, and she knew me. I became the person she knew. My feeling for Helen was not a matter between my mother and me, but it absorbed what had for so long stood between my mother and me, so that the remaining barriers could at last drop, to reveal entire the straightforward and fitting love my mother and I had for each other. The madness went out of it, at last, and we loved each other simply as sons and mothers have loved each other all the days of the world.

I did not know it then, but there were only four months left for my mother. She and I were given just four months of wisdom after a lifetime of folly, four months of peace and a measure of serenity. Four months! It seems so terribly short a time, and on sad days I imagine what it might have been like to have five months, or six, or another forty years. Four months was hardly time enough for us to register the truth of this new relationship we had found. I am profoundly aware that had my mother's lethal cells multiplied more rapidly we might never have had those months. A fate as arbitrary as the weather, which served to take my mother away, gave us with equal indifference that almost holy time before she went, the Helen time, when we could live in the compass of our pleasure in each other, while I had for myself the pleasure of Helen.

All happy families are not the same; nor are all happy lives the same. The day my mother died, I thought of saying something about Helen, but by then it was too late. I did not want my mother in the world Helen and I took for our own, but I suppose also that in those final months, I wanted to have the joy of my mother unmarked by the drama of my own changes. I wanted to keep separate things separate. There were a thousand empty reasons for not stirring things with my mother any further, but in the end, she must have known this as she knew so many other things. 'Would you love me more if I were a boy?' Helen had asked me; a week later, she said, 'Would you love me more or less if your mother weren't ill?'

'It's not about my mother,' I said. 'It's about you. About you only.'

'Even I', said Helen, 'am smart enough to know that that's not true.'

It was humiliating to have her say that. 'If my mother weren't ill,' I said, 'I'd have more time and energy for you, and I'd be able to love you as much as you deserve.' This sounded like the right answer.

'But I might have to be a boy,' said Helen.

'I like your being a girl,' I said. It seemed not to matter any more, and I was tired of talking about it, tired of thinking about it, even.

'Well, we've both agreed on that, then,' said Helen. 'I like being a girl. A woman. Not a boy. I like being with you as a woman. It's something private, something of our own, something you haven't been squandering all over town for years and years.' She paused. 'Pirate,' she said, with a smile. 'I adore your mother in her way, but I wish we could sail away and not worry about her for a swashbuckling month or two.'

This conversation taxed me more than I realized. All my life I had feared my mother's death, and now that it was coming I had to give myself over to that fear. Sadly, it overwhelmed everything else. What Helen and I had was both too happy and too difficult to last through the consuming sadness, too enormous, too frightening, too much of a seeming answer at a time when I was figuring out how to live without answers. She and I had both tangled our love too entirely with my mothers' illness. Swashbuckling was not on the cards. My mother was dying, and I was careless with Helen in the face of that, and she was hurt, and for a while things were uncomfortable between us. Helen and I never actually broke up, but we paused. I paused, anyway. All along I had had to choose between joy and sorrow, and I now selected sorrow gladly because I believed that joy would wait for me around the corner. I think that in the end Helen understood that. I think that in the end I understood that myself. Loneliness is the only and terrible thing; and I had a cd coming out, and a party to plan, and a mother dying. I had made up with Bernard, and now spoke to him from time to time in an effortless fashion. He was an old friend and nothing more; but my easy conversation with him made me believe that romantic love was easily repaired, that cracks in love could be painted out after the fact. I assumed that Helen would be there later on. Besides, I was exhausted, so exhausted that I could hardly think or move or feel, and Helen was hungry for feeling, for all that feeling I had wasted earlier on Nick, that wasn't there to give any more. These changes of mood and self wear us out.

How, then, to reconcile the surface and the depth? How to reconcile England and America, the love of men and the love of women, childhood and adulthood, joy and sorrow, the glamorous and the substantive ways of life? It seemed too often to me that the surface of my life was a work in lacquer, exquisitely wrought to conceal the simple but cavernous fact of a wooden box beneath; or on better days it seemed that a watery surface was so churned with waves and turbulence as to give only a passing hint of the infinite stillness below. This is what I imagined: a surface that gave way only by degrees, a surface as transparent as what lay under it, a surface that was like a glassy and exquisite introduction to depth itself. This is what I imagined: that you could slide from level to level, from surface to depth, by slow and gradual measures, never losing sight of your passage, so that from the greatest depth you might gaze up infinitely far and still catch the hues of the sky, so that from the surface you would see at least the vague and hulking forms of the rocks on the ocean floor. This is what I imagined: a life that was both beautiful and full of meaning, a life that encompassed what I had felt for men and what I had felt for women, a life as innocent as birth and as wise as age, a life made glorious not by the joy that comes of pain avoided, but by the joy that lives intimately with the unavoidable kinds of pain. I dreamed of a life in which the control at which I had arrived in England met with the power of my feelings in America, a world in which what was heavy encompassed some measure of lightness, and what was light, all the weight of insight. It was not compromise that I imagined; it was not a limpid pool or a fresh pond that I wanted, but the sea itself, for a flashing instant as clear as knowledge.

VIII

An Almost Perfect Party

I can remember how, as the long afternoons of that spring drew to a close, I would from time to time ask my mother what she was doing in the evening, and how she would tell me of some engagement that, under previous circumstances, would have sounded dull or remote or too adult for my attention; and I can remember how she would say, casually, as if it didn't matter, 'You're welcome to come along,' speaking in a tone half way between question and comment, between a favour granted and a favour requested. 'You're welcome to come along,' my mother would say, and I would feel – I think we both would feel – that strange enormous quality that time could take on between us, and I would decide to go along to dinner with some rather remote friends of my parents', or to a benefit for some good cause, and I would cancel peremptorily whatever considered plans I might have had for the evening.

Frequently – this is the way with seating plans – we would go off to some lovely restaurant and sit far apart. I would spend the evening in insignificant conversation with those members of my parents' outer circle who were the evening's novelty. What I remember is that feeling of being within reaching distance of my mother, that neither of us had had to part from the other just yet. When at the end of such an evening we would get back to my parents' apartment, I would go in and sit at the foot of my mother's bed for hours, talking about the marginal people, the restaurant, whether her duck had been good, whether the mint sauce on the chocolate torte was a big mistake (my mother insisted that sauce was made by folding toothpaste into crème anglaise), about whether I had spilled something on my tie and about whether it was likely to come out if I rubbed talc on the spot ('For heaven's sake,' my mother would say. 'Just put it out for the dry cleaner. Everyone but your grandmother gave up on those tricks twenty years ago.') We would go on talking, and from time to time my mother would say, 'It's getting late; I should go to sleep,' and I, inventive in those precious moments at the edge of night, would ask questions that reached as far back as her childhood, or beg advice, and, sustaining her interest in an absurd line of topics, would keep her awake and even – so it often seemed – alive for an hour or more. In a clear tone she might have used to give driving directions, my mother would answer my questions. They were often questions she had answered many times before, but she gave me those familiar answers a last time, so that I could remember them. We would keep time at bay for a little while, by being together, until finally it would get so late that my mother couldn't stay up any longer. Near midnight – and my mother, rigid in her ways as a wrought-iron fence, had never stayed up until then unless there was an occasion – I would heave myself out of that bedroom and go downtown and practise obsessively or talk on the phone, doing anything to keep the time full enough so that I did not need to be reminded that in such a way at a future time we would say good-night and mean all the nights that there had ever been or would ever be.

Sometimes in my dreams, my mother is standing at the front door of that apartment and saying to me, 'You're welcome to come,' and I am racing, with my heart pounding, to some banal social event, at which to sit feeling as whole and entire as an unpeeled orange, watching my mother across the table, some simple bits of jewellery flashing when she moves her hands or shakes her head, talking about the sauce on the chocolate torte. Eventually, I run out of my own dreams and find myself back in my own apartment, and I do not think so much of the voice with which my mother would say that she loved me, or that she missed me, or that she was worried about me. I hear instead that offhand way she had of saying, 'You're welcome to come,' and I wonder whether I will ever again be welcome to go anywhere, really, in the way in which I was welcome to come to dinner with my mother's college roommate and her husband.

During this period, the period before my cd came out, the period when I was always welcome to come with my mother wherever she went – during this period my mother became steadily sicker. When one therapy failed they tried another. As the therapies blurred, my mother railed against them less and less. I told her that her fighting spirit seemed to have gone out of her. 'What will come of fighting?' she said. In that clear spring, one of the treatments caused her hair to fall out again, though the doctors had promised that the risk of that was almost nil. I spoke with her every hour the day it happened. 'It's coming out in handfuls,' she said. 'Bald again. Like a freak show. And it's giving me a rash too. Harry, I'm becoming disgusting.' I tried to contradict her. 'I disgust myself,' she said.

Once more the wigs came out, now trimmed to something closer to the length her new hair had been reaching. Her tremor had by that time become terrible and it was increasingly difficult for her to walk. She had to steady herself on an arm to go outside, and sometimes she had trouble even with the short distances within the apartment. Once she fell down while I was there, just after dinner. I heard a bang, and then I heard my father's voice, like the bewildered voice of a child. 'Harry, Harry, Harry, Harry,' he called, over and over as I ran into the room. By the time I got there she was propping herself up. 'Don't come in, Harry,' she called out as I got to the door. 'You don't need this memory.' When she stood up she was bleeding slightly from a cut on her face. She turned to me and to my father. 'Excuse me,' she said, and went into the bathroom, and closed the door. When she came out, the wound was gone. On feet she could not trust, she walked across the room and got into her side of the bed. 'I get all the fun of being ninety while I'm in my fifties,' she said, and laughed. 'Thank you Leonard. Thank you Harry.' My father was still holding the paper he had been about to read when she fell. 'Anything in the news?' she asked.

Some days she had to stay in the hospital. Most days she was at home. I was up at the apartment constantly; Freddy had a summer job at a lab and was living with my parents. My father's hours at the bank got shorter and shorter. Meanwhile, my mother could eat less and less. The doctors had suggested some crackers that were supposed to settle her stomach. She would sit down at the table with a plate of them in front of her and smile at the rest of us. 'Would any of you care for a dog biscuit?' she would ask wryly before she started to eat. Still she continued, on nights when she was able, to go out with my father. She continued to have lunch with her friends.

'You shouldn't push yourself so hard,' my father would say to her, but she would brush him off.

'There doesn't seem to be much of a floor show on in the bedroom all day,' she said. 'I might as well distract myself.' Laced through that tough stance, which she used to propel herself through the days, was a softness delicate as the silk left behind by a new butterfly. She told me over and over again, afraid perhaps that I would forget, how much she loved me. She had always told me that with what she did and the way that she was, but now she said it in so many words. She told my father and Freddy how much she loved them. Some afternoons, she would describe everything she had ever imagined for me, cataloguing the pleasures and pitfalls of every stage of life in sequence; it was as though she wanted to pack into the little time that remained to us all the wisdom she might have dispensed over the ensuing decades. I tried to remember every detail of every day, as one tries to remember the nature of heat on the last day of summer. I spoke to Helen from time to time, but I did not sleep with her; I imagined that I was only a mind and a heart, that I had left my body as entirely as if it had been laid in earth.

Helen was crisp. 'There's no point arguing with you now,' she conceded on the phone at one point. Later, she said, 'You haven't been very nice to me, Harry. Why did you go and start all this if you didn't want to follow through with it?'

I said I was sorry. I said that it was beyond me, that it was all beyond me. I said that I was feeling too overwhelmed to cope.

'There's nothing to cope with,' she said. 'It's just me. Helen. I'm not so overwhelming.'

'This is not an easy time for me,' I said.

'You're being egotistical and selfish,' said Helen. 'And childish.

And it's not just circumstances making you that way. Underneath all this profound engagement with human drama, you're still as impossible as ever, like a little boy, like you were when I first met you, years and years and years ago.'

'I don't mean to be impossible,' I said. 'But right now, it's all of us. It's just the way we are. Everything's falling apart, and it all feels impossible.' I drifted out of the last sentence. 'I don't know what to do. I don't know how I got to be this way, how things got to be the way they are now.'

She looked at me curiously. 'Well, I do know,' she said. 'You would also know, if you really tried to think about it. You've bought into the myth of your own perfect family. That's your biggest problem. You've bought into it hook, line and sinker. And it is a myth.' I looked at her, and she put her hands on my shoulders. 'Harry, can't you see that? Can't you see how muddled things were, even before your mother got sick? Look at the evidence. Bernard, and then Nick, and now me – you're a cripple, Harry. You can't love anyone; you can't let anyone love you. Is that what makes you a perfect part of this perfect family? Is that what comes of your mother's perfect love for you and your perfect love for her and all the rest of this "everything's perfect" routine? You have to be able to move on from it all, Harry. Perfect families let you move on. You want to be happy with a boyfriend? Find one. Be happy. You want to be happy with a girlfriend? Find one. Be happy. It doesn't have to be me, but it has to be some real person, someone who's got perfections and imperfections, some girl or some boy. You have to be able to make it with someone, and sustain it. You have to give up on the myth.'

'Helen, Helen,' I said. 'Not now. It's not time now. My mother is dying. You know that. You knew that when we started this whole thing a few months ago. It's taking a toll. I can't meet everyone's demands all at once.'

'That's just it,' said Helen. 'It's so sad to be locked into all these demands, to think that reciprocal demands are what makes love. Love should give you more than it takes. Right now, your mother is dying. Later your mother will have died. You can't just hide behind that forever. We're all dying, lambchop. Your mother is just doing it a little bit faster.' And then she stopped and looked at me long and hard. 'It's not that I don't see the way of love that you and your mother have,' she said. 'I can't try to talk about whether it's valid or invalid because it's just what's true, and it's who you are, and the world is full of lonely people, and you aren't one of them, and maybe that's the biggest success anyone can hope for. But sometimes I look at you and I think it's as though you've chosen a boat carved from diamond with sapphire masts and sails of rubies and emeralds for your journey across the sea. It's breathtaking to watch it cutting through the waves, but it's a stone boat. You have to be crazy to choose a stone boat. Anything else would be easier to sail, Harry.'

The date of the release of my cd was drawing closer, and my mother said she was counting the days. Meanwhile, we had to attend to the party. There was a great deal that she had intended to do but in the end was unable to do, and so she left more and more of it to me. 'Elegant, Harry,' she said. 'I hope this is going to be an elegant party. I hope you're not getting carried away with yourself, and that it's not going to be too showy. Remember that parties are about the guests, and that the flowers and the setting and the food should be so beautiful that they almost disappear. If they overwhelm the people, it's not a good party.'

I had been to enough of my mother's parties to know that. But I had such glittering aspirations of my own; I wanted a party that was as romantic as *Love in the Afternoon*, in which every detail astonished. It was my mother, extravagant in her way as the day is long, who told me to tone it down. And she also remembered all those sensible details that my mind skipped over. 'Don't serve the herbed chicken in lettuce leaves,' she said. 'The leaves break and people spill the chicken down their fronts.' Later she told me, 'Don't serve anything on skewers; people end up holding the skewers and they don't know what to do with them.' Another time she said, 'Make sure there are flowers in the ladies' room, but make sure the arrangement isn't too big. Nothing is more irritating than flowers that take up all the space where you want to put your handbag.' But when I asked (for the third time) which of two salads she thought sounded better, she put a hand on my arm; that new tone crept into her voice, that last four months tone of hers. 'Harry,' she said. 'Don't keep worrying about the salads. Either salad. It doesn't matter.'

I quoted her back to herself. 'It all matters,' I said.

She turned on me a funny look, a new look. 'No,' she said. 'It doesn't. Very little really matters. Life is . . . a lot of the things I used to think mattered – I was wrong, Harry. A lot of them really don't matter at all.'

When I looked at her with an expression of surprise, she laughed. 'Serve the tomatoes,' she said. 'I like tomatoes.'

In the end, my mother was too weak to do more than give advice. I threw my own party. It was as though I were in training for the parties to take place after her death, because it was not my kind of party, not like the party I had almost thrown for Bernard. Some days my mother and I still argued, but she would cut short the arguments.

'If you make up your mind that you're dying, you're sure to die,' I said once, when she was being negative.

'I don't think you want to sound so hard,' she said. 'I love you, Harry; I'm trying my best to do what will make you happy. Don't take such a hard tone with me.'

I was in a bad mood that day. 'You don't love me,' I said accusingly. 'You're obsessed with me, and you keep trying to drag me down into your illness. You don't love me at all. If you loved me, you'd stop striking these dramatic poses all the time and keep on fighting this cancer.'

All she said was, 'I wish it were up to me that way.'

By the time I got my first advance copy of the cd, I had been at enough production sessions so that I knew every second of my own performance by heart and was thoroughly sick of it. I had seen the cover art, and I had seen the designs, and when the messenger came over with the thing itself, I felt no thrill, not even a tremor. I went uptown, and found my mother propped up in bed.

'Hi, Harry,' she said. 'I thought you were doing errands all day today.'

I held out the cd. 'It's the first copy,' I told her. 'It's for you.'

She took the disc in her hand and for a long minute she sat and looked at it. The sense of occasion I had not had on seeing it an hour earlier came now. My mother turned the cd over and over, and she clicked the box open and looked at the disk itself, as though she could read its sounds with her eyes. 'This is really it,' she said at last, in a voice of satisfaction. 'I made it through. I made it through long enough to see it.'

'That's really it,' I said, and it was as though I had not known, until then, what it was.

'When you were little,' she said, readjusting her pillows and sitting up very slightly, 'you were afraid of so many things. You were afraid of the dark, and of playing games, and of thunder, and you were afraid of other children. I recognized all that fear in you, because I was in some ways a very frightened person myself. There are so many things I never did because I was afraid – jobs I never had, people I never met or got to know. I didn't want you to grow up frightened, to be a frightened person. I used to say to you, "Think of life as an adventure." Do you remember?' She looked down at the cover photo, me at the piano. She read the little biography on the back of the cd, and then she looked at the photo again. 'And you believed me, even though I didn't really believe that myself. *You* believed me. Step by step, you did more and more things, and you began to talk to other children. It was so hard to push you out into the world. And then you began to do it on your own. I just watched you and held my breath. I wanted to think that you could set the world on fire.' She looked at the cd. 'And look. Look who you've turned into,' she said. Then she looked directly at me, and she smiled. Her face was full of joy. 'Look who you've turned into!' she repeated. 'I don't know when or how it happened. All that worrying I did, and now look who you are.'

I smiled. 'It hasn't been reviewed yet,' I said.

' "Think of it as an adventure," I used to say to you,' said my mother. 'And you did. And so your life became an adventure, a wonderful adventure. Performing in all these places, making records. When you were nine, you said you were going to be a great pianist, and I worried that life might disappoint you. And now – ' She paused and then she smiled at me. 'Now the world *is* on fire. You've set it on fire, Harry.'

'Should we go through to the library?' I asked. 'We could listen to it.'

'I'm sorry,' she said, letting herself back down on her pillows. 'I'm feeling very weak today. I think I'd better stay in bed. It's my copy, though?'

I nodded.

'I'll listen to it later. Maybe I'll feel stronger this afternoon.' She sounded suddenly crisp. 'Listen, you've got a lot to do today if you're going to throw that party Wednesday. You said yesterday you had a thousand errands. You'd better get going.'

'I guess I should,' I said.

'I hope one of your thousand errands is getting a haircut,' she added. 'You look like you're planning to entertain a family of hedgehogs up there.'

The day of the party broke radiant and clear; I looked through the large windows of my architectonic loft and saw nothing but sunshine stretching in every direction. I had scheduled the day to the minute. I called my mother and asked how she was doing, and she told me that she was fine and that she would be at the party an hour after it started. 'I don't know how long I'll be able to stay,' she warned me. 'I'll stay for as long as I can, but it may just be half an hour or so. But I'll be there for long enough to say hello to everyone. You keep calm.' I called Helen, who confirmed that she would meet me at my apartment at 4.45. I got my hair cut. I shaved slowly and carefully. I spoke with the florist twice, and settled the question about the tall urns. I went out and bought champagne in case close friends wanted to come back to my house after the main event. I collected my watch (my parents had given me that watch for my twenty-first birthday) from the repair people, with whom it had spent a month. I telephoned some very close friends to make sure that they would arrive on the early side. I spoke with the caterer and tried to confirm the number of guests, but by that time the totals had run away from me. There were so many people who had said that they might be bringing friends, and so many others who had said that they would not be bringing friends, and so many who had called and virtually invited themselves, and so many who had been oddly unavailable.

'Don't let yourself wind up with rooms full of marginal people,' my mother had said. 'If you're having a party, invite only people whose presence at it will make you happy, because those are the people who will have a good time; with them, it will be a success.' In fact, pretty much all of my good friends were coming. Pretty much all of Freddy's good friends were coming. Almost all of my parents' good friends were coming. Nearly everyone any of us cared for was going to be crowding on in.

Only one of my mother's friends responded with regrets and didn't come. Later, she was to say that she hadn't understood how close my mother was to the end, but even so – she must have known that this was to be the last of my family's astonishing parties, the last one at which my mother would quietly lend her air of grace and so make of the flowers and the food and the company something miraculous beyond the simple measure of festivity. I suppose that different people live in worlds of different priorities, and to her this was simply a party, and not very import- ant. She was the sort of person who had never understood why we poured so much energy into the flowers and the food and the invitations and the tablecloths. Perhaps she didn't believe that we all inhabit a flawed world beyond our control, and that to extract from that world of flaws a moment closer to perfection than daily experience is a great and noble thing. Her friendship – her remarkable friendship, for she was a remarkable friend – had of course been manifest constantly in phone calls and letters and visits, was of course a matter of sensation and emotion and laugh- ter and tears. But it would also have been a part of a collective of love that could for a few hours be brought into one room, and surrounded with peonies, and made wholly palpable.

I talked about it with Helen in the afternoon, while we were getting dressed for the party. I was upset. 'Stop being petulant,' said Helen. 'She's a good friend to your mother, and she's been a good friend in the ways that matter. It's going to be an astonishing party, but it's just a party. Try not to get so out of control about it. There's no point having a fabulous party at which you have a bad time. And if it is your mother's last party – she'd also like you to have a good time. If you can't have a good time for yourself, or for me, then have one for her.'

We were both getting dressed at my apartment. Helen had bought a suit of fiery pink watered silk and black velvet for the occasion, and she had amazing shoes with large black rosettes on them. I had had a suit made of dark blue worsted with an almost imperceptible stripe; it was double-breasted, and the trousers had narrow legs. But I had had a hard time choosing a tie; and in the end I had settled not on something new, but on a tie that my mother had given me in my Christmas stocking when I was perhaps eleven years old, a tie with a tiny pattern of bridles and stirrups and prize ribbons on it, a tie she would have bought in Paris on one of those long Paris shopping afternoons that made her forever young. It was the first truly beautiful tie I had ever owned, and I had kept it for all these years, and it had never faded and (miraculously) it had never been spotted, and it had remained in perfect shape and condition. The deep violet of the prize ribbons was as rich as it had been that childhood Christmas morning when I had opened the box, and the elaborate turnings of the bridles and stirrups were still as exquisite and intricate.

I had assumed that my mother would give all her finery a last outing, but when I had gone uptown a few days before the party she had said no. 'I've had my super-diamond days,' she had said. 'Look at me,' she had gone on, and I had looked at her. 'I'm wearing a wig. I've lost weight. I can't wear anything that presses against my scars. I can't wear makeup. I can't wear high heeled shoes, because my sense of balance is completely gone. I'd look like a clown in a dress that was too much dress with diamonds all over the place.' I had interrupted her but she would have none of it. 'I've got a very simple dress and my double rope of big pearls and the earrings your father gave me this Christmas. It's a cocktail party, Harry. A big cocktail party, with a buffet supper, but still really a cocktail party. I'm going to wear what's appropriate for me to be wearing to a cocktail party right now. Everyone I care about who's coming to this party has seen me all dressed up before.' And she had shown me the dress she was planning to wear, a simple, loose black dress with trails of brilliant flowers falling down it, like fresh snowflakes or chance tears, flowers in red and blue and pink. On the hanger, that dress had looked like nothing, like a shapeless bolt of silk, like a dressed-up bathrobe. My mother had watched my face. 'Harry, it's appropriate,' she had said.

Helen called in to me while I was showering. 'You know that it's almost six o'clock,' she reminded me as I inhaled the steam. 'You said you wanted to be uptown by six o'clock.' And so I suddenly realized that I was late, despite all my careful planning, or perhaps because of it. And then I began to panic. I finished my day's second shave in a mad rush, and cut myself slightly under my chin. I leapt out of the shower and got dressed and put on the wrong shirt. Helen was all ready, sitting in divine calm on one of the black chairs. She had poured herself a glass of white wine, which she was not drinking, but she sat holding it and watching as I dressed myself. 'I think you've missed a button,' she called out to me as I put on my shirt. 'Calm down, Harry,' she said a minute later. 'The knot in your tie looks like you're trying to strangle yourself.'

By the time I was ready I was sweating slightly. Robert had come down to pick us up and take us uptown. In the car, I dropped one of my cufflinks behind the seat; and when I put my hand back to get it, I broke the band on my gold watch. It was too late to do anything about it. The party was called for 6.30; we arrived at 6.25. Helen had given up on trying to keep me calm, and sat erect and dignified, but with one arm draped around my shoulder.

The party was in a small museum uptown that my father had hired through the bank. The rooms were lit with tiny candles, which had all the soft candescence electricity lost us. The musicians were at the top of the stairs, and as we walked in they started to play a trio by Schubert, the E flat, that I had chosen with them one long afternoon a few months earlier. The many separate buffets had been put into the various galleries, and the food had been arranged with fantastic care, as though each shrimp were an apostle placed for the Last Supper. I had had all of the tablecloths made of heavy dark red watered silk, and there they were on the buffet and cocktail tables. I had at first wanted a brighter fabric, but my mother had said dark red would go better with the occasion and would distract less from the flowers, and the tablecloths were right. The waiters were all in place, in white jackets with gold buttons. Two of them stood near the door with silver trays and tall flutes of champagne.

Over all of it, like the arms of God, arched the flowers. I have never seen flowers like that, before or since. I had told the florist that I wanted lilies and roses, and he had thrown in delphiniums and a few other flowers I knew less well. I had told him twice that peonies were my mother's favourite flowers, and he had promised to have some selected especially for the party. I had not told my mother about the peonies; they were to be like a private letter. When she saw pink peonies, she would know that the party was not only her party for me, but also my party for her. These peonies were like great pink cabbages; they were like upholstery; they were like feathers. They had in them pinks that faded and grew into each other, a pale pink like laughter and a medium pink like sunrise and a deep pink that could have been the colour of truth. Roses, of course, possess a multitude of petals, but a rose opens itself up and in the end leaves you with a fine core of pistils and a stamen, its petals strewn around it. You can get to the centre of a rose; the petals run out, like anything else you can count. But peonies – there is no end to the petals once a peony finally gets going. That tight bud of a peony is like the clown car at heaven's circus, the petals, then, the smiling faces that pour like infinity into the ring. A peony begins to open and then the petals keep piling from the centre, and there is no end. Also, peonies have, still, their season. In this era of forced and artificial growing of things, so many flowers are with you in spring and autumn and winter and summer, but peonies have their month and then are heard from no more. How right my mother was, to say that the tablecloths should be dark red and the rooms lit with candles – because these winter assumptions seemed like only a becoming modesty before the June splendour of the peonies. I had promised my mother that the party would not be flashy or ostentatious, and everything about it was restrained except these flowers, which were as unabashed as the Ritz Hotel.

'It's the most beautiful party I've ever seen,' Helen said to me as we walked through. I was in a haze, or a daze. 'Come on,' she said, and led me to the top of the great sweeping staircase. And there we stood, and greeted the guests as they arrived, in ones and twos and sixes and sevens. It was as though each of them were escorting a memory. Friends from my childhood came in, people I had known since just after I was born. Elementary school walked before me, and high school, and summer camp, and college, and conservatory. Friends of my parents who had never changed came and reminded me of a life I had once led and of the life I had once supposed I would lead. Friends I had met through Helen came. Friends from England and from Russia and from Germany and from other countries came, piano friends, to remind me of all the adventures I had had in the ten years previous. People I knew too well and people I hoped to know better filed in in troops and tangles. Nick showed up; I'd invited him but had never had a response, and I'd assumed he wouldn't come. 'God, Harry,' he said as he looked around. 'Helen! Christ!' he said. 'You look like – wow!' And then he drifted off into the galleries. 'God, is this your life?' he asked, and then laughed; from the corner of my eye I could see him starting to pick up one of the waiters. Bernard also came. He had told me that he wanted to come, but he had said until the last minute that he might make it or might not. We had continued to talk from time to time by phone, and I was very pleased when he arrived. I introduced him to Helen at the top of the stairs. 'I hope we'll get to chat later,' he said, as he politely moved into the big gallery, where he spotted some other friends who had come from England. All the people at my party were dressed as well as they could be; some looked beautiful, the others closer to beautiful than I had seen them before. The soft light, turned pink as it reflected off all those peonies, made each one look calm and joyful. I continued to greet the arrivals, while the air behind me echoed with delight.

Exactly an hour after the party began, Helen put her hand on my arm. 'Look,' she said, and I looked down the long sweeping flight of stairs. I saw my mother. She was wearing just what she had said she was going to wear, but now that the dress was off the hanger it seemed – not more elaborate, because it was as simple as a paper bag – but more elegant than anything that anyone else had worn. I had told my mother that there was an elevator to get her to the second floor, where the buffets were, but every guest had proceeded up those stairs and my mother had apparently decided to do the same thing. My father and Freddy walked just behind her, but she was, for the first time in weeks, not leaning on my father's arm. Later I learned that she had eaten nothing for two days because she wanted to be sure that she had no further digestive problems, but if the lack of food had made her weak, something else had made her strong. I did not move from my place at the top of the stairs; I stood there with Helen and waited. One step at a time, regal as the Queen of Sheba, my mother climbed that staircase. The long rope of pearls swung slightly as she walked, as though it were telling time. She had a smile on her face, a smile as much of her eyes and her hands and her shoulders as of her mouth, a smile of love and of triumph, a smile that reminded me more than anything of the smile she had in her wedding picture, the smile of being glad in every ounce of her being to be where she was. Friends were still arriving, and several walked up the stairs with her. I couldn't hear them clearly from where I stood, but I saw her throw back her head when she laughed at something one of them had said; and as friends of mine arrived, I heard her greet each of them by name. When she finally got to the top of the stairs she kissed me and she kissed Helen. She was not out of breath, though she leaned for a moment on the top of the bannister to steady herself. Then she looked around and her eyes followed the lengths of the galleries in either direction. She took a glass of mineral water from one of the waiters. 'I'm going to find a place where I can sit,' she said. I told her there were some chairs in the far gallery on the left. 'What a beautiful party, Harry,' she said.

Helen said to me at one point that evening. 'You know what you should do? You should go and lock yourself in the bathroom for a minute. Just for a minute. Clear your head. It'll make it easier to remember what's happening.' But though I set off in that general direction, I was derailed by friends, and spent the evening orchestrating and breaking down conversations. From time to time I would go to the room at the end, the one with the four great bunches of peonies, where my mother was sitting and holding her quiet court. All my mother's friends were there, and some of my oldest friends. Everyone was speaking softly, not about anything of great moment, and there was a quality to the light in that room like nothing I had seen before, and in that light everyone seemed to be young, and my mother's face had that freshness that it had held in my childhood. When I went into that room I saw that my mother had been right, that the tablecloths and the food and the champagne and even the peonies had almost disappeared in the face of these tides of love. My father looked sad much of the time, but my mother had a look I had not seen in a long time, not the Lake Como reckless look, but something simpler than that, as simple as her black dress with the bright flowers on it. She had gone to this party determined to keep up the front of fun for me and for her friends and for my friends and for Freddy's friends, but in fact she was no longer keeping up a front at all. She stayed for almost three hours, longer than she had been out in a crowd in months. When she left, she did it almost silently. 'I can't stay any longer, Harry,' she said to me. 'Robert's going to drive us home. I hope you're having a good time. I've had a lovely time. Just lovely, Harry. It's the most elegant party I've ever been to. The best party.' And she went off to take the elevator down.

Helen stayed with me most of the time, though she occasionally drifted off, and once I turned around to spot her on the other side of the room talking to Nick and Bernard. At the sight of the three of them I gave in to a sadness that had gone away until then.

I stared at Nick and for a split second I wanted him to come up to me and push me back against one of the tall urns, as he would have done four months earlier. For a minute, I felt a terrible sense of loss, a sheer physical emptiness that I thought only Nick could fill. Bernard, standing beside him, looked like the livable past. I wanted to take his hand and go into the garden and eat some of the nicer hors d'œuvre and talk about everyone; I wanted to ask him what he thought of all my New York friends, as though they were a display I had mounted for him. I wanted to fall into the safe world Bernard and I had occupied; when I looked at him I felt a nostalgia twice as strong as my passion for Nick. And then Helen. What I felt for Helen was effortless. Helen looked to me like a life preserver, and I wanted to sail away with her held securely in my arms.

'Look who I've introduced to each other,' she said to me with a laugh when I approached. Nick had just slapped Bernard around the shoulders by way of response to a passing remark. I talked to them all for a minute, about something that was little more than nothing. Then I took Helen and headed with her across toward one of the buffet tables.

'I love you, Helen,' I said.

She shook her head. 'No, you don't,' she said. 'It would be lovely if you did, but you don't.' She smiled at me, a sad smile. 'Where's your mother?' she asked. I said that my mother had just left and I said that I hoped everyone was having fun. I said that I hoped she, Helen, was having fun. 'Listen,' Helen said. 'Maybe someday you will.'

'I will what?' I asked.

'Love me,' she said. 'Or have fun. Or both.' And then someone else came along to greet us, and we lapsed into sociability.

I have been looking at the photos from that party. There are seven pictures of my mother, the only seven pictures that were ever taken of her in a wig. She is laughing in most of them, though in one she is staring out with a look that is not quite a look of laughter. She is with her laughing friends. The other pictures – there must be four hundred other pictures – show the friends and the flowers and the pinkness of the light. There are a lot of pictures of me, and I am laughing in all of them. It's easy to remember that my watch was broken, that I always felt that I was neglecting someone, that my mother was ill, that Nick was flirting with Bernard, that Helen told me I didn't love her. It's easy to remember all those things. It's harder for me to remember how I came to laugh so much and for so long. The pictures of me at that party seem as remote as the pictures of my mother, but I know myself well enough to know, looking at them, that I was not pretending. I can tell, looking at them, that I too must have had a wonderful time at that party; it must have been one of the happiest events of my life.

I remember an ordinary day uptown, some years ago, before my mother got sick, when she said to me, 'I look in the mirror in the morning and I see a fifty-year-old woman. When I was your age, I thought that by the time I was fifty I would have turned into a whole different person, a whole different kind of person, a fifty-year-old person. Now I look in the mirror and I see a fifty-year-old woman looking back at me, and I wonder, how did I get to be fifty? And I don't understand why no one ever told me that I would just go on being myself, that I would just eventually find the same old me aged fifty, with grown children and a marriage and houses to run and the essence of my life behind me.'

I remember that I was bewildered, because no one at that time seemed more clearly adult to me than my mother. I think that she must have spoken that day in a voice edged with fear and regret, because when I recall those words they seem to me to be the saddest words in the world. Some days, I myself feel so old, so full of knowledge that would once have eluded me; but on other days I feel young, and seeing the face of someone past adolescence, I feel a sinking terror, a fear that my mind will never catch up with my body, that time is sliding away from me, and that I am not changing as quickly as the moments do. Lately, those days have come to dominate. I look at the photos of myself from that party and this is what I see: I see a young man in the middle of a party as stunning as the feast day of an ancient king. I see him surrounded by many friends and a few lovers. I see him looking as though he is entirely in control, negotiating his family and overseeing the waiters and making introductions; he is evidently the master builder who has constructed everyone else's delight. I see him utterly at ease, and clearly very happy. I see someone of vast competence, looking out at me from clear confident eyes. I look at him and I wonder who this young man is, not yet thirty, so sure of himself and of the world. I wonder what it would be like to be on top of the world like that, to have so much of what youth dreams maturity might hold. I look into his clear blue eyes and I envy him, because he is so full of laughter, because he seems not to know about or not to mind the effort life is, because he has the face of someone who has all the things that I have always wanted, but who couldn't possibly care less about them.

IX

Inside The Shell

Three days after the party we went up to the country for the weekend. The weather was clear again; indeed, the weather that month was as impeccable as though our lives were being filmed. My mother had ordered all the food, as always; she could not cope much with the oven or the stove, but she could do quite a lot sitting down, and Freddy and I did the rest at her direction. We talked about the party, and she told me what a splendid party she thought it had been. I asked her what she had thought of the food, tomatoes and all, but she said that she had had nothing to eat. 'Half a glass of water,' she said. 'That was all. I was afraid I might have problems. And once it began – I wasn't hungry. But everyone told me how delicious the food was.'

Later that afternoon, she said, 'Your cd is really very good.' She sounded almost surprised. 'The Rachmaninoff sounds strong, like you mean it. And the Schubert is very poetic, very light. That's your best piece, that Schubert.'

'Do you remember that day?' I asked. 'I called you from the recording studio before I played. You were going in for a treatment.'

'Yes,' she said. 'That was when they had me on Agent Orange. You sounded terribly tense; I didn't think you'd play well that day. But I was wrong.'

On Saturday afternoon, my father set up the card table near the door to the terrace, as he often did, and my mother started a jigsaw puzzle of a painting by Monet. I stood behind her and watched her sorting the edge pieces from the centre pieces for a little while, then came around the table and knelt at its far side. 'I love Impressionism,' my mother said, 'but Northern Renaissance is a lot easier in a jigsaw puzzle.' I made a mental note to try to find a good puzzle of a Northern Renaissance painting to give to her. For a while neither of us spoke. My father and Freddy were sitting on the terrace talking about a medical question raised in the paper, on which they strongly disagreed. 'Your friend Nick came over and introduced himself to me,' my mother remarked casually.

I was instantly on the defensive. 'Well, then, there he is. I guess you didn't talk to him for long, but even so you've got to admit that he's charming and smart and very attractive,' I said.

'I'm sure he is,' said my mother, joining two sections of the edge of her puzzle. Her eyes were focused down, on some mostly blue pieces she had grouped together. 'Harry. Charming and smart and attractive is all very well. But maybe you should look for nice for a change?'

I snapped back. 'I'm pretty nice,' I said. I don't know why I said that.

My mother looked at me, and she reached out her hand and put it on mine, on the edge of the table. Her voice took on that softness again. 'Oh yes, Harry,' she said. 'You are. You're one of the nicest people I've ever known.' And she looked straight at me, as though it were she who needed to hold onto what she was saying, to help her remember me.

I stood up then, because I was determined not to cry in front of my mother. I went out onto the terrace. Perhaps it seemed brusque. Freddy and my father were still debating. 'You'll never win with Dad,' I said. 'You're in a losing battle.' My mother called out her agreement from inside.

On Sunday, we had breakfast on the terrace. There was melon and there were fresh berries and there was newly squeezed orange juice. My mother had made something eggy and delicious with blueberries and cinnamon, one of her breakfast specialities, and bacon. There was cake, and there was a fresh brioche. There was a variety of cheeses. The table was set with the breakfast china, with the pattern of yellow ribbons waving on it, and various serving dishes. My father had picked a handful of wildflowers that morning, and had put them in a blue jug, and they were at the middle of the table. Freddy had his camera, and he wanted to take pictures, since this typical Sunday would not be many more times repeated, but my mother refused to be photographed with the wig. 'You'll have enough of those pictures from the party,' she said, and settled the matter.

The weather had continued cinematic. 'Look at all this,' said Freddy, gesturing at the sunlit food.

'We do live beautifully,' I said into the air.

My mother laughed. 'Have you boys just noticed?' she asked.

'No, but – ' I paused.

'Come on, Mom,' said Freddy.

'It's not so hard,' my mother said in her soft voice. 'Living beautifully is not so hard. So many people –' she began. She looked across the table for a minute. 'We'd live more beautifully if someone replaced that chipped sugar bowl,' she finished. 'Do any of you want another slice of brioche?'

In the afternoon, she did the crossword puzzle with a blue felt-tip pen. 'Do you know what I did?' she suddenly volunteered.

We all turned around.

'A couple of months ago I went out to lunch, and I put on that diamond pin of Grandma's. Do you know the one I mean? With her monogram done in little stones?'

My father looked confused. 'You know,' Freddy said to him. 'It was square. Grandma always wore it in the winter.'

'Oh, yes,' said my father. He looked at my mother. 'I don't think I've ever seen you wear that pin,' he said.

'I've only worn it two or three times in my life,' said my mother. 'But I wore it out to lunch that time, on that blue jacket, and I think I left the pin on the lapel when I sent the jacket to the dry cleaner. I'm so annoyed about it. I thought I might have brought it up here, but it's not with my jewellery and it's not in my box in New York.'

'Maybe if you call the dry cleaner they'll have it,' I said.

'No, I'm sure it's gone,' said my mother. 'I didn't wear it much, of course. But someone else might have worn it someday. Your grandmother loved that pin.'

In the late afternoon, she and my father and Freddy got into my parents' car, and I got into mine, to drive back to New York. It wasn't until I was alone in the car that I felt afraid. I turned on the radio as loud as possible and tried to bang out time to the music. I switched from classical to rock to light FM and back to classical, trying to figure out how best to block my mind. By the time I was half way to the city, I knew that I could not go back to my apartment. I thought about going to my parents' apartment, but that option was also intolerable. I couldn't bear to stop at home even to collect a razor and a toothbrush, so I headed for Helen's instead, even though I knew that she was having friends over for dinner.

I arrived just as Helen and her friends – they were all acquaintances of mine, people who had been at the party – were sitting down to dinner. When I rang the bell from downstairs, Helen guessed who it was. 'Come on up,' she said.

The elevator was impossibly slow.

'So how was your weekend?' Helen asked when I got upstairs. The others all looked at me, politely expectant.

I found myself telling them about what we had had for breakfast, and then I started to talk about the jigsaw puzzle. I kept interrupting myself, as though I were several people all talking at once, and as I went on I got faster and faster and faster, as though I were several people all being played on fast forward. 'I don't know,' I said. 'It could be one month or two months or six months, but it's not going to be forever. She's not going to go on like this forever,' I said. I had to go on talking, in front of all these people. Helen was rubbing my shoulders as I talked, and I knew that I was being incoherent, but my voice wouldn't stop. As some people sob uncontrollably, I talked uncontrollably. I didn't know what I was saying. I couldn't even hear myself.

Helen interrupted after about twenty minutes. No one else said a word. 'What you're saying is that you want her to die soon,' said Helen.

I didn't stop. I went on and on. I said, of course, that I wanted my mother to live forever.

'She's not going to live forever,' said Helen. 'You know, it's not going to be a relief when she dies. It's going to be pretty awful.'

I went on talking and talking and talking. No one else said

anything. I felt that I was taking up the entire room, squeezing everyone back into the silence of the walls.

'It sounds terrible,' said Helen, 'It's a terrible thing to say, but I hope, for your sake, that she dies soon.'

We all stayed over that night. I asked the others not to leave, and by the time I asked them it was already late, and so we all camped out in solidarity on Helen's floor. I lay on the floor like a tightly strung bow, and then suddenly I fell asleep, into a turbulent sleep full of dreams, an exhausting sleep, in which it was as though I had gone on talking and talking and talking.

There is a silent time when you wake up, and another before you fall asleep. There are moments of silence during a shower, or while you brush your teeth. There can be silence if you drive in a car alone. I found the silence unbearable at all these times. On Monday morning, I woke up at Helen's apartment. She had left, and so had the others. I'd slept through everyone's leaving. I called my mother on the phone and we talked about nothing. Then I went over to my parents' apartment, in principle to pick up a package my mother told me had arrived.

A sofa had also come back that morning. My mother had been systematically reupholstering things that spring. She'd had all the curtains cleaned, some of them changed. She'd had the restorer in to treat all the wood surfaces in the house. She'd had the kitchen ceiling repainted. My mother was getting things in order. 'Your father would never cope with any of this,' she said. 'If I get all these things done, he's got a good five years of the apartment looking all right, and by the time five years have gone by, I hope he'll have found another woman.' So that Monday, the sofa came back. I thought it looked great; I have a feeling my mother was not entirely content with it. But it was good enough. She couldn't very well have it redone again at this stage.

I helped arrange the pillows. 'That looks fine,' she said.

We went into the kitchen and I made tea. We took it back to her bedroom.

We talked about her current treatment. She said that she was having more tests in the afternoon. 'The fun never stops,' she said.

I told her that I had stayed at Helen's.

'Helen is a really good friend,' she said.

Suddenly, I started to cry. I could say that it was very complicated, that it was about everything, and of course it was about everything too. But in fact I started to cry in simple mourning for my mother, who was there in the room with me. I started while she sat across the room, and then I walked over and sat down beside her and buried my head and wept on her shoulder. For a long time she stroked my hair. 'Harry,' she said. 'You will be all right, Harry.' I shook with tears, as I had cried when I was very little. It was a kind of crying I had almost forgotten. 'Harry, you've been working yourself up into hysterics,' said my mother. 'I know that you'll miss me, Harry, but you can go on and you will go on, because you don't have any other choice. I understand why you're sad, Harry, but not why you're so overwrought. There's nothing to be afraid of.' I held on to my mother's fragile body, the shadow of a body that she had then. 'There's nothing to be afraid of,' she said again. 'You have such a good life, Harry. You've got to get on with it and live it.' Still I cried. 'This has gone on long enough,' my mother said quietly, almost to herself. 'You've all got to get on with your lives.' Then she pushed me gently away. She put a hand under my chin. 'Come on, Harry,' she said. 'Pull yourself together. Let's make ourselves some lunch.' And she stood up, and led me along the hallway to the kitchen. Janet was doing the cabinets. 'Janet, is there some of that salmon left?' my mother asked, and we made toast.

The verb 'to die' is one of the few that is only readily usable in the past and future tenses. We accept, he died last year, and we can easily accept, we will all die someday. But the present tense, I die, you die, he dies – that should be cancelled right out of the language. And to have to use the verb in that tense not for a single moment but for weeks and months and then years: that is altogether intolerable. We tend to think, furthermore, that 'to die' is a verb of the instant, like 'to dive'. It is a thing that takes almost no measurable time. One second you are on the board, looking at the water, and the next second you have left the board behind you and taken the plunge. So with many deaths: one second you are alive, and the next second you are dead. Science defines death in this way, and on your death certificate indicates a particular moment as the moment of death. But sometimes the verb 'to die' is more like the verb 'to age', and is a thing that happens by terrible and slow and imperceptible degrees. My mother was not given a chance to age in that manner, and was, by way of inadequate compensation, given an experience of death as gradual as a life span.

On Tuesday night, we all had dinner together, in the kitchen. My mother had made chicken. She was not feeling at all well, and was off to see the stomach specialist again the following day. I had plans to meet friends that night, and had said that I could stay only until nine o'clock. My father wanted me to have no plans, but I had done enough rearranging of my schedule and I put my foot down.

Freddy pulled the wishbone out of the chicken. 'How about it, Mom?' he asked, offering her one side.

'If wishes were horses,' she said, and they each pulled, and she won. 'Look at that,' she said.

'It doesn't matter,' said my father. 'I'm sure you both wished for the same thing.'

'I don't think so,' said my mother cryptically. And she put her half of the wishbone at the front of one of the shelves above the kitchen table.

At nine o'clock sharp I stood up to leave the apartment. I kissed everyone goodnight. 'Always running off to something,' said my father.

'Leonard, let him do what he likes,' said my mother.

'I suppose you're leaving all the dishes for Dad and me,' said Freddy.

I pointed out that I had done more than my share of the dishes over the weekend in the country, while Freddy had been on the phone endlessly with that friend of his who'd moved to Chicago.

'I'll do the dishes,' said my father in a tone of mock heroism. 'Just stop arguing.'

'Go on, Harry,' said my mother. 'You're keeping your friends waiting.' And so, though I suddenly wanted to stay, I went.

The next morning, Wednesday morning, my mother went to see her last doctor, for a test the details of which seem too miserable to tell, a test whose lack of dignity, in a day when my mother had, above all else, an unsullied sense of her own dignity, seems to make it irrelevant. The truth of that day lies not in what she endured at the hands of that gastroenterologist, but in the quiet, unyielding, and generous determination with which she was to carry off her death itself. Because that day, Wednesday, after seeing the doctor, in the late afternoon, my mother killed herself.

In real life, people do not have deathbed scenes. Deathbed scenes are a matter for grand opera, and you will perhaps recall that my mother hated grand opera. I can remember her joking about women who stumble across the stage singing for an hour while the knives turn in their hearts; it was one of her synecdoches for the absurdity of the form. But my mother had a deathbed scene as grand and rich, as well-conceived and as stunning as *La Traviata*'s. Like some Butterfly loosed on Manhattan, she plunged her many knives into her own ravaged frame, and having done that she sang like the sea itself, as though the lifetime she had saved and felt and known had suddenly all come to repeat itself, until we felt, finally, that love was in the room with us, an object no more substantial than her last breaths, but so strong that it would stay with us for all our lives.

On the Wednesday my mother died, the implausible weather finally broke, and it rained and it rained and it rained and it rained. I remember that this seemed like a dark omen when I woke up in the morning, as though the clouds had come to tell me something I would have preferred not to know. But I remember feeling also that the rain seemed protective, all that water flowing down around us, and that my apartment seemed strangely dry and safe in the downpour. I remember sitting inside with all the lights on, thinking that I needed more and better lamps. I played the Schubert over, the piece on my cd, which I was to play for a concert two weeks later. I tried to play it just as it was on the cd, but I found that the piece had changed for me, that it had become softer and less clear. I put down the lid of the piano, and decided that I would rearrange all my closets, bring to the apartment the fullness of order, the order that had degenerated into chaos during the weeks before the party. Seldom have I been so meticulous and so thorough: I chose each hanger for each pair of trousers, put the suits at the left side, the winter things far to the right, arranged my neckties in a chromatic progression.

Did I have a sense of foreboding on that damp morning? Is there anyone in the world who, recalling the events, has not had a sense of foreboding on the day of his mother's death? I had had a sense of foreboding every day for a month, and on that day I had a strange sense of peace, a sense that the time had come to put everything in place. Was I hoping for my mother's death? The thought made me ill. And yet it cannot be denied that what we have anticipated with dread for too long comes to seduce us. I wanted to put pain behind me, and though my mother's death in fact would only change the shape of my pain, it would be at least an end to her pain, an end to the pain outside my knowledge or ability to affect. I wanted my mother to live forever, but if she could not live forever, I wondered whether it wasn't time for her to go.

That is not to say that I was prepared or even comprehending when she called at three o'clock. 'Hello, Harry,' she said. 'How are you?'

I said that I was OK, and that I had been rehanging the closets. 'And how are you?' I asked.

'It wasn't good news this afternoon from that doctor,' she said, and paused for a moment. 'I think this is it.'

I felt a strange surge of terror, and excitement, and also panic, and also a sudden blankness. 'Do you mean – ' I started. I tried to think of words.

'I think you'd better come uptown,' she continued. 'I'm going to call Freddy now.' Then we hung up. I spun around. I was in a bathrobe and wearing glasses, my hair all standing on end; I had not bothered to get dressed before attacking the closets. Should I just throw on something fast and rush uptown, or should I have a shower first and try to calm down? I couldn't bear to waste any of my mother's remaining minutes on earth, but I also wanted to spend the last evening I would spend with her feeling, in small external ways, my best; she hated it when I didn't shave. I wanted her to remember me as she most liked to see me. I rushed into the bathroom to wash my hands, and the phone rang. I couldn't decide whether to pick it up, and I almost left it, and then I grabbed it, and it was my mother. 'I thought it might be easiest if I sent Robert down to get you,' she said. 'I'll send him down now, and you can collect Freddy from the lab on your way uptown, and you boys can come up here together.'

So I had time to shower and shave after all. My hands were shaking so badly that I could barely hold onto the soap, and the razor was tricky. My contact lenses were almost impossible. Haste makes waste, I thought, trying not to jab myself too many times. I stood in the shower and tried to lose myself in the rush of the water, tried to find repose in the splashing of the water, rubbed shampoo into my hair. I felt physically sick.

I was rubbing conditioner into my scalp when I suddenly felt again the urgency of time, and so I rinsed my hair quickly. I wondered whether Robert was downstairs yet, and worried that I might be wasting minutes I could have been spending with my mother. I rushed to get clothes to wear. And then there was a moment of puzzlement: what to wear to head uptown for my mother's death? As I looked at my clothes, each item seemed to me marked either as something I had bought in accord with and tribute to my mother's taste, or as something I had bought in resistance to my mother's taste. I might have organized my closet that morning by putting the clothes she liked on one side and the clothes she disliked on the other; the items she liked well enough but would never have chosen for me could have been ranged in the middle.

I put on khaki trousers and a blue oxfordcloth shirt, nothing ostentatious, not items we had talked about at any length, year-old and comfortable, but clean and freshly pressed and neat. I stared in confusion at my sweaters, and then suddenly saw the green sweater she had knitted for me. I'd never worn it much, because it itches slightly, and because I'd had a fear of wearing it out: I started saving that sweater when it was made, even before my mother got sick. It seemed like the right thing to wear that day. It occurred to me then that I would probably be the one to choose the clothes in which my mother would be buried.

I became aware again that I was wasting time, and I went downstairs. I stood inside the glass doors to my building and stared at the steady grey pulse of the rain. Robert wasn't there yet. The traffic was moving agonizingly slowly. Finally, he pulled up. He of course didn't know what was happening, so I ducked through the rain, got into the car, and tried to seem sunny as we drove uptown. Freddy was waiting on the corner outside his office, and we hugged each other. 'This is too weird,' he said, and I agreed. 'I don't feel anything,' he said, and I realized that I was numb, completely numb. On the way to my parents' apartment we had a conversation that was only half in code, so as not to give away too much to Robert; but we didn't keep much secret either.

We inched our way north through the slow traffic. Robert naturally drove us up to Madison Avenue. Whether it is the most convenient route or not, Robert still drives up Madison Avenue rather than Park or Third, because it was always my mother's preference. That training ran deep. I can remember how, when I was little, she would say: 'Leonard, let's drive up Madison. And don't drive too quickly; I want to see what's in the windows.' And my father would grumble something about shop windows, but he would drive up Madison, not too quickly, and my mother would watch out her window as though she were at the movies, at a movie version of her own life. So on this day too, true to his training, Robert drove us up Madison Avenue, in the rainy day traffic, until we were finally there.

How many times had I gone upstairs on that same elevator in much that same way and come into the front hall, where the light was on? How many times had I gone from the front hall through the big wooden door into the back hall, how many times called out greetings (because my mother hated for people to come in and not call out their hellos; she said it was like thieves in the night). So this time, Freddy and I walked in the front door and we called out hello, and heard the echo sounding through the hall. And then we walked along that hall (my mother had lately recarpeted it in green, as part of her scheme to get the apartment into shape) and in my parents' room (I still seem to call it my parents' room; that was the last day that I did not have to reproach myself and say instead that it is my father's room) – in my parents' room were my parents. My father looked shocked and so grief-stricken; his whole face was tensed, as though his jaw and neck were being held together only through the strain of muscles beneath the skin.

But my mother looked much as she had looked for months. She was sitting up on the pink loveseat at the foot of the bed, her back erect, and she had a magazine in her lap. 'Hello, boys,' she said. It was the last time she ever said that. 'Hi,' we said. She had on her little bit of non-allergenic makeup (still from the doctor's appointment? was it just what she had worn to go out for the day, or had she touched it up before we arrived?) and she was wearing a nightgown with pink roses on it, and with lace around the neck and the arms. It was not one of the amazing silk nightgowns she saved for European trips; it was just a nightgown, in her favourite colour, with flowers. It was the kind of thing my mother wore, the kind of thing she always wore, that she slept in from my earliest childhood. She was wearing a long pink bathrobe, and one of her white turbans, very fresh and clean, carefully straight on her head. She looked so much herself that I could hardly bear to see her; nor could I turn my eyes away.

Had she said in the hospital room, one year before, that she was already dead? She had repeated, insistently: can't you see that the woman you loved is already gone, that I am only a shadow, that she isn't here anymore? But the day she died, that was altogether untrue. She was never more entirely present than she was on that last day in her bedroom. On the day my mother died, it was as though all the richness of her character that provident nature had saved to be slowly dispensed over the following thirty-two years (had she lived as long as her own mother) was suddenly poured out in the space of three or four hours. It was almost blinding, so dazzling you could hardly look at it, a distillation of her capacity to love. Never have I loved anyone so much, or felt so loved, as I did in those few hours.

Freddy went and sat beside her on the loveseat, and I sat down on the floor at her feet. Freddy took one of her hands, and I took the other. My father sat opposite us in his red chair. The three of us who were not my mother were full of anxiety, but my mother behaved as though this were only another ordinary matter in the course of family life. 'How exactly does this work?' my mother asked, and my father dutifully looked again through the booklet with the directions for ill people who want to kill themselves. He said that according to the booklet it was the usual practice to have a light meal about forty-five minutes before taking the pills. Freddy kept interrupting. 'This is just too weird,' he said. Then he said, 'Are you sure you want to do this now?' and my father and I were more or less in tears.

My mother said to Freddy: 'It's really time now. I think you know that.' And then she said, 'I think we're all being a little bit melodramatic, don't you?' And she said, 'I guess we might as well get started and go eat something, if that's what the directions say to do.' And she stood up and led us into the kitchen, her long pink bathrobe trailing out behind her. Freddy and my father and I trailed along in her wake like clouds. 'Who wants an English muffin?' she asked. My father said he couldn't possibly eat anything, and my brother also ate nothing. I had had nothing to eat all day and I was desperately hungry, and though I felt sick, I had a feeling that I would feel sicker later on, and I had an English muffin.

Freddy and I set the table and my mother sat in her place at its far end. We kept up a stream of non-talk: who wanted tea and where had the potholder gone and did everyone have a napkin. Freddy took a box of cookies, left from the previous evening, and he put it on the table. My mother looked up at him, a look full of affection and a lifetime's frustration, lessons still untaught but worth another chance, and she said, 'Freddy. For the last time. Please. Would you put the cookies on a plate.'

We all laughed (it seems incredible that we all laughed, but it's true) and Freddy put the cookies on a plate. 'Just for you, Mom,' he said.

My mind was crowded with something ridiculous. I couldn't decide whether to tell my mother that I had broken a dessert plate the previous weekend in the country. It seemed like such a small matter, the dessert plate; I had intended to buy a replacement and just quietly take it up to the house. She would never have known. Why, then, tell her now? But I suddenly regretted every detail of my life that I had never shared with her, every misdeed, every calculation to which I had not immediately confessed. I have repeated as though it were a mantra that my mother knew me, but at that moment I wanted to tell her everything there was that she didn't know, to hold onto the absoluteness of her. And I wanted her to forgive me, though that dessert plate was a small matter to forgive. I don't know what the total is of the things I did that made my mother unhappy. At that moment, she would have forgiven anything. I knew that the dessert plate was so unimportant as not to be worth mentioning, and I never mentioned it; but in my dreams, I can still see that plate shattered on the white marble floor, the fragments high-gloss in their glaze, with dull edges of rough white.

The period in that day about which I am most fuzzy is the period in the kitchen. I made my mother's chamomile tea, so pale it was hardly more than water, the way she liked it. I ate a muffin. I was aware, as I put on not too much butter, that it was the last time I would ever do what I knew was best for myself in deference to her watchful eye. Freddy had put out the cookies in their box, but I knew not to put too much butter on my muffin, and yet I also knew that a well-toasted muffin must have enough butter to make it delicious – an amount my mother had demonstrated to me in my early childhood.

She buttered her own muffin.

I said that there were a thousand things I had still to ask her. 'I'm not ready for this yet,' I said.

'We're all as ready as we're ever going to be,' said my mother. 'If you have things to ask me, then ask me now, Harry. I'll do my best to tell you.'

I couldn't think of anything. For some reason, I asked her how to make oatmeal. She said to follow the directions on the box but use milk instead of water, and to add a little bit of cinnamon. 'And keep stirring,' she said. 'Don't let it get lumpy.' Freddy asked how to make roast chicken. 'Boys,' she said. 'Most of my recipes are written down in that blue notebook. Whatever isn't in that blue notebook you can ask Janet about; she knows how I cook most things. Otherwise, use a cookbook. The world is full of good recipes.'

Freddy looked up at the shelves over the table and saw the winning half of the wishbone still sitting there. He reached over and picked it up. 'What did you wish, Mom?' he asked.

'I wished for this to be over as quickly and as painlessly as possible.' My father began to cry again, but my mother smiled. 'And I got my wish.' She looked back down at her English muffin. 'I got my wishes so often,' she said.

There was a pause.

She turned to me then. 'Harry,' she said. 'There's one thing I haven't had time to do, and I'm telling you because you'll remember and your father and Freddy won't. I had the arrangement of dried flowers that goes in the front hall in the country redone, and I haven't picked it up yet. It's at that dried-flower shop near the antique dealer where we bought your desk, and it's supposed to be ready this weekend. Please try to get it before the end of the month, because if you wait all summer, it'll get kicked around in their storage area and it'll look awful.'

I stared at her for a second. 'Yes, of course,' I said. 'I'll get the flowers.'

'They're being put in that same ceramic pot that they've always been in,' she said.

'OK,' I said. 'Don't worry about it. I'll recognize them.'

'I'm sorry,' she said. 'I thought I had a few more weeks. I didn't think I had much time, but I thought a few more weeks at least. Still, I've done almost everything. I'm probably forgetting something, but you'll all figure it out.'

The cookies were on a plate but no one was eating them.

'When I'm gone, you should make sure that you get rid of my

clothes and my personal things as quickly as you can. Don't distribute my belongings to your friends or my friends or even to Janet. You don't need to see them wandering around. I don't care what you do with them, but get them out of here sometime this month. I know that it will be unpleasant, but it will be a relief to get them out. My jewellery should be left in the safe. It's for my daughters-in-law. Don't bury me with any of it, except my wedding ring; it would be a stupid waste. And don't you boys give it to the first girls you think you like. When you have real relationships that are forever, then you can give it to those people.'

We all nodded.

'Shall we go back to the bedroom?' asked my mother, and she stood up. As though in a trance, we all followed her.

She took off her bathrobe and got into bed. She arranged her pillows for the last time in that odd way she had of arranging her pillows, and she said she was a little bit cold, and asked for her blanket. It was that same blanket that she had kept taking to the hospital, the plaid blanket with the squares in different colours.

'What's next?' she asked my father.

My father studied the booklet for a moment, though in fact he'd read it a thousand times and knew it almost by heart. 'You've got to take the antiemetic,' he said.

'Freddy,' my mother said. 'Go and get me a glass of water, would you?'

Freddy remembered the cookies. 'No ice, no lime, sparkling water in a stem glass?' he asked.

'Thank you, Freddy,' she said. And he went and got the water, and my mother took the antiemetics.

'Now we have to wait about forty-five minutes,' said my father.

'Isn't this strange?' said my mother. 'Here we all are together again, going through all of this. I feel as though tomorrow we're all going to be sitting together and talking about it, making it into a family routine about how we weathered another disaster. It seems so unreal to me, the idea that I'm not going to be here.' There was a strangeness in her voice. 'I hope you're not going to be angry at me about this,' she said. She looked at Freddy and she looked at me. 'I think it's best for me, and for you boys, and for you, Leonard.' She paused.

'Losing you can't be best for me,' said my father.

'This has gone on long enough,' said my mother. 'You've all lived through enough, and you have to get on. If I had a choice, no one would be losing me, but there isn't any choice now. I just meant that I hoped you wouldn't be sorry afterward that you had all been here today. I thought about doing this when you were all out of the house, but I thought it would be such a horrible surprise. And then I thought about doing it just with you, Leonard, but I thought you two boys might feel . . .' her voice trailed off. 'Left out,' she finished, with a sort of shrug.

My father interrupted. 'I couldn't have gone through this alone,' he said.

'I know,' said my mother. 'I knew that too. So I decided this was the best way to do it. But it's a terrible thing for you boys to have to go through, and for you Leonard, a terrible thing for you to have to remember. I've tried my best. I really have.' She drifted off into silence.

'You seem so calm,' Freddy said. 'You seem so in control. You're about to die, Mom, and you seem completely in control.'

My mother nodded. 'That's the way I've lived my whole life, Freddy, and it's not a bad way to live. Think about it. You too, Harry.'

My father had started to cry again.

'Don't you feel frightened?' I asked.

'Frightened?' My mother looked puzzled. 'No, not frightened. The only thing I'm afraid of is that this may not work, that I may take all those pills and then wake up again. Aside from that, I feel only sad. I feel terribly sad,' she said. 'I feel as though I'm leaving sooner than I'd planned to. But in many ways I feel as though I do have the bulk of it all behind me, as though I've had the real experiences of my life. I've run the race.' She paused again.

'I wanted you to be here to see me run it too,' I said plaintively.

'Oh, yes, Harry,' she said. 'That's what I wanted too. I wanted that more than anything.'

There was a brief pause. 'I'm glad you made it to my party,' I said, rather idiotically.

My mother smiled. 'Of course, Harry,' she said, as though we were discussing the scheduling of a lunch engagement. 'I wouldn't have missed your party.' Then she looked across the room. I was sitting with her on the bed, and Freddy was rubbing her shoulders, which she'd said were stiff. My father was in his red chair on the other side of the room, weeping quietly. 'Leonard,' she said, and she reached out her arms. 'Come here, Leonard,' she said, and my father slowly crossed the room and came and stood by her head and held her hands in his. They looked at each other.

'I wish it weren't raining,' I said.

'Oh, I'm glad it's raining,' said my mother. I remembered that it had been raining the day we left Lake Como, ten months earlier. It was always my mother's ideal to have a holiday of unrelenting sun, and then to have the rain begin the day we left. It should rain the day you leave, she used to say, because it makes you feel more ready to go home. Was it coincidence that my mother killed herself on a wet day? The day she went to the doctor and got bad news happened to be rainy, but I think I had known that she would choose a wet afternoon; I had come to be afraid of the weather itself. Our lives are shaped when water hangs in the air.

'Maybe each of us should get a minute alone with you,' said Freddy. 'Just a minute.' I said that I thought it was a good idea. My mother said that would be fine. So Freddy went first. My father and I waited in the hall while they talked. I don't know what they talked about.

Then it was my turn. I went into the bedroom and closed the door. 'Harry, I want to make sure you know this,' my mother said in a strong, stern tone of voice, a tone I had not expected.

'What is it?' I said.

'Harry, what happened to me is genetic.' My mother paused. 'You had nothing to do with this illness. Make sure you know that, and that you believe it. It was terrible, what I said to you that week, and it was untrue. You have to believe me. It was untrue and I know that it was untrue. You didn't make me ill. You did help to make me well for the periods when I was well, and to keep me alive through these two years, which, awful though they've been, I wouldn't have missed for anything.'

I saw in that moment how much I had made her suffer over what she had said during that first hospital visit. I saw how much I'd made her suffer for years and years, and I felt terrible about it; but it was too late to change it. I thought about telling her about the dessert plate. I thought about telling her about Helen, but it was too late also for that, and it would have seemed absurd and theatrical. So I just went over and hugged her. 'I love you so much,' I said. 'I know I've been stubborn sometimes, but I hope you know how much I love you.'

'And I hope you know that I love you, Harry. I'm not obsessed, or anything else. I love you, plain and simple. I always have. I always will. Now go and open the door.'

My father stepped inside but he didn't close the door.

'Leonard,' my mother smiled. 'I have nothing to say to you that you don't already know. I've said it all to you over and over again.'

'We've said it all,' agreed my father in a dim voice, and he crossed the room, and Freddy and I filed in behind him. He sat down on the edge of the bed and he held my mother tightly for a moment. Then he let her back down onto the pillows, very softly, as though she might chip.

'How long has it been since the antiemetics?' asked my mother. I'd known she was going to ask soon.

'It's been an hour,' said my father.

'So it's time for the pills,' said my mother. 'Any more instructions?' It was Wednesday evening at 7.30. Exactly a week earlier, to the minute, she had arrived at my party.

My father went back to his red chair, where the booklet lay. 'You're supposed to try to take them with alcohol,' he said. 'You need to take at least twenty-five. They suggest thirty.' He shook his head. 'You've got sixty of them,' he said. My parents were always thorough. 'Can you take thirty pills?' he asked.

'If I can take one pill, I think I can take thirty. I'm not so sure

215

about the alcohol. Freddy, could you get me some more water, and maybe a small glass of something alcoholic?'

'How about vodka?' said Freddy.

'Vodka will be fine,' she said.

Freddy went off to get the water and the vodka. My father went to get the pills from the bathroom. I sat at the foot of the bed and stared out the window at the endless rain.

When Freddy and my father came back, my mother said she couldn't swallow the pills lying down. So she sat up and opened the bottle, and poured the pills out onto her plaid blanket. Then she began scooping them up, three at a time, like jacks, and putting them in her mouth and swallowing them with the mineral water. When she had taken thirty pills, she tried to swallow some of the vodka, but she choked on it. 'We're going to have to hope that this works without that,' she said. 'I've never had straight vodka before. How can people drink that stuff?'

I often think that I will never be able to escape the terrible image of those red pills strewn across that blanket like a handful of confetti. When I close my eyes in fear so as not to see something terrible, what I see in the chaos inside my own eyelids is those thirty red pills. In traffic at twilight, they are there ahead of me in the rear lights of every car. When I see fireworks, I find in the last of the falling stars from some glorious explosion the image of those pills again. When I see the hands of models, nails lacquered to reflect the light, I remember. And every night, as I look for sleep, I find them imprinted in my mind like thirty red lights that say stop, stop, stop, stop, over and over and to no one and to no avail.

She said that she was uncomfortable and asked me to get her another pillow, and I got it for her, and then she lay down again, and I straightened out the plaid blanket, and for a long time Freddy sat beside her on one side and I sat beside her on the other side and held her hand, and my father sat back on his red chair, crying. And then she began to speak. I noticed that the hand I held had on her wedding ring, which was the only ring she wore. My mother had always spoken easily, but now she seemed to speak in a new language, a language of transfiguration. At first she spoke quickly, but as the drug settled in it became a slow monologue.

I said to her, 'You look so fragile.' Freddy and my father were silent.

And she said, 'I am fragile.' She reached up and touched my arm, and then sat up slightly. 'That's the sweater I made you,' she said in a tone of surprise, and readjusted the shoulder slightly. 'It's good to see you in that sweater. It's a nice sweater, Harry. Enjoy it.'

'You gave us such a wonderful life,' I said. 'The trips and the parties and –'

She interrupted. 'Oh, Harry, I hope you remember more than the trips and the parties,' she said. 'I hope you remember something else. You were,' and she paused, as though she were looking for a word. When she spoke again, she put an enormous weight onto each syllable. 'You were the most beloved child.' She looked straight at me. 'We waited so long for you. No child was ever loved more than you.' She paused again. 'Until you were born I had no idea that I could feel anything like what I felt then. Suddenly there you were. I had read books all my life about mothers who bravely said that they would die for their children, and that was just how I felt. I would have died for you. I hated for you to be unhappy. I felt so deeply for you whenever you were unhappy. It was so much worse than to be unhappy myself, it pulled at me so terribly. I wanted to wrap you up in my love, to protect you from all the terrible things in the world. Maybe I sometimes protected you too much, but I always did it because I loved you. I wanted my love to make the world a happy and joyful and safe place for you.' She squeezed my hand, so gently that it was almost imperceptible. 'Harry, Freddy, I want you to feel that that love is always there, that it will go on wrapping you up even after I am gone. My greatest hope is that the love I've given you will stay with you for your whole life.' Her voice took on a softer tone, almost at the edge of incredulity. 'I loved you so much. And you always returned that love. I never knew why, why I loved you so much, or why you should love me. It was something that was just there, and it was the most wonderful and amazing thing in the world.

'And then you were born, Freddy. I felt it all over again. I felt twice as much as I had known I could feel.' She looked away, and called out for my father, and he, almost reluctantly, came to sit on the side of the bed. He took her left hand. I curled up farther down the bed, so that several times she had to ask me to move slightly so she could stretch out her legs. Freddy and I held her right hand together. 'First there was you, Leonard. All my childhood I was this little girl who thought she was unlovable, and then you came along and you really loved me. When I met you, you made me feel like a person. I wasn't a person until I met you. I didn't know it, but I wasn't, I really wasn't. And now I've had thirty wonderful years. You just accepted me exactly as I was, and loved me as exactly who I was. You supported me through fights, and miscarriages, and worries, and panic. You always told me I was right, even when you didn't think so.' A shiver ran down her spine. 'I would gladly have given decades of my life to be the one who went first. I can't imagine what I would have done if you had died before me. You are my life. For thirty years you have been my life.'

Her voice trailed off for a minute. The drug was beginning to set in, and her speech was slowing. 'I always felt important when we went out together. You always made me feel important. It wasn't the jewellery and clothes. When I went out with you, I was carried along by your love. And then you were born, Harry. And then you, Freddy. Two more came along, and then there were three people who all really loved me. And I loved you all so much; I was so overwhelmed, so overpowered by it.'

She turned her head and looked at my father. 'Leonard,' she said. 'Leonard, don't forget that your life is in other people. I know you, Leonard. I'll be gone and you'll try to bury yourself in the office and work and you'll crowd up your mind. I've told the boys and I've told all our friends. You have to find someone for yourself. You could live for another thirty years, Leonard, for as long as we've known each other. Don't waste that time.'

Then she looked at me. 'Pull yourself together, Harry,' she said.

'You've been letting yourself go to pieces these last few months. You've got to get your life in order and get on with it. Everyone's mother dies, sooner or later. Don't sit around feeling sorry for yourself: you're brilliant and talented and you have wonderful friends, and you're a good person, and you should have a good life. And don't lose yourself in ridiculous teenage crushes. Wait for someone who cares. Harry, there will be someone who cares.' She paused. 'Don't think that you're paying me some kind of tribute if you let my death become the great event of your life and you fall apart. The best tribute you can pay to me as a mother is to go on and have a good and fulfilling life, and to love someone who deserves and returns your love.'

She turned her head again. 'Freddy, you have to let go a little bit. You're like me with all that control. You have to let go a little bit and let someone love you, and make a life for yourself. The only thing I regret right now is that I've spent my whole life looking forward. Don't do that. I've had so many of the things that everyone else only dreams of, and I haven't always enjoyed them as much as I should have. Enjoy what you have. All of you. Life is – ' she paused. 'Life is so sweet.'

She paused again, for longer. 'I'm so proud of both you boys and I love you so much. I'll go on loving you even when I'm not here; I'll love you your whole life. I'll come sit on your shoulder, the one Grandma isn't on, and stay there forever.'

And then there was a sort of struggle, as though she were negotiating a few last minutes with her own heavy eyes. She looked at my father again. 'I've been so lucky. Ever since I married you, I've been so lucky. I wouldn't want to change my life with anyone else's. I have loved completely, and I have been completely loved, and I've had such a good time. I might want to change my death, but even with this death, I wouldn't want to change my life for any other life in the world. There are so few people who can say that.' She looked up. 'I love this room,' she said. 'I love this colour pink. I've loved lying in here, afternoons, nights. It's like being inside a shell.'

Her voice was becoming faint, as though she were speaking through water. 'I've looked for so many things in my life,' she said. 'So many things.' She stopped and she moved her head very slightly to one side. 'And all the time Paradise has been in this room with the three of you.' She closed her eyes for a minute. I thought they might not open again, but they did. She looked straight at Freddy. 'Thanks for the backrub, Freddy,' she said. 'Thanks for taking care of Dad.' And then she closed her eyes again, for the last time. For a while we all sat there on the bed with her, waiting, wondering whether she was going to say anything more. After about ten minutes, my father stood up and crossed the room and sat back in his red chair. 'Oh my sweet wife,' he sobbed. I looked at my watch. It was 10.30. At exactly that time, a week earlier, my mother had quietly left the party.

Freddy and I stayed on the bed for a few more minutes, looking at each other. Then he stood up and crossed the room, and went to sit on my father's lap. My eyes and my mouth were dry. I looked at my mother, lying there and breathing steadily. It seemed incredible to me that none of us was waking her up, that we weren't doing anything about the fact that she was dying, that we weren't trying to stop it. I wanted to reach out and shake her by her shoulders; she would probably have looked up at me and perhaps then she would have said something. I wanted to call an ambulance and take her to the hospital and get her stomach pumped. I thought she was wrong, that even if she had only two months of agony left they would be better than this.

But I didn't do anything. I just sat there and held her hand. Occasionally I said something. I didn't know whether she could hear me or not. It didn't matter. There wasn't anything left to say.

At the end of an hour, I finally stood up and crossed the room to where my father and Freddy were, and threw in my lot with the living. 'How long does this take?' I asked my father, who I thought should be making sure that things proceeded in an orderly fashion. He handed me the booklet, as though he no longer had any responsibility for it. The booklet, however, did not say how long it took for the pills to work. We had somehow, all of us, assumed that it took an hour or so, but here we were an hour later, and my mother was still breathing peacefully and regularly.

'We can't just sit here watching,' said Freddy.

'I don't know what else to do,' said my father. 'Look at her,' he said. 'She's still so beautiful.'

'Well, let's at least get out of this room,' I said, and I led them down the hall to the kitchen. My father sat on a chair and continued to cry. Freddy and I washed the dishes from the light meal we'd had earlier.

'Anyone want a cookie?' said Freddy, but no one did, so he put the cookies back in the box and put the plate in the dishwasher.

'Does someone want to go back and see what's happening in there?' asked my father.

There was a brief silence. I focused on rearranging the glasses on the upper rack of the dishwasher. 'I'll go,' said Freddy. My father and I stared at the walls until Freddy came back a minute later. 'Same as before,' he said.

I took out a pad. 'All that stuff she said was incredible,' I said.

'Your mother was such a remarkable woman,' my father began, and then started to weep again.

I was suddenly businesslike. 'Let's try to remember as much as we can,' I said. 'I want to write down as much as possible, so we can remember it.' I began listing things as I remembered them. Freddy came up with some others that I had already forgotten. My father also volunteered a few. It never occurred to me to write down what I had said to her; now it saddens me that I remember her last words so well, while my last words to her have vanished.

'The first night your mother and I went out,' my father said, 'she recited Yeats to me.' My mother had had a joke about that first date. She used to say that she had recited Yeats because she couldn't think of anything to say. But my father was not in a jokey mood. 'I'd never been out with a girl who did anything like that.' He paused. 'It was something about dreams,' he said.

Freddy and I, who had known the story since childhood, chimed almost in unison, 'Tread softly, because you tread on my dreams.'

My father looked at us in surprise. 'Yes,' he said. 'Yes that was it.' And he seemed to drift off into thought. 'I guess someone should check again,' he said.

I went this time. My mother was still lying there, just as she had been, breathing softly. I had realized by then that I was going to have to spend the night uptown. I wanted to call Helen. I wanted to get out of there. I wanted to get away from my whole family. I wanted to wake my mother up, but I also wanted her dead, wanted it almost enough to kill her, because I couldn't stand any more waiting. My mother had been right. It was time for it to be over. If it hadn't been time in the afternoon, it was certainly time now. I went back to the kitchen. 'Nothing's changed.' I said.

My father studied the booklet for a few minutes. Freddy went back to his room and got a big file with all the letters and birthday cards and postcards and funny notes my mother had ever sent him, and he dumped it all over the kitchen floor. 'I want to find something she wrote to me,' he said. 'For a eulogy.'

My father shook his head. 'I could never deliver a eulogy,' he said. I looked at my list of sentences, the last words on the yellow notepad. My father coughed. 'Boys,' he said. 'It says here that sometimes the pills don't work, and that if they don't take effect and you think the patient is waking up you should try to smother him under a pillow, as he will be too weak to fight back and will in that way die as planned.'

I remembered my mother saying that the one thing she feared was waking up, and though I still wanted in some ways to wake her myself, to get something more from her, I knew that she had closed her eyes when and as she had meant to close them. I knew that she would hate waking up and having her life end in a mess. I looked at my father blankly. A minute earlier, I had thought about killing her.

'If someone has to do it, I'll do it,' said Freddy staunchly.

I looked at my father and waited for him to decline that offer, but it didn't happen. 'Thank you, Freddy,' he said. 'I just couldn't.'

I went back and checked again. I thought her breathing was becoming slower, but I wasn't sure. I went and sat by her side, and made some more meaningless remarks.

When I got back to the kitchen, Freddy was arranging everything in piles. 'Look at this,' he said, and passed me an old letter that had been sent to him at summer camp. 'And do you remember these?' he said, and showed me a series of postcards my mother had sent one summer from a trip to Scandinavia with my father.

It was nearing midnight. 'It's been a long time,' said my father. 'I'll go and check this time,' he said, and he went back, but he returned within a few seconds. 'I think you're right, Harry. I think her breathing is slower. But it's not much slower.'

I said that I thought we should eat something, but my father and Freddy both refused, and I in fact felt too sick to eat anything myself. I started trying to write a eulogy. 'Should we call any of her friends?' I asked.

'Not yet,' said my father. 'Just in case something goes wrong. I think we should wait until she's really dead before we do that.'

'Do you know what arrangements need to be made in the morning?' I asked.

'Your mother and I figured it all out,' said my father. 'We're going to have the funeral on Friday. We'll have to go tomorrow and work out the details. Maybe you boys can phone our friends tomorrow. I'm not sure I could bear it. I'll call a few people, maybe, but I can't face that list. Your mother had so many friends.'

An hour later, everyone agreed that we should try to eat something. There was soup in the refrigerator, that my mother had made a few days earlier. I heated it up. My father cried into his bowl, but he finished it. 'This is the last time I'll ever have your mother's soup,' he said.

It took four hours for my mother to die. Freddy was the one who finally found her dead. No one had had to smother her. I never looked at her dead. I could hear her voice saying, 'I don't want you to have this memory.' We had to get the death certificate and call the funeral home. While we waited for the relevant people to show up, I played the piano. First I played Scarlatti, whose work I never play in concert. My first serious teacher had told me that I should work on Scarlatti because it would give me discipline. Then I played Beethoven, and then I played the Schubert. My father came into the living room and looked at me playing. It would be touching to say that I had never played that piece better, but in fact I knew even as I played it that there was, finally, too much emotion, that Schubert had got lost in all my emotion, and that I was playing badly. My playing was not so much an interpretation as a conquest. Nonetheless, I kept on, through the whole piece, because I thought that if I stopped I would go crazy. My father and Freddy stared at me blankly. I put in repetitions that Schubert never wrote, and I pounded on the piano hard enough to break a hammer and I stopped playing only when the doorbell rang, and the three men from the funeral home came in with a stretcher on wheels.

Then I stood at the side of the hallway and told them to be careful of the wallpaper as they wheeled it back. I noticed that my mother had died on a day with an even number, that her death certificate would list an even-numbered day, which I felt was rather like her.

After the men from the funeral home had left, my father distributed sleeping pills. We did not take the leftover red pills; we took ordinary sleeping pills, the kind my parents kept for jetlag. Still, there was something sinister about my father's standing at the door to his room with that bottle, distributing those pills, taking one himself before getting into the bed in which my mother had died an hour earlier. 'I hope you get some sleep,' my father said. Then he closed the bedroom door. I went into my old bedroom, where I had last slept the afternoon Nick broke up with me, and eventually, under the influence of the pills I had taken, I drifted off into a silence of my own.

X

Our Venice

When I woke up the next morning, my mother was dead. This was incredible to me, and it remained incredible to me, and it is still incredible to me now. During the ordinary daylight hours, I have come to accept that my mother is dead; but in the earliest part of the day I still have the sense of bewildered disbelief that woke me up the morning after her death. She said, on the day she died, that she could not believe that we wouldn't all be sitting around afterwards discussing how we had weathered another family storm, and I feel that way myself. So much of the reality of events always came from her; if she and I could compare notes about her death, I would perhaps accept it, but since she and I have not been able to talk about it, it remains obscure and dreamlike. In the early mornings, it seems no more plausible than that the earth is round. I acquiesce to the general wisdom according to which these things are true, but I do so in contravention of every natural instinct and of the evidence of my heart.

The morning after my mother's death I woke up to a world changed beyond recognition. Hanging in that world as though suspended in water were my father and my brother. We met in the new blank space of the kitchen and ate a silent breakfast. The silence was not one of anger or even of sadness; it was a strange pervasive silence almost like snow, a silence that coated everything and took away the shapes and forms, like the silence of the newly deaf. Without breaking that silence, we talked about what needed to be done. I agreed to phone my mother's friends. Freddy agreed to go with my father to identify the body. My father called to make the technical arrangements for the funeral. We agreed to meet at noon to make together whatever decisions we needed to make together.

It is often said that there is nothing so terrible as to be the bearer of bad news, but this is untrue. Every time you convey some sorrow of your own, you are borne up by the dismay you bring to other people, which makes your own sensations more full and more rounded. It is painful to make others sad, but their sadness also places and contains and validates your sadness. I called all my mother's friends and many of my own friends that morning. I did not chat with anyone; I gave the news to each of these people and explained that I had many calls to make, and hung up almost at once. This telephoning was a powerful business: I felt that I reached into each of these men and women and brought forth their grief. Of course everyone was shocked, everyone but the very closest members of my mother's inner circle. 'But last week,' they all said, 'at the party,' they all said, and I said only that she had died quietly and at home and as she had wanted to die.

That afternoon, we went to the funeral home to choose a coffin. There were dozens of designs available, and the choice reminded me of shopping for furniture with my mother; I could hear her voice criticizing busy designs and fussy craftsmanship. Freddy and I walked through the display room, and at last I saw a coffin of very simple design, made of beautifully grained wood, highly polished, with elegantly finished corners. It reminded me of the piano at home. I said I thought it was the right one, and my father and Freddy conceded that it was. Then the director of the funeral home (how do people become the directors of funeral homes, I wondered) took us into his office and said that everything would be taken care of and that the coffin would be brought to the chapel where the funeral was to take place. He asked whether we wanted to have flowers at the funeral.

'Oh yes,' said my father. 'She would have wanted lots of flowers.'

The director of the funeral home suggested calla lilies.

I said that my mother had always hated calla lilies.

'I like calla lilies,' my father said, but Freddy pitched in with me.

'Mom used to say they were the ugliest flowers on earth,' he said. 'Like plastic coffee filters.'

The director of the funeral home wondered whether we had

any other particular ideas, and brought out a book with glossy photographs of funeral wreaths.

I looked at Freddy and he looked at me. 'Pink peonies,' I said. 'The only flowers for this funeral should be pink peonies.'

The funeral director asked no further questions about the peonies. He wrote down our instructions. He wondered in what clothes we wanted to bury my mother.

My father broke down at that point. 'She had such beautiful clothes,' he said. 'We have closets and closets full of clothes at home. What clothes? How can we possibly choose clothes?'

But I had seen this question coming for a long time. I put my hand on my father's arm. 'I'll take care of it,' I said.

'Thank you,' my father said, and stared off into space for a minute.

I assured the director of the funeral home that I would bring the clothes up later in the afternoon.

We arranged all the other details and returned home. I went into my mother's enormous closet and found among the hundreds of dresses and suits and skirts and blouses the dress she had worn to my party, the black dress with the trails of brilliant flowers falling down it, like fresh snowflakes or chance tears, flowers in red and blue and pink. I picked out a pair of stockings and black shoes and put them all together in a bag and took them up to the funeral home.

Then we all sat down to write eulogies. Freddy had done a lot the previous evening, while my mother lay dying. I had sketched out drafts of one kind or another on and off during the preceding six months, but they all seemed banal to me. My father headed back to his bedroom to sit in the red chair and write.

'I suppose we should ask someone to read these at the funeral,' he said in passing.

'I'm going to read my own,' said Freddy.

I wavered.

'I couldn't possibly stand up there and read,' said my father.

'I'm going to read my own,' said Freddy. 'If you want me to, I'll read yours too.'

'If you're sure you can do that,' said my father, 'then you might as well. But I wouldn't plan on that. Funerals are terrible. I don't know how I can even get through the day.'

I wavered. Freddy looked at me. 'I'll do yours if you want, Harry,' he said.

I said that I would have to wait until the morning to decide. 'If I can, I'll read my own,' I said. 'If not, I'll let you do it.'

Then I sat down and wrote my eulogy. It was four pages long, double-spaced, and it was about my whole life with my mother, and it took me fifteen minutes to get it down on paper. It was like typing out something I had memorized a long time before.

I took sleeping pills again that night, and woke up the next morning with a start. Friday, the day of my mother's funeral, was my mother's kind of day, pure springtime, the sun bright and strong and the skies clear with a few tiny puffy clouds scattered down near the horizon as though their sole function was to underscore the extreme blue of the heavens. My father was weeping in the kitchen when I went in to make tea. Freddy was being stoical. I took a long shower and got dressed carefully. I had found the shirt I had had made for my party, that I had forgotten to wear ten days earlier, and I wore it that day. My gold watch had been repaired, and I wore that as well. During breakfast, I reread my eulogy, and I read my father's, and I read Freddy's. None of them was as simple or pure as my mother's last words, but they were just as urgent.

We were to fight and argue, the three of us, through much of the summer that followed, but on the day of my mother's funeral we could not let go of one another. My father's misery was so terrible and so immediate that neither Freddy nor I could look away from it even for a minute, though it also weighed on me to feel that I had to support a grief besides my own. Freddy and I walked on either side of my father as we headed down for the funeral. We went through the great bronze doors with the merciless faces of Old Testament sages carved in them, and we passed through the main sanctuary, and we came to the chapel where the funeral was to take place. I had made perhaps fifty telephone calls the day before, but sad news travels with astonishing speed. Hundreds of people had come to the funeral. All my mother's old friends were there, and all of my friends, and all of Freddy's friends. People who worked with my father were there. Janet was there, and Robert, and the man who used to do my mother's hair, and the woman who did her nails, and the seamstress who altered her clothes, and the doctors who had got to know her during her illness. The children of her friends were there, and the parents of some of my friends, and people with whom I had worked, and people with whom Freddy had worked. Friends of my grand-mother's, people I had thought long dead, were gathered in a few pews near the back. Our relations were there, even the cousins whose names I could never keep straight. It was a sea of faces. 'She was so wonderful,' I heard, and 'She was so kind to me,' and 'What a magical woman she was.' Of course people do say those things at funerals, even at the funerals of people who are not wonderful and not kind and not magical, but I believed then and believe now that that mass of people had come to the funeral because they had all in fact been touched by my mother; and I wondered as I looked around at them where my mother had found the time to be so wonderful and kind and magical to so many.

The three of us stumbled up to the front row of the chapel, and after various people had come up to us and embraced us, the funeral began. I looked up at the soaring pilasters and at the high points of the ceiling and at the dark colours of the stained glass. I heard the beginning of the service. I thought it was impossible that my mother could be in the polished wood coffin at the front of the room, under its wreaths of pink peonies. I noticed that the peonies were not as pink or as full as the ones we had had for the party, and realized that I should not have let the funeral home arrange for the flowers. I noticed that the coffin seemed short, as though they would have had to crunch up my mother to fit her in, but I decided that this was probably an optical trick played by its proportions.

We were approaching the eulogies. My father wept steadily, and his breath came in sudden gasps. He looked sideways at me.

'You aren't going to be able to read a eulogy,' he said. 'Let Freddy do it.'

I didn't say anything. Lofty religious words floated over our heads. The time arrived. Freddy stood up. 'Are you coming?' he whispered to me.

As I looked up at the pulpit from which we were to read, I had a sudden image in my mind, so clear that the Gothic arches and the stained glass and the hundreds of mourners seemed to disappear. I saw my mother, dressed in the same dress she was wearing inside that closed coffin. I saw her walking up that long flight of stairs at my party. She was not leaning on anyone. With – as it had turned out – a tumor almost entirely obstructing her digestive track, and another one wrapped around her spine, with a body ravaged from chemotherapy and lack of food, with a grasp on life as fragile as memory itself, she was climbing one step at a time, and as she climbed she was laughing and laughing and laughing. I saw her rope of big pearls swinging back and forth, and then I saw how her eyes lit up when they caught mine, and how she stopped laughing to smile, that particular smile that was my smile, that smile that had never changed, that she had smiled at me since before I had begun to remember. In that moment my funeral tears stopped. Then I reached farther back, to my childhood, and I heard her saying, 'When the time comes, you do what's necessary. You do what's appropriate. You do what's right. That's part of what it means to grow up, Harry.' And I felt that I owed it to her, at the very least, to stand up myself and say to all these hundreds and hundreds of people what she and I had always known and they, perhaps, had not.

So Freddy and I walked up together, and climbed the steps to the pulpit. We held onto each other as we climbed those steps. I thought of my mother telling us, when we were little, that she had had two children so they could love each other. 'If you boys don't stop squabbling, I'm going to leave you on the steps of the foundling home,' she would sometimes say in exasperation. I thought how pleased she would have been to see us together in this way. 'Don't worry,' Freddy said to me. 'If you have a problem, just pass yours to me and I'll finish for you.'

But I didn't have a problem. I had dreaded having to stand up in front of everyone, without some genius composer's music to shield me; but once I was there I wanted the time to last forever. I had been told that my mother was in the coffin down below me, but in the deepest part of my mind she was just where she had said she would be, sitting on my shoulder. I spoke slowly and with great certainty, giving each word as much weight as I could. The party the previous week had been so joyful as to be almost a lie: there had been no space at it for the terrible grief and anguish of my family. This funeral was so sad as to be again a lie: I needed to bring into it some of that quality of joy that my mother had brought to me and to all these others. I spoke for less than five minutes, and it was no time at all, but it was also a time as long as eternity.

Then Freddy read his eulogy, and I noticed that he had captured things about my mother that I had not captured. And then he read my father's eulogy, which was not so much about my mother's character or qualities; it was like the scream of a wounded animal, long and relentless, the scream my mother had not produced when she died.

Helen came along to the graveside, and after the burial, when they had lowered my mother into the earth, I turned and saw Helen through the glistening air, and I heard again my mother saying to me, 'Helen is a good friend.' I could not demand more comfort from my father or my brother because they were busy demanding comfort of their own, but I could turn to Helen and collapse, and so I did that. Helen came back to the apartment with us, and she stayed almost all the time during the weekend, while we received mourners. People poured and shifted through the house. My father wept in front of everyone, and I disliked that intensely. Freddy and I comported ourselves like hosts, and introduced people to each other, and made sure that everyone was comfortable. Every night, when the people left, my father would tell us, Freddy and me, that we had to stay to help him to get on with his life. 'You can move back into this apartment,' he told me.

I said I would stay through the weekend, and that beyond that I would not even consider it.

He told me that I was selfish and impossible.

I told him that he was selfish and hateful.

Freddy told us that we had to stop battling. He reminded me that I had promised my mother that I would help to take care of my father.

I said that I would take care, but that I would not go on sleeping in that apartment.

Like an old man, my father shuffled back to the room in which my mother had died a few days earlier, the only room he had to sleep in, and lay down by himself in that big double bed. It was as though he was locking himself inside a shell.

And I went into my old room, to sleep. As I waited for sleep, half way to dreams, I thought that a part of me had been ripped out of my body. I know that science has appointed the brain as the seat of all our emotion, but the dull ache of loss has never sounded around my head in the small hours of the night. It is in my chest that it speaks, and it is around my lungs and in the coursing of my blood that I feel as though I am being torn apart. In that half-conscious state, it was not my mind that had been yanked so unceremoniously from my body, but my heart; and when I woke up the next morning, it was in my chest that I seemed to be missing some crucial part of myself, and to be no longer more than a shadow of what and who I had been.

Sunday saw the last of the condolence callers. That night, when all the people had left, I packed my things to go back to my own apartment and I went into my parents' room to say goodbye. My father was sitting on the bed, his bed, and looking at my mother's handbag, which she had left sitting next to her night table, where it had always been. Either Freddy or Janet had come in over the weekend and closed the book that had been open beside her bed, and put away the glasses that had sat on top of it, but the handbag was just where she had left it.

'Look at that,' said my father.

I was going to meet Helen and she was going to come down

and help me settle back into my own apartment. I thought I would explode if I didn't leave soon. The walls were pressing close; I saw that if I stayed with my father, I would become as old and as lonely as he. That prospect enraged me. I picked up the handbag and put it on the bed.

My father put his hand on the bag.

I picked it up and turned it upside down and shook it, so that everything in it fell onto the bed. My mother's wallet, her silver pillbox, her lace handkerchief, a square powder compact with an amethyst on it, a few blue felt-tipped pens, a couple of photographs, her ring of keys: all these things went tumbling onto the bedspread; and with the others came also, to my astonishment, the diamond pin that had been my grandmother's.

My father and I both stared at it.

'That's the one she thought she'd lost,' said my father.

'That's it,' I said.

We looked at it again, as though it were a meteor fresh from the outer reaches of the galaxy.

'Freddy,' I called, and Freddy came running in from his room. 'Look,' I said.

Freddy looked down at the bed. 'What do you know,' he said. 'It's that pin. So it didn't go to the dry cleaner after all.' He leaned over and picked it up. 'Remember how Grandma used to wear this all the time?' he said. 'When I think of Grandma, I think of her in this pin.'

My father began to cry again. 'If we could only let her know that we'd found it,' he said.

Freddy crossed the room to put it away, and he opened my mother's jewellery box. Placed neatly on the tray that held her everyday earrings, the top tray in the box, were three envelopes. One was addressed to me, one to Freddy, and one to my father. It was Sunday night. The condolence calls were over, and we were about to begin the struggle of life without my mother. We found her letters all together; it was as though she had planned this detail too.

To me and to Freddy she said what she had said before she died. She told us that she loved us and that we had to get on with our lives. To my father, she wrote simply this: 'My dearest Leonard: What a sweet life we had together. How happy you made me. You made me feel beautiful, you made me feel cherished, you made me feel safe and protected. Above all you gave me the bliss of knowing always that I loved and was loved. You are in my heart always.'

I read my note over, and then I set off downtown. Helen met me at the door.

The process of holding onto someone who is dying and the process of holding onto someone who has died are as alien to each other as love and indifference. I had argued with my mother in the weeks before her death, but for those first months after she died she was in my mind an angel, and I had no purchase on the reality of our relationship. I played memories over and over until I eventually made them tedious even to myself. Every day I talked on the phone with my father and argued. Then I called Freddy to tell him how impossible my father was. Sometimes his line was busy, when my father was calling him to complain about me. Freddy was implacable and even-tempered; some days I thought this must mean he had loved my mother the least of us all, but some days I thought it meant he had loved her most.

In the weeks after the funeral, Helen provided endless comfort, but so too did my many other friends, and I felt that I was living in the luxury of their sympathy, and that sympathy so preoccupied me that sometimes I lost for a little while any sense of my own sadness. As the months went by, however, that sympathy seemed to fall away. I went to England a few times; friends in New York and friends in London had never seemed more different, though the meaning of their friendship came in the end to parity. The English say to you frankly (Bernard said it too): it will take you years and years and years to recover from this. The English say to you: it would be in poor form for you to tell me too much about your suffering. The English say to you: the thing to do is not to express your pain. The English say to you: you're being very brave and good not mentioning that you are at a pitch of anguish, pretending that life is fine, and that's just what you should go on doing.

The Americans, on the other hand, say: let it all hang out. The Americans say: tell me what is in your mind and on your mind. The Americans say: whatever you are suffering I want to be part of; I want to suffer it with you. And the Americans listen to you for one or two months with an intensity of focus before which the fragile constructs of your sorrow crumple. After two months, when Americans ask how you are, you say, as you would to the English: I'm fine. You say that because if you say anything else you will be called on to explicate it and unravel it and include the person to whom you are responding in it. You say that because you make people too uneasy if you say, simply: I feel that life itself has lost its purpose. You say that because people don't know how to respond if you say: I feel so worn out that I have stopped answering the telephone. America and England are both terrible countries for mourning, but perhaps there are no countries that are better. At least in England people give you some credit for pulling yourself together; in America people only assume that your suffering was never so great in the first place, that if things weren't fine you would say so.

I tried to explain this to Helen, and she stopped me. 'Don't you see,' she asked, 'that there's nothing else to do? That there's nothing for people to say, no matter why it is that they're not saying it? At the beginning, you had this terrible thing happen to you. Your mother died. It was straightforward and concrete and anyone could respond to it. It was outside of you. It was an event. But what you have now is something very different. You have this sorrow that is simply a part of you, that isn't an event at all. There's nothing to say about it; all people can do is to love you as you now are, with this pain that has become a part of you. They can't keep responding to it as though it were a thing of its own. It's like the way people love you while you grow older; they don't keep telling you how sorry they are that you're growing older, or keep saying that they really like you and how it must be awful for you that you're becoming old. It's just you. It's just who you are. You're someone else now than who you were before, and your friends are as fond of you as ever, or maybe fonder than ever. Stop complaining about it. What you're getting is as much as anyone has any right to expect.'

I thought about that, and the months passed. I saw Helen often, but I could not quite bring myself to push our friendship back into that physical realm where it had dallied at the end of winter, and I thought that I had world enough and time to think of such matters later on. I was, of course, quite wrong. In the autumn, Helen found a new boyfriend, a sweet man who clearly adored her, and though she continued to offer me her friendship, I saw that I had in some very fundamental way missed my chance. The man she had found was less difficult than I, less demanding, more devoted to her; I look at him and I look at myself and I am reminded how very sensible Helen is. These days, I see her once every couple of weeks, and though we are always glad to see each other, she is not at the centre of my life; I miss her terribly. I am forever struggling not to be angry at Helen and her boyfriend. I have found boy-friends and girlfriends of my own, but as I am not sensible like Helen, they have mostly appeared and disappeared like dots on a disk of snow. Sooner or later, perhaps, I will really fall in love with one of them, and that one will last. I suppose that someone will be the one who cares, and for whom I care; but this is scant comfort right now. Helen gave me so much time, more time than I could possibly have deserved, even under the circumstances. I know that. I am the one who wasted it.

I wasted a lot of the time I had with my mother as well. Is forgiveness ever fully conscious? Insofar as it is, I forgive my mother here and now for whatever she may ever have done that I may have failed to forgive, even for her death. Today it is a Tuesday, and the sun is out (how prone I used to be to the weather! how happy such days as this made us!) – and I forgive my mother as though I were spokesman for the very gates of heaven, as though I could paint forgiveness to stretch from my childhood to the place among the constellations where right now, perhaps, my mother is smiling her particular smile and struggling to articulate one of those little, passing insights that give life its foil of meaning. I have learned now that loss and forgiveness come only too readily to join each other, like shy and sorry partners at a crowded dance. As my sense of loss settles and becomes more clear each day, so too does my desire to forgive rise up and overwhelm me, until I feel I could forgive not only my mother, but also the terrors of war, the cruelty of illness, the mystery of life and death. In the end, long after a death, when your pain has become fully a part of you from which there will be no separation, as integral as your sense of humour or of self-worth, you find that the pain has brought with it its reverse. For it is also the case that all the joy that came before that pain, which had seemed foreign, or inaccessible, or temporal, or forgettable, also becomes an inalienable part of you. Then the act of memory does not entail recollection of events or circumstances; then everything you do is a part of your act of memory, and every bit of your daily life, no matter how trivial or banal, becomes a form of tribute. Already, some kinds of memory of my mother are fading. I cannot remember so well as I once could what her voice sounded like, or how she walked, or the smell of perfume and fur that came with her into the house on a winter day. I have gone on with my life, and I busy myself with ordinary negotiations, with playing the piano, with Helen, and with other friends, with lovers, with taking care of my father, with Freddy. From time to time I plan and throw a party. You get on; you get on with life because there is nothing else to do. The new experiences do not fill the void this death has left, but they lie beside it, and, as they accumulate, form banks around it to make it less terrible. My mother said the day she died that she had wanted all her life for her love to wrap me up and make the world a safe place for me, and I imagined then that her love was made of masses of cotton wool in which I could roll and luxuriate. But my mother's love is no longer outside of me; it is within me. It is not made of cotton wool, but of bones. What the world sees are skin and eyes and the soft shapes of flesh; but that unknown and unknowable part of me that holds together the rest, giving it worth and meaning, is the part that my mother gave to me. I have built myself upon it. The little memories that are the stuff of this book are almost meaningless by comparison to that. The credible life I lead does nothing to belie the wonder of this truth beneath the surface.

Until October of the year my mother died, I lived shrouded in a pure and immutable mourning, and I saw all the world out of focus. But one crisp afternoon, when I had gone out to do neighbourhood errands, I chanced to hear from someone's passing car window a song from the forties. I caught only half a minute of music before the light changed and the car sped away, but that half minute brought back to me a memory of Venice. Before our first family trip to Italy, when I was six, my mother had said, 'Rome is overwhelming, and Florence is beautiful, but Venice is like fairyland.' And though in the month before that trip she had told me about Medicis and museums, about the Pitti Palace and the Arch of Constantine, she had refused to say more of Venice than that: 'Venice is like fairyland.' And so for me Venice was forever fairyland.

When I was perhaps twelve, my mother and I went there, for reasons I no longer remember, without my father or my brother. I think it may have been that my school vacations and Freddy's were out of alignment, and that we could not all travel at once. On the last day of that holiday, my mother and I went for a long walk, which took us through some of the southern parts of the city, and then led us into San Marco itself. We would have had to walk only another two minutes to get to the hotel. My mother was tired; it was the end of the afternoon, the hour at which she always went back to have a bath. But I was so full of delight at being in Venice – and it was our last day – and she suddenly turned to me and smiled, and suggested, to my astonishment, that we not return to the hotel yet, that we sit instead for a few minutes in one of the cafés of the square.

It was a sudden gift, a gift of time I would not have thought to ask for: her afternoon bath was sacred. And yet there it was. We walked together across the piazza, spurned Florian, and went through to the piazzetta, because an orchestra was playing there, and because we could see the sunshine on the water. It was a beautiful day, clear, with a slight breeze, and we sat at an outside table and talked and felt the air and the sun and the freshness of the water beyond us, and listened to the sentimental music of the orchestra. Did they play the song I was to hear from a car window a few months after my mother's death? Perhaps they did; certainly it was that music that returned this Venetian day to me. What I remember about sitting there at the café, while my mother sang along to some of the tunes and played out the rhythms of others on the table, abstractedly, with one hand, and talked to me, about what time we would have dinner, and about her first trip to Venice when she was in college, and about friends and small events: what I remember most about it is that I was, at that moment, completely happy. It was the most simple, easy, unlaboured sense in the world. I felt that there was nothing I wanted on earth that was not mine, that to be there in that café, eating – who knows what I was eating – perhaps ice cream, talking to my mother and listening to the faint strains of music and the man whistling at the next table, watching the pigeons group themselves around a few scattered tourists – it *was* fairyland, as full of enchantment as any promise my mother had ever made. She of course looked beautiful, and she too was happy, and I was a part of her happiness as much as she was a part of mine, and so our happiness seemed to form a sort of cloud of magic in which we sat, like the lucky Queen and Prince in a fairytale. I saw – or rather see in retrospect – not simply that it was a lovely moment, but that I was unscathed, in a way that I was soon to lose and will never reach again. For an hour or two, I felt a total and absolute rapture that nothing could mar. And what is most astonishing to me is that I didn't have any inkling then of how rare such feelings were. I thought that this was simply what life was, that every childhood was full of such love, that everyone in the world went on much as I did, felt what I felt, knew what I knew. I understood by the time I was thirteen that I was lucky to get to Venice for spring vacation, but I had not the slightest idea of how remarkable it was to grow up in the constant radiance of my mother's affection. Nor indeed did I know, then, that I had already embarked on a course of exchanging easier for more difficult pleasures, that my mother's love was one of the most difficult pleasures of all, that I had been paying for it for years and would go on paying for it forever. I did not guess, then, that emotions so profound and so far-reaching might come only to those who were willing to suffer (I do not remember being asked if I were willing), that I could have such tremendous joy only if I gave up the anodyne pleasure of ordinary freedoms. I did not know that those children who grew up outside of this passionate empathy might live to the end of their days on the easy satisfactions of the manifest world, while for me love itself would remain so perilous, so engaging and so entire as to be almost inconceivable.

Acknowledgements

This is above all a novel about love, and the outpouring of affection qua editing that came from friends was profoundly moving to me. First and foremost, I must thank the close readers of every draft: Amanda Smithson, Katherine Keenum, James Wood, Mary Marks, and Maggie Robbins each ploughed through version after version. Others gave wonderfully close responses to single drafts: Fran Kiernan, Jane Mendelsohn, Betsy Joly de Lotbinière, Julie Sheehan, Christian Caryl, Dorothy Arnsten, Claudia Swan, Brian D'Amato, Claire Messud, Rachel Eisler, James Meyer, Thomas Caplan, Dana Cowin, Sue Macartney-Snape, Harold Bloom, Lydia Phelps Stokes Katzenbach, Michael Lee, Talcott Camp and Carl Halvorson. Howard and David Solomon both read this closely, provided useful critical suggestions, and supported me in the writing of a story that was not without pain for them. There are three people who deserve particular thanks for giving me a vision that is at the heart of this book: Maggie Robbins, Sue Macartney-Snape, and Talcott Camp. They have been better friends than I deserve. Finally, I must thank Carolina Sherman Salguero, the bravest soldier of them all, who lived through all the terrible moods of this undertaking, and managed not to give up on me despite them. Without her, I would never have been happy enough to be able to write this book.